Praise for Cheryl St.John

"The characters are delightful and
inspire anticipation for the next story."
—*RT Book Reviews* on *The Wedding Journey*

"This well-written, sweet love story
has lots of romance and adventure."
—*RT Book Reviews* on "Mountain Rose"
in *To Be a Mother*

"St.John's books are emotionally charged
and her characters are well rounded."
—*RT Book Reviews* on *The Preacher's Wife*

Praise for Debra Ullrick

"Ullrick skillfully uses her heroine's dilemma to prove
the power of moving on from the past
in this delightful story."
—*RT Book Reviews* on *Groom Wanted*

"The hero's journey from what he thinks he wants to
God's revelation of what he really wants and needs
makes for a lovely story."
—*RT Book Reviews* on *The Unlikely Wife*

"Ullrick pens a wonderful, sweet romance
with ⟨...⟩ aracters."
⟨...⟩ *Unexpected Bride*

CHERYL ST.JOHN's

love for reading started as a child. She wrote her own stories, designed covers and stapled them to form books. She credits many hours of creating scenarios for her paper dolls and Barbies as the start of her fascination with fictional characters. At one time Westerns were her preferred reading—until she happened upon LaVyrle Spencer's *Hummingbird* in her local store. After that she couldn't read enough romance, and the desire to create stories of hope and forgiveness was born.

Cheryl loves hearing from readers. Visit her website at www.cherylstjohn.net or email her at SaintJohn@aol.com.

DEBRA ULLRICK

is an award-winning author who is happily married to her husband of thirty-six years. For more than twenty-five years she and her husband and their only daughter lived and worked on cattle ranches in the Colorado mountains. The last ranch Debra lived on was also where a famous movie star and her screenwriter husband chose to purchase property. She now lives in the flatlands, where she's dealing with cultural whiplash. Debra loves animals, classic cars, mud-bog racing and monster trucks. When she's not writing, she's reading, drawing Western art, feeding wild birds and watching Jane Austen movies, *COPS* or *Castle*.

Debra loves hearing from her readers. You can contact her through her website, www.debraullrick.com.

Colorado Courtship

CHERYL ST.JOHN

DEBRA ULLRICK

Love Inspired

Recycling programs for this product may not exist in your area.

™ LOVE INSPIRED BOOKS

ISBN-13: 978-0-373-82948-4

COLORADO COURTSHIP
Copyright © 2013 by Harlequin Books S.A.

The publisher acknowledges the copyright holders of the individual works as follows:

WINTER OF DREAMS
Copyright © 2013 by Cheryl Ludwigs

THE RANCHER'S SWEETHEART
Copyright © 2013 by Debra Ullrick

www.LoveInspiredBooks.com

Printed in U.S.A.

CONTENTS

WINTER OF DREAMS

Cheryl St.John

This story is dedicated to my beautiful grandmother, Sarah Mellissa St.John, who by example taught me to call on the name of Jesus in times of trouble, to love unconditionally, to laugh a lot, to cry a little and to always see the good in others.

O death, where is thy sting?
O grave, where is thy victory?
The sting of death is sin; and the strength of sin is the law.
But thanks be to God, which giveth us the victory
through our Lord Jesus Christ.
—*1 Corinthians* 15:55–57

Chapter One

Colorado, January 1899

Mr. Hammond's telegram had assured her, due to the mild winter, that the train would have no problem reaching Carson Springs mid-January. Violet Kristofferson unfolded his message and read it again, her gaze stumbling first over the name she'd chosen. She would have to remember. Bennett. *Violet Bennett.*

She'd barely been able to eat the entire way, even though train stations between Ohio and Colorado often had decent restaurants or a nice café next door.

Her stomach tightened now at the prospect of living and working among strangers in a place she'd never been, but she'd had little choice—her situation in Ohio had forced her to take action.

The heavy gray sky outside the steamed-over windows didn't bolster her mood or her confidence, but some time ago the conductor had announced their destination only an hour hence. A single stove glowed in an attempt to heat the railcar, but all day her feet had been numb from the cold. Absently she checked the delicate gold watch that hung on a chain around her neck and discreetly adjusted one leg, then the other, eager to stretch. She would sleep like a baby once she was finally able to lie down with a comfortable mattress beneath her.

The rhythm of the wheels changed, and the car slowed fractionally. Passengers straightened in their seats in anticipation of the stop.

Violet wiped the window with her mittened hand and studied the landscape. Horses and cattle huddled in clusters, dotting the white expanse of snow. Scattered houses came into view, situated closer and closer together the more the locomotive slowed. The train turned a last bend, climbed an incline and chugged into the town.

Carson Springs was larger than she'd anticipated, a combination of stone, wood and brick buildings, most of which she could only see from the back. The train rolled alongside the station, blocking her view of the town. A large canopy covered the platform, wisely protecting it from the elements. From her window seat Violet strained to see the men and women waiting for arriving passengers, unable to guess which might be her new employer.

She waited her turn, descending the stairs behind a portly woman wearing a fox coat and a large plumed hat. Making her way to an open space on the wood platform, Violet stopped to get her bearings. Her breath came out in puffy white plumes. Her feet ached.

Nearby the porters unloaded and stacked trunks and valises.

Violet scanned the crowd. A tall man in a black coat

and hat separated from the others and made his way toward her. "Miss Bennett?"

"Um." Startled at hearing the unfamiliar surname, she composed herself. "Yes." She didn't want to be found, and her real name was too distinctive. "I'm Miss Bennett."

He removed his hat, revealing an unruly shock of russet-brown hair. "I'm Ben Charles Hammond."

"How do you do?" She offered her hand, and he held her wool-covered fingers for the briefest of moments in a polite greeting.

"I hope your journey wasn't too unpleasant."

He had a strong jawline, arching brows and friendly gray-green eyes. She liked him immediately. "Not at all. The accommodations were more than adequate, thank you."

"If you'll point out your luggage, I'll take it to the carriage."

"There's only one carpetbag. The other two are crates. Fairly large ones. I don't expect you to manage those on your own. I can hail someone—"

"Let's have a look before you count me out."

"I didn't mean—"

"I know you didn't." He adjusted his hat on his head. "Point them out."

She indicated her belongings and picked up the bag. He hauled one of the crates to his shoulder, and she followed him through the thinning crowd to a black carriage with a boot on the rear. He stored the load and went back for the second. Meanwhile Violet admired the sleek black horse harnessed to the carriage. Taking a few steps forward and cautious of the layer of dirty snow along the curb, she tugged off her mitten to stroke the animal's shiny mane and neck. The heat and texture of his hide was familiar and comforting. She could almost smell the stables.

Mr. Hammond stowed the rest of her belongings, folded down a step and waited beside the carriage until she joined him. Quickly pulling on her mitten, she accepted his outstretched hand. Climbing up from the other side, he took the seat beside her. "You like horses?"

"Yes. My father used to take me riding."

"There are saddles and tack in our stable. Henry takes care of the horses. He'll help you if you want to ride. Maybe you can get Tessa to join you once the weather's nice."

"I would enjoy that, thank you." Tessa was his sixteen-year-old sister. Violet had been hired to do the cooking for him, his sister and his other employees. He'd suggested she take an interest in Tessa as well, being a companion of sorts as time permitted. "Will I meet her today?"

"Yes. She's waiting at home."

Once they'd moved past the main street of businesses, where wagons and buggies traveled and townspeople went about their day, he drove the carriage several blocks along a street of two- and three-story homes until they reached a cross street, where he turned to the right.

"I expect you to take time for yourself," he said. "Attend church with us—or another church if ours isn't your preference. Sunday will be your day off. Tessa and I will either fix our own meals or eat in town. You're welcome to join us if you're not tired of us by then."

"That's thoughtful of you."

Mr. Hammond was polite and seemed kind and generous. It appeared her concern had been for naught.

The buildings on the north side of this street backed a wooded area. A row of enormous attached brick structures came into view. Behind them stood a matching carriage house and a small wood-frame stable. The sign in front of the first building they passed indicated it was a furniture maker's. "Do you make furniture?"

"No. My father did, but I sold the business to Walter Hatcher in 'eighty-five. Two doors down is where we live."

Her interest was definitely piqued now. Whatever he did, his company obviously thrived. "One of these is your home?"

"And my business," he replied.

A low hedge surrounded the next two connected buildings, where white shutters framed the windows and white arched doors indicated entries. There were two sets of doors on the front, a double set on the right.

They drew close, and a fancily lettered iron sign caught her attention:

Hammond Funeral Parlor
Ben Charles Hammond, Undertaker & Stone Mason

Undertaker? Violet's heart hammered and, though she'd had little to eat for days, her stomach threatened upheaval.

He'd brought her to his *funeral parlor?*

A dusting of snow fell now, and the smell of smoke curling into the sky from two chimneys was strong, but she barely noticed.

She fastened her gaze on the portion of the structure

at the right. Double doors, wide enough for…coffins.
"You're an undertaker?"

"Used to be Hammond and Son until fourteen years
ago when my father passed on. Now it's just me. I have
help, of course. Too much work for one person to handle."

She guessed him to be no older than his mid-thirties,
so he must have been quite young when he'd taken over
the business. He helped her to the ground, where she
stood unmoving while he unloaded the baggage. From
around the end of the building, a young man joined
them, removing his wool cap and giving Violet a lop-
sided grin.

"This is Henry," Mr. Hammond told her. "Henry,
Miss Bennett."

"How do, Miss Bennett."

"Help me take her things upstairs, will you?" Mr.
Hammond asked.

Violet hadn't answered. She stared at the other portion of the building—right beside where she was expected to work and live and *sleep*. Were there—what did
Mr. Hammond call them?—lifeless clients in there now?

Henry grabbed a crate and carried it into the house.

"A lot of people have an aversion to my occupation," Mr. Hammond said. "Is it going to be a problem
for you?"

"It's just—well—you didn't mention it in your telegrams."

He hefted the other crate onto his shoulder. "I didn't
think you'd come if I did."

She stared at his retreating back.

Ben Charles made a concerted effort not to grunt or
sweat, since he'd been adamant about his ability to lift

and tote Miss Bennett's belongings. The young woman had apparently packed bricks and planned to add an addition to his home while she was here.

He'd fully expected her revulsion regarding his profession and his home, and it had only been a matter of time until he'd seen the reaction on her face. "Henry will return for your bag," he called over his shoulder.

He experienced a slim measure of guilt for not telling her up front, but she wouldn't have come. And they needed her. He'd been relieved to find someone to take over the kitchen and he'd been eager for her to arrive. He hadn't known what he'd expected, but the pretty doe-eyed Violet Bennett wasn't it. There was something too vulnerable about her. Something that made him shudder when he thought of her traveling alone.

As soon as he'd seen her, he'd felt guilty that he hadn't gone to get her, as he had for Tessa when she'd come home from boarding school last year. "Thank You for keeping her safe, Lord," he whispered.

He stopped on the landing midway up the stairs and looked back.

She stood in the enormous tiled entry, staring up at the ceiling where cherubs cavorted with plaster ribbons, then studied the shining oak stairs and banister. She glanced at the east wall of the foyer, and he read the questions on her lovely face. She wondered what was on the other side.

He imagined he saw her shudder.

Henry passed Ben Charles on his way back down and greeted Miss Bennett. "I'll be right back with your bag."

She looked up, caught Ben Charles watching her and quickly composed her features. As long as she was a decent cook, a person of good moral character—and

Tessa liked her—he intended to do everything in his power to keep Miss Bennett here.

Violet gathered the hem of her traveling skirt and climbed the stairs, her aching feet protesting. At the top was an open room with an arched and draped window facing the rear of the house, and framing a white-blanketed lawn and the copse of trees beyond. The room held floor-to-ceiling shelves of books and assorted plush furniture.

"Tessa!" Mr. Hammond called, startling Violet.

"No need to shout, Ben Charles. I'm right here." A slim young woman stood from one of the chairs facing the window and rested a book on the seat she'd vacated. Her rose-colored dress was nicer than anything Violet owned, though it was simple in design. The girl walked forward.

"This is Miss Bennett."

"Pleased to meet you," Tessa said, without a smile. "Your room is ready. My brother gave you the one next to mine."

Violet followed her, and when Tessa stepped back, she entered first. Two windows opened to the west, taking advantage of the side of the structure away from the funeral parlor, thank goodness. At least she would be on the opposite side.

A small fireplace burned, warming the room and adding a comforting hiss. The walls were papered with a pale peach wide scrolling pattern. One wall held a bureau. Handkerchief drawers held lamps and the top a trifold mirror. On the opposite wall stood a tall armoire with carved roses adorning the doors and drawers.

The head of the bed, with its white wrought-iron spindles, stood between the windows, and a calico spread in colors matching the throw rugs was topped with comfortable-looking pillows. A plump chair stood near the fireplace.

The room was so bright and welcoming, Violet had difficulty imagining it as part of the funeral parlor.

"Can you start tomorrow?" Ben Charles asked from behind her.

She turned to face him. "What about supper this evening?"

"We'll make do like we have been."

"I'm here now, and we will all need a meal. I'd feel better if you let me start right away."

"You'll get no argument from me. Poke around the pantry and the kitchen. As soon as you want to shop, either Henry or I will take you. There's a tub and running water in the water closet across the hall. Also a small coal stove to heat a kettle of hot water. I'll start the stove now."

"I can't imagine I'll want for anything." The accommodations were far more luxurious than anything she was used to.

Henry entered with her bag. He set it down and used a hammer he'd brought along to remove the lids from the crates. Once he'd finished, she thanked him and he exited silently.

"Tessa will help you unpack." Ben Charles turned and left the room, closing the door behind him.

Tessa studied the door with an uncertain expression.

"You don't have to stay." Violet sensed her discomfort and she wondered how Tessa felt about Violet coming to live in their home. "I can take care of my things if you want to run along."

The girl took a few steps into the center of the room. "I don't mind."

She remained quiet as Violet opened the bag and stacked clothing on the bed.

"That's a pretty watch," she said finally, as Violet placed her undergarments in a drawer.

Violet stopped to touch the timepiece she wore. "It was my mother's."

"Has she passed on?"

Her brother had used the same phrase. "Yes."

"My mother passed on when I was a baby. And I was only two when my father died."

"You were still just a baby," Violet said. "Your brother raised you?"

She nodded. "We had Mrs. Gable to take care of us until a few months ago. Her sister got sick, and she went to take care of her family."

"Was this her room?"

"No, she stayed downstairs. Ben Charles said this room hasn't been used much at all. He painted the ceiling and had the wallpaper replaced."

Violet took out several books and a few framed pictures she'd wrapped in clothing.

"Are those of your family?"

"I don't have any likenesses of my parents. These are pictures of horses I saved from magazines. I'd like to hang them on the wall if you don't think your brother would mind."

"I'm sure he wouldn't." Once Violet had set down the frames, Tessa looked at the pictures. "You're fond of horses?"

Violet nodded. "They're incredible animals."

"There are several in the stable." Tessa stepped to the window. "There are two in the corral now."

Violet joined her and held back the curtain to gaze out at the horses. "Both are black."

"They're all black. Ben Charles says they look smart pulling the hearse."

Violet let go of the curtain.

"Surely after your trip you're ready for a bath. I'll go check on the hot water and fill the tub," Tessa said.

The best part of her bath was warming her feet. Violet could have stayed in the tub the rest of the day, but the water cooled and she finished bathing. Less than an hour later she let her hair dry by the fire before dressing and making her way to the kitchen. She carried her stack of white aprons, in hopes of finding a convenient place to store them.

Though the house was forty years old, the kitchen held the original charm, but boasted an icebox and two electric pendant lights hanging from the ceiling. Violet tested one by turning the key above the bulb. Incandescent light filled the room. In the town where she'd come from, only stores had used electric lighting.

Turning, she discovered a stove she'd seen only in the Montgomery Ward & Co. catalog. With shiny chrome edges and ornate trim, the range was conveniently waist high with a reservoir in the back and a narrow shelf above. She hoped it wasn't fueled by gas. She'd read about those and the idea didn't sit well. Hesitantly she checked behind, to her relief seeing nothing out of the ordinary. She had enough new things to learn. On closer inspection she found ashes inside and a supply of evenly cut wood in a cubby on the brick wall. The supply could be stocked from a small door on the outside.

Through a long window she surveyed the tidy dooryard, spotting no garden or any type of animal. After familiarizing herself with cupboards and the pantry, she made a list. In one cupboard she discovered a row of shapely narrow bottles filled with dark liquid, and recognized the cola drink from magazine advertisements.

"A refreshment is in order after your journey."

She turned at Ben Charles's voice. He wore dark trousers, with galluses crossing his shoulders over a white shirt. His hair looked as though he'd run his fingers through it in lieu of a comb. He seemed more approachable this way, less severe. She had an inappropriate urge to reach up and push a lock of hair from his forehead. Her fingers tingled, so she clasped her hands. "Perhaps a cup of tea," she answered.

"Tea if you prefer. Or you might join me in a glass of cola?"

She wanted to taste the drink. "Yes, thank you."

"Grab a couple of glasses." He took a pick and mallet from atop the icebox, opened the insulated door and knelt to chip ice.

Violet brought him a bowl, and studied his wide flexing shoulders as he filled the bowl with ice slivers, then stood and filled both glasses. He'd lifted her crates as though they were light as a feather, which she knew they weren't. With a bottle opener he took from a nail inside a cupboard door, he removed the metal caps. The hissing sound surprised her as much as the mist that rose from inside the bottles.

Ben Charles filled both glasses halfway and foam rose on the surfaces of the liquid. After waiting a moment he filled them the rest of the way and handed her a glass.

She met his gray-green gaze for a moment, before taking the drink. Her fingertips brushed his, warm against the cold glass.

The bubbles tickled her nose before she could get her lips to edge of the glass. Startled, she drew back.

Her employer lifted his glass and took a long swallow, his Adam's apple bobbing above the collar of his white shirt.

Violet took a dainty sip, blinked at the carbonation and then drank a swallow. The overpowering bite and syrupy sweetness took her by surprise. Her eyes watered. "Oh, my."

Ben Charles grinned, his full mouth inching into a smile that revealed his teeth and an appealing dimple in his cheek. "Is this your first cola?"

"You must think me very unsophisticated."

"Your reaction is charming." He nodded toward the pantry. "Did you find the supplies adequate?"

"I'll need a few things, but for the most part the pantry is well stocked."

"Good. The iceman comes by every other day, and the dairy truck stops early each morning. Set the empty bottles outside the back door the night before. When you need wood replenished, leave Henry a message on the chalkboard."

Violet noted the wood-framed chalkboard near the door. "Everything seems quite efficient."

"Things run smoothly when they're organized. Having you here is going to take a big load from my shoulders. I'm not much of a cook." He finished his drink. "Can you manage supper with what's here?"

"Yes, of course. I'll shop tomorrow. I was wondering…"

"What were you wondering?"

"If it might be possible to keep a few chickens."

He appeared to think for only a moment. "I don't see why not. If you want to take care of them."

"I wouldn't mind. I need eggs to make good coffee."

He looked at her with a puzzled expression. "Coffee?"

"Äggkaffe," she explained. "I learned from my Swedish father how to make coffee."

"All right. As weather permits I'll see about constructing a coop out of the wind."

"What time would you prefer to have your supper?" she asked.

"We're used to eating at six."

She gave a nod to confirm. "Six it shall be."

"I'll leave you to your work," he said. "If you need anything, Tessa is no doubt still upstairs reading and I'll be right next door." He set his glass in the basin, and pointed to a door she'd assumed led to a cellar. "Through there."

He strode to the door and opened it. Violet imagined cold dank air seeping from the other side, but all she saw was a chalkboard just like the one in this room before he closed the door and was gone from sight.

A shiver ran up her spine.

A connecting door.

Everything about her new job had seemed so perfect only moments ago. But now she knew there was a door connecting the place where she'd be spending the majority of her time to the funeral parlor.

Somehow she had to learn to ignore that door and

do her job. It was her only choice. Back in Ohio there were people who believed she'd started a fire that had destroyed the bakery where she'd worked.

Her employer had made it clear a year ago that he wanted her to marry his son. Wade Finney had been in trouble so many times, Violet had lost count. He constantly caused an uproar at a local establishment or came to work reeking of alcohol and stale tobacco. Sometimes his friends showed up during work hours and enticed him away from his job. Wade was trouble and she'd held no intentions of marrying him, but his father had constantly pressured her to give Wade a chance. All he needed was a good woman to settle him down, he'd say.

Wade was an only child and Mr. Finney had reminded her often that the bakery would go to his son and whomever he married. While Violet wanted nothing more than to own her own bakery, a life with Wade wasn't an incentive.

And Wade hadn't wanted any part of her either. He despised the bakery and everything related to it including her. On that fateful night only weeks ago he'd climbed the side of the boarding house where she'd been staying, broken her window and burst into her room.

Violet had been terrified that he'd come to hurt her. He'd been drinking, and his threats had held a tone she'd never heard before. He'd grabbed her by the hair and yanked her to the window. In the moonlight thick smoke had curled into the night sky above the bakery two blocks away. "You soaked your apron with kerosene and used the matches you keep in your bin. You hate me enough to burn down the bakery."

"I didn't! I've been right here."

"There are witnesses who saw you near the building only moments ago. My father will believe you set the fire."

Violet's heart had pounded in terror and confusion. "Why?"

"Get dressed," he hissed. "Do you have a bag? I'll send the rest of your things to the station in Pittsburgh. Send for them using the name Tom Robbins."

Trembling, she'd taken the dress she'd pressed from a hook. "Turn around. Why are you doing this?"

While she'd dressed he had taken her clothing from the bureau drawers and had shoved it into the valise, then had held up the bag and swept the surfaces with his arm, dumping her belongings into a jumble on top.

She'd perched on the chair and hurriedly pulled on her stockings and boots.

He'd grabbed her hand and roughly shoved something into it. "I'm not going to marry you. I'm not going to be stuck in that bakery for the rest of my life."

"I never had any intention of marrying you."

"But you were too cowardly to tell my father that. He'd have convinced you eventually."

"No. No, I—"

"Buy a ticket to somewhere far away. They put people who start fires in jail."

Violet had stood in the alley behind her boarding-house, tears streaming down her face. Lights had come on in the windows, and at first she'd thought other boarders had heard the commotion in her room and on the stairs, but as her head had cleared the sounds of people in the street had alerted her. The fire had been discovered.

And Wade was going to make sure everyone believed

she was responsible. For a confused moment she'd considered staying and pleading her innocence. She hadn't done it—surely the truth would come to light.

A window had opened overhead, and a voice had called down. "Violet? Is that you? What are you doing in the alley?"

She'd been standing in the dark with her bags packed for flight. Like a guilty person.

Violet had turned and run.

Now she had no choice but to make this work. Either make a go of it here or leave and hope for something else. She glanced around the Hammonds' kitchen, her gaze touching on a glass-front cabinet filled with blue-and-white plates and platters. She took in the long uncovered window that let in the light, her aprons stacked on the table.

After starting the stove, she pumped water into a kettle and set it to heat for dishwater, then found a drawer in the pantry and stored her aprons.

She could do this. She *would* do this. She had no other choice.

Chapter Two

In his bright sunlit office Ben Charles ran his finger down a column in the open ledger on his desk. The numbers weren't adding up today, and the problem was due to the pretty little distraction he'd picked up at the train station.

He'd prayed about hiring someone to help out after Mrs. Gable had resigned to care for her sister. The woman had been with them since Tessa's childhood. She'd been a part of his and Tessa's little family. He'd been sorry to see her go, and not only because of her cooking and housekeeping abilities. Her cheerful countenance had been sorely missed these past few months. Tessa needed another female around.

He'd been impressed with Violet's replies to his ad, but after meeting her he wasn't confident she had the maturity he'd been counting on. He had a good ten years on her, if not more. Only time would tell if she had what it took to run the place—or the stamina to stay. If God had directed her to them as he'd prayed, then Ben Charles had to believe she would work out. He and Tessa had both grown up in a home where the undertaker lived and worked. For Ben Charles it had been his father, for Tessa that figure was himself. The way they lived was normal to them. A death meant carrying out the duties required for a service and a respectful burial. There was nothing uncomfortable or repelling about it.

In his experience people appreciated his calling and stuck closer than brothers during their time of need. But as for friends and marriage prospects, they kept their distance.

Only once had he thought he'd met someone who understood his work and who would make a good companion. He'd been very young, very naive. Madeline had been interested, but only in a perversely curious fashion. He'd been an oddity, someone her friends whispered about, someone with whom keeping company drew attention, and she'd liked that.

Afterward he'd even wondered if she'd shown interest on a dare, if, after their evenings together, there had been curious inquiries. While hope had sprung to life in his heart, he'd been no more than a passing peculiarity to her. She'd married a banker and moved to Denver. And he'd learned his lesson. He stuck to business, devoted himself to his sister and his work, and didn't aspire to be like other people.

At five-forty he closed his ledger, capped the bottle of ink and headed next door. The smells emanating from the kitchen made his stomach growl. He'd missed a meal at noon and eaten only a handful of pecans at his desk.

Violet started when he entered the room through the connecting door. "Sorry," he said.

"I didn't know whether to set this table or the one in the dining room, so I set that one for you and your sister, and I set places for Henry and me in here."

He glanced at the two plates on the long wooden

table. "Unless you prefer to eat in here, I'd rather you join us in the dining room."

Her expression showed her surprise.

"Is that a problem?" he asked.

"No, sir. It's just—well, employees eating with the family is unusual."

"We're an unusual family." He dipped water from the reservoir into a small pitcher. "I'll be back down in just a few minutes." He climbed the narrow back stairs.

Tessa wasn't in her favorite place at the other end of the hall near the front stairs, so he called out.

She poked her head from her room. "I'm ready for dinner."

A few minutes later, washed and wearing his jacket, Ben Charles pulled out Tessa's seat and waited for Violet to return and take hers. She blushed as he held her chair. "Everything looks and smells delicious."

"It's only scalloped potatoes and ham. Not much effort involved in opening a jar of green beans. I did make biscuits when I saw the crock of honey."

Henry had seated himself before Ben Charles had entered the room, and his expression showed appreciation for the feast on the table.

Ben Charles reached for Tessa's hand and she took his immediately. Henry bowed his head. Violet looked from one to the other, then followed their lead.

"Thank You for Your generous provision, Lord," Ben Charles prayed. "We're thankful for Miss Bennett's safe journey and her presence here at our table and in our home. I pray her transition into this household is smooth and that she feels welcome."

He was praying about her? The only person Violet remembered hearing pray was the reverend who performed her father's burial service, and his stilted language had sounded nothing at all like the conversational tone Ben Charles was using to speak to God. The heat creeping into her cheeks would no doubt give away her embarrassment at being singled out.

"Keep us healthy, Lord," he continued. "And bless the abundance of this food to the nourishment of our bodies. We humble ourselves in Your presence and rejoice in Your grace and mercy. It's in Jesus's name we pray. Amen."

"Amen," Tessa and Henry chorused. Henry picked up his fork. Tessa spread her napkin on her lap. Violet was slow to raise her head, and when she did, she didn't meet Ben Charles's eyes. She leaned forward to serve the casserole.

Ben Charles inhaled the aroma of the steaming creamy potatoes on his plate. "Where did you learn to cook like this, Miss Bennett?"

"Both of my parents were excellent cooks," she replied. "My mother worked for a family for years, and when I was small she took me with her. As she cooked she used to share stories about her family and her childhood. All her recipes were in her head, and she'd add a pinch of this or a handful of that as she talked."

Tessa gave her an encouraging smile. "Those sound like good memories."

"They are. My father was a baker. After Mama died and there were only the two of us, I helped him before and after school. Father was precise and businesslike while he measured and mixed."

"Your parents are no longer living?" Ben Charles asked.

She set her fork on her plate and sat with her hands in her lap. For a moment he didn't think she'd answer, but then she said, "Mother has been gone since I was small. My father became ill several years ago. He was forced to sell the bakery and I took care of him. After his death nearly two years ago I worked for the man who bought our bakery...until recently when—when it closed."

The pain of her loss was plain in her voice and expression. "It's always difficult to lose a parent, whether we're children or not." He took a sip from his water glass and glanced at Henry. "Miss Bennett will need to shop. If weather permits tomorrow, please have the carriage ready in the morning."

"Yessir. It snowed some this afternoon, but nothing to keep us from going out."

"Tessa, it might be nice if you joined Miss Bennett."

His sister quirked an eyebrow. "To buy food?"

He'd had this sort of thing in mind when he'd hired Violet, and he might as well start pushing his plan now. "Maybe there's something else you need. You might introduce her to the seamstress. You two can look at fabric and buttons or whatever it is ladies do."

Tessa and Violet exchanged a glance. "Yes, of course," Tessa replied.

"Do you live here, too?" Violet asked Henry.

"No, I have a place at the south end of town. Sometimes I bunk here if the weather's bad, but not often." He helped himself to another heaping serving of the potatoes and ham. "You're a fine cook, Miss Bennett."

A quick smile lit her features, bringing a new sparkle to her eyes.

Her smile was gone too soon. Ben Charles considered how to elicit one himself, and then realized what he'd been thinking. He used the opportunity sitting across from her to enjoy an assessing look. Her dark hair was sleek and shiny, and she wore it loosely contained on the back of her head, with practical tortoise-shell combs holding it away from her face behind each ear.

Her narrow brows arched gracefully above expressive dark eyes fringed with black lashes. Her ivory skin was a becoming contrast. Her appearance might easily lead one to think she was delicate, but the air of confidence and strength with which she handled herself hinted otherwise. He admired the courage she'd shown by coming to a place she'd never been to work for people she'd never met.

She lifted her gaze. "I didn't have time to prepare a dessert. But there are jars of peaches, and I hoped one of those might do."

"Sounds perfect," he replied. "We can get to know each other better over coffee." He glanced at Tessa. "And tea."

Tessa gave him an affectionate smile that said she appreciated his attention to her preference for hot sweet tea. She spent too much time by herself, and he hoped Violet's presence was going to change that. Though she'd kept much of her unhappiness to herself, she'd been teased and shunned in school, due to living beside the funeral parlor. Once he'd learned the extent of the cruel treatment, he'd removed her immediately and sent her to a boarding school out East.

She'd been painfully homesick and begged him to let her come home—and so of course he had. A tutor came four days a week to guide his sister with her studies.

Violet served the peaches, steaming cups of coffee, and placed a Wedgwood teapot filled with steeping tea within Tessa's reach.

Ben Charles sweetened his coffee and turned his attention to Violet. "You must be tired after digging right in as soon as you arrived."

"I'm thankful to have this job."

"You said the bakery where you worked closed?"

She stood and refilled Henry's cup, then glanced at Ben Charles's, which was still full. "The tea should be done."

Tessa filled her cup. "It smells good."

Violet had changed the subject, and he surmised that closing what had once been her father's business was an uncomfortable topic. He sipped his coffee thoughtfully. "Is there anything you want to ask us? I want you to feel at ease."

Her cheeks were flushed, probably from her chores and the tension of serving her first meal. At last she lifted her gaze to his. There was deep vulnerability in the dark abyss of her eyes, an uncertainty that touched his heart. The same bone-deep protectiveness he felt toward his sister reached its possessive arms toward her.

She wanted to say something, so he waited.

At last she parted her lips to speak. "What time would you like breakfast served?"

He drew on inner reserves to find a shred of detachment, which had never been his strength. "Henry and I will eat in the kitchen at six. Tessa usually wakes later, so keep a plate warm for her."

This relationship wouldn't work if he couldn't keep his objectivity. He could already see the flaw in that plan.

Everything about Violet intrigued him.

Chapter Three

A night's sleep stretched out on the comfortable bed in sublime relaxation did wonders. Violet was rested and had breakfast on the table at six. She sat to share the meal with the men, and had finished eating when a loud chime rang from the front hallway.

Ben Charles pushed back his chair and stood. "That's the bell next door. I'll get it."

He returned a few minutes later. "Guy Chapman passed on during the night."

A death.

Violet strove to keep her composure, but panic rose in her chest. A myriad of sensory images—memories—curled around her heart like a squeezing fist. She forced her body to relax and she took several slow deep breaths.

Ben Charles resumed his seat. "That was his son. I'll need you to assist me in bringing him back this morning," he said to Henry. He glanced at Violet. "We won't be but an hour. Henry will return and drive you to town."

He spoke of their chore in a matter-of-fact manner, not at all as though they were headed out to do something unpleasant. This was his work. She had to get used to it. After the men had gone, Violet did her best not to think about their task, but she happened to glance out the back window as a pair of the magnificent horses pulled a long black hearse from the carriage house. After that she avoided the windows, in case she might glimpse their return.

Tessa arrived to nibble at the bacon and a piece of toast while they waited. "Who passed on?" she asked.

It was only a conversation. She was in a warm kitchen, safe and sound. "Someone by the name of Guy Chapman."

She nodded. "I went to school with his granddaughter."

"Were you friends?"

Tessa poured tea into a cup. "I can't say we were. She was one of the girls who made a show out of avoiding me as though I had a disease."

Violet studied her with surprise. "Why did they avoid you?"

"I'm sure you can figure it out."

Taken aback by her reply, Violet considered the girl's words for a moment. "Because of your brother's occupation?"

"And the fact that we live here. Some people think it's morbid."

"I suppose they do." Violet thought of Tessa as a child, and tried to imagine what she'd experienced.

"They taunted us and called my father and Ben Charles hatchet men and body snatchers, things like that."

"That's cruel. So you don't attend school any longer?"

Tessa shook her head. "Ben Charles removed me. He sent me to a boarding school, but I was homesick and begged him to let me come back. He rode the train all the way to Pennsylvania to get me."

"He loves you very much."

Tessa looked up from her cup, thoughtfully. "Yes, he does." She shrugged. "I don't really care what others think of us. Ben Charles is happy doing what he does, and I'm happy living here with my books."

The connecting door opened, and Violet jumped a foot from the seat of her chair.

"The wagon's ready," Henry called.

"We'll be out front in a moment," Tessa replied.

Violet took a deep breath to calm her racing heart and stacked their cups beside the enamel dishpan. "I forgot to ask. How do I pay for the purchases?"

"We have accounts at the stores," Tessa replied.

"I'll just get my coat and boots."

The sky was blustery, and the wagon offered no protection from the bitter-cold wind. Even though they huddled behind the seat, Violet tied a wool scarf over her face and Tessa held her rabbit fur muffler to her nose and mouth the entire way.

Their first stop was the mercantile, where Violet handed her list to the man who greeted them. "Ben Charles told me he'd hired a new cook," the bald man said. "I expected you'd be older."

Amused, she smiled. "I'm Miss Bennett. Pleased to meet you. Henry will load our items."

She and Tessa browsed the aisles, adding a few things to their purchases. A group of white-haired men sat around a potbellied stove. "That you, Tessa Hammond?" one of them called.

Tessa introduced Violet to the gathering.

"Heard old Guy went to glory durin' the night," Frank Turner said with a shake of his head. "Is he out at your place?"

"Ben Charles is attending Mr. Chapman now," Tessa told the elderly man in a comforting voice.

The old man nodded. "Yeah. Old Guy never liked the cold weather much. His bones was achin' something fierce this winter. Think he'd a had the sense to die durin' the summer."

Tessa didn't respond to that, but she nodded and said her goodbyes.

"Tell Ben Charles to take real good care of Guy now."

"I'll do that."

Tessa and Violet stood near the door, pulling on their gloves and scarves. "They seem to like you just fine," Violet whispered.

Tessa met her eyes. "They're older. They've had more experience getting to know our family. And no doubt they see the inevitability of needing an undertaker sooner than later."

Violet blinked, but after her initial surprise Tessa's deduction made sense. "Where to now?"

"The seamstress is down a few doors." Tessa led the way out.

Marcella Wright seemed surprised to see Tessa. "You bought a new wardrobe before you went off to school, so either you've grown or you've brought your friend for measurements."

She made introductions. "Violet needs a few dresses."

Violet's cheeks warmed and her gaze skittered to Tessa's.

"My brother instructed me to make sure you ordered several."

"Let me have your coats." Marcella asked Violet to step behind a screen and remove her dress, so she could measure her. Violet had purchased a few ready-made dresses, but she'd sewn the rest of her clothing, so this process was foreign.

"It's all right," Tessa encouraged.

Violet stood straight as the woman took measurements and recorded them in a slim journal. A fire crackled in a woodstove, keeping the little shop warm.

"Now for fabrics and colors," Marcella said, with an excited smile. "I have ideas for combinations that will go with your lovely dark hair and eyes. What is your ancestry, dear?"

Violet touched the bolt of fabric the woman pulled out. "My father was Swedish."

"That explains the faint accent, but not your hair or skin."

"Well, my mother's mother came from Ireland."

"Yes, yes, of course. Tessa, I'm thinking of the dress we made you with the puffed sleeves and the gathered bodice. The skirt is chocolate sateen and the bodice a soft ivory. That style would look lovely on Miss Bennett, but with a spring-green skirt and a print blouse and sleeves. The tails of a faux demijacket nestled at her hips would be striking, don't you think?"

Violet agreed with a nod. "It sounds lovely."

"And you definitely need something in a rose-red," she said to Violet. "I have the perfect princess pattern. The skirt would be a solid, the sleeves and yoke in embroidered sateen, with fitted forearms—and fur at the collar, I'd say. The front buttons up on one side, rather than down the center. I'd add a snip of fur on a matching hat, as well."

Marcella's eyes shone with excitement as she described styles and fabrics. She showed Violet a pattern from an afternoon dress she'd been wanting to create, but she hadn't known the appropriate lady to carry it off.

Everything she mentioned sounded expensive, but Tessa didn't blink an eye. When Marcella went to her stockroom for trim and buttons, Violet whispered, "I don't know about the expense of all these dresses on your brother's account. I'm only the cook, and I've just arrived. I haven't earned my way yet. I don't know that I'll ever earn enough to pay for all this."

"Ben Charles said not to let you leave without ordering dresses for church and shopping and social events."

It seemed like a lot of fancy clothing for a cook.

"You're part of our household now," Tessa told her, as though she knew Violet's thoughts. "You represent the Hammonds."

Violet had never imagined the prestige of her new position. While part of her was uncomfortable with this treatment, another side of her was childishly thrilled with the attention and acceptance. She wanted to be worthy of the Hammonds' faith in her.

That afternoon Violet put away all the supplies and took another look at the pantry and each of the items it held. Delighted to discover three cookbooks, she pored over the recipes, making notes. She prepared the turkey she'd purchased from the butcher by brushing it with oil and rubbing it with thyme before roasting it in the oven. While the bird baked, she prepared stuffing with leeks and wild mushrooms, cooked corn pudding and made cranberry-walnut relish. Her rolls turned out perfectly, and she stored them until supper.

The sideboard and cabinets in the dining room held tablecloths, heavy silver, ornate trays and enough dishes to serve a banquet. She set the table and trudged out in the cold to find evergreen boughs, graceful twigs and berries for the centerpiece. After adding candles, she stood back and admired her handiwork.

She checked her timepiece, removed the turkey from the oven and ran upstairs to change.

"There will be one more for supper," Ben Charles said as he passed through the kitchen a few minutes later. "Hugh Senior is helping me today, and I've invited him to join us." He stopped before he reached the stairs. "Something smells awfully good."

"Probably the turkey," she replied.

Hugh Senior was a man several years older than Ben Charles, but his hair was still dark. Ben Charles explained simply that the man helped him on occasion. As each person entered the dining room, his or her face showed surprise and delight at the feast.

Tessa stared until Ben Charles pulled out her chair and prompted her to sit, so the men could take their places.

"I haven't seen the table look like this since my mother used to set it," Ben Charles told her. "These were her things."

"I hope it was all right to use them," Violet said uncertainly.

"It was more than all right," he replied quickly. "What use are nice things if they're not enjoyed? The china has been gathering dust."

"Oh, I washed everything," Violet was quick to assure him.

"I had no doubt."

Ben Charles sliced the turkey, and Violet spooned cranberry relish over each serving as the plates were distributed. They passed the other bowls and the basket of rolls before Ben Charles took Tessa's hand and prayed. "We lift up Gus Chapman's family to You, Lord," he said. "I ask that you bestow peace and comfort on them this day and in the days to come. Give them strength to trust You and abide in Your love during this difficult time."

Violet had never heard anyone speak to God the way Ben Charles did, as though God was a real person, as though He was listening and truly cared. *As though his prayer made a difference.*

Her employer's genuine concern for the family of the deceased man unexplainably touched her. Peace and comfort had been elusive commodities in her experience. What if someone had prayed those words for her when her parents died? *Would* it have made a difference? Could Ben Charles make the same request for her all these years after her mother's death or was there an expiration on petitioning God?

She didn't think about her mother often, yet she answered questions about her methodically, without letting memories invade the locked-off portion of her heart and mind where she kept pain and reality at bay. Ben Charles's words and example were a steel chisel prying at the seams of her guarded sanity.

She didn't like the feeling. But she liked being here.

Her supper was an enormous success, and she accepted praise for her efforts. "I don't know that you should have set the bar so high this soon," Ben Charles admonished with a grin. "Now we know what you're capable of doing."

"It's a pleasure to cook for someone who appreciates the effort," she answered. "It's no hardship to cook in your kitchen."

"You didn't have to eat any of the meals we fixed before you got here," Tessa said. "A fancy stove doesn't cook a good meal itself."

"You can ask me to work anytime you need help," Hugh Senior said to Ben Charles. "I ain't had a meal like this since Rosie and I ate at the hotel in Denver on our honeymoon." He set down his fork and ticked off numbers on his fingers. "Twenty-four years, it's been."

Violet raised her brows in surprise. "Now, that is a compliment, Mr. Senior. But don't let your wife hear you say that."

The men looked at each other with amusement. Finally Ben Charles said, "Hugh's last name is Crabtree. Everyone calls him Hugh Senior because his son's name is Hugh Junior."

"Pardon my mistake. Do you have other children?"

"Goodness, yes. Three others, plus two sons-in-law and three grandchildren. Hugh Junior is the youngest and my only boy."

"Hugh Junior has a way with horses," Henry said. "If ever there's a problem with one of Mr. Hammond's animals, Hugh Junior knows what to do."

They finished the meal and Violet served a warm cobbler she'd made from dried apples. Tessa declined her serving, but Henry raised his dessert plate for her portion.

Tessa helped with cleanup and dishes while the men

went next door. Violet was uncomfortable with the extravagant expenses of the clothing they'd ordered that day and hoped for a moment to speak about it with Ben Charles. She remained in the kitchen, her attention on the adjoining door, long after dark had enveloped the house. Using only an oil lamp on the table for light, her imagination took over with what lay beyond that door.

Finally it opened and her employer stepped into the kitchen. "Violet. You're still here."

"I was waiting to speak with you."

"You could have come found me."

Her gaze skittered to the door and back. "I preferred to wait. Did Mr. Crabtree go home?"

"Yes, quite a while ago."

"Would you like a cup of coffee?"

He glanced at the cold stove. "I'm fine, thanks. What did you want to talk about?"

"Tessa and I went shopping today, as you know."

He nodded.

"She let me know you wanted me to have several dresses."

"I hope you weren't offended. You may already have enough clothing."

"I don't have appropriate clothing, and I'm not offended. I understand I have a place in your household now and I should look my best in public."

"Were you able to select things you'll like?"

"Yes, of course. My concern is the cost. I've only begun to earn my keep and wages. I shall be indebted to you for the cost until I've been here long enough to repay it."

"I won't hear any more talk of indebtedness," he said.

"Our terms of your employment included food, lodging and clothing."

"I thought perhaps a few work dresses would be included, not such lovely—and expensive—things."

"Do you need work dresses, as well?"

"No, I can wear my own."

"All right. Your wages are your wages, Miss Bennett, to use any way you see fit. Food, a room and clothing are my concern. A position like this requires a sacrifice many women aren't willing or able to make. You've already relocated in an unfamiliar place. Your schedule will revolve around ours for as long as you're in my employ. You've made a big commitment to my family, and I don't take that lightly."

He made it sound as though she was doing him a favor, instead of the other way around. Of course he didn't know she'd never lived anywhere so nice or had as many choices for meals or used such efficient appliances. There wasn't a cook around who wouldn't move lock, stock and barrel to work in this home.

Still, it was an extravagant expense. "Well, then I thank you."

"Have you made yourself familiar with the rest of the house?" he asked.

She tried not to react, but a growing fear in the back of her mind wouldn't leave her alone. She'd fought the panic earlier, but she didn't dare get any closer to the place where he worked. If he wanted her to clean the rooms in the mortuary, she might have to leave.

Had she seen the entire house? "Not yet."

"You've barely had time to get settled. Maybe tomorrow you'll look around. We don't get the place dirty, so a little dusting is all that's needed most of the time.

Tessa takes care of her own room, but I would appreciate it if you dusted mine and changed sheets on the beds. You may send out bedding and clothing to be laundered. And, Violet?"

"Yes, sir?"

"Please make yourself at home. Use any room you care to and help yourself to the books. There is sufficient lighting in the parlor if you do needlework."

"Thank you, but…Mr. Hammond?"

He nodded to show he was listening.

Wind buffeted the panes of glass in the long window.

She took a deep breath. "Do my duties extend to cleaning next door at—at—where you work?"

"Goodness, no. Someone from town comes once a week to clean the mortuary—more often if we're especially busy. I should have thought to tell you that. I wasn't thinking."

Relief washed over her at his reply. Once he'd said good-night and gone upstairs, she poured herself a pitcher of warm water and turned down the wick until the oil lamp snuffed out. She felt as though she'd escaped the guillotine. She didn't think there was enough money in the Carson Springs bank to get her to clean the funeral home.

When she reached the upstairs hallway, she paused before the door to her room. Voices came from the other end, where the library was, as brother and sister conversed pleasantly. She listened for a moment, not eavesdropping, but learning about their family. Ben Charles chuckled, and the deep sound resonated to where she stood, creating an empty ache in her chest.

She admired what they shared. She mourned for the loss of family. They had lost parents, too, but they had each other. Something she would never know. She let herself into her room and turned on the light using the wall switch. Lamps on either side of the door lit the room.

She admired the relationship between Ben Charles and Tessa. Other siblings she'd observed had been young and squabbled most of the time. Perhaps the difference in their ages made a difference. Surely him taking on the responsibility of raising her had changed everything. Ben Charles was devoted to his young sister. Violet thought of how they held hands as he prayed for their meals. Tessa spoke of him with pride and honor, as she would a beloved father. She looked at him with love and respect in every glance. Theirs was an enviable relationship.

Violet may not have had anything comparable in her life, but she had other things to appreciate. Her employer and his sister were kind and gracious. It seemed this job was hers for as long as she wanted it. Her room was cozy and felt like home already. And she didn't have to dust the dark side.

She felt bad for thinking of it like that, but when she thought of what Ben Charles did next door, her attitude darkened and her imagination ran amok. His occupation obviously provided a luxurious home and many comforts for his sister and employees—and he seemed to genuinely enjoy what he did.

That didn't mean she would ever be comfortable with his profession or the mortuary next door, but it didn't look as though he was going to force a closer proximity on her. She was happy right here, and she had no intention of getting any closer.

As long as the situation remained as it was, she was going to do just fine.

Chapter Four

Violet didn't want to disappoint her employer, who plainly took for granted she'd be going to church. She had no idea how to decide which one to attend, so if a man like Ben Charles attended the Carson Springs First Christian Church, she figured it must be all right. She wore the dress she'd traveled in, because it was the newest, and she took special care with her hair. She had saved a tiny hat that had belonged to her mother, so she pulled it from its box and adjusted it on her hair, securing it with a long pin.

Violet studied her reflection in the mirror, trying to remember what her mother had looked like, wondering if she resembled her. She had only a few mementos and had been fearful she'd never see them again, after her unexpected flight from Ohio.

Her belongings had been stored, awaiting her arrival, when she'd used the name Wade Finney had given her to claim them. While she was still angry and resentful, she was thankful for that small favor. The fistful of money he'd thrust at her had been enough to pay for a room until she found a job, to buy a few pieces of

clothing for travel and to send telegrams. Ben Charles
had paid for her train tickets and wired her money for
expenses to get here.

Already the fire seemed so long ago. She and her
father had both grieved over selling the shop to the
Finneys and now it had gone up in smoke. At least her
father hadn't lived to see the destruction. Violet got her
coat and carried it downstairs.

She'd made biscuits the night before, so they each
ate one with a cup of tea before heading out. It had
snowed again during the night, and in a few places the
snow had drifted over the road. More than once Ben
Charles took a shovel from the boot and made a path for
the horse. The main street through Carson Springs had
been cleared, making the rest of the trip less difficult.

Ben Charles removed his hat as they entered the
church, and his hair was damp from exertion. He took
a handkerchief from inside his jacket and wiped his
forehead, then hung their coats in a cloakroom before
coming back and escorting them into the sanctuary.

A few older men spoke to Ben Charles as they made
their way forward. About halfway toward the front of
the narrow building, he stepped aside and ushered them
into a row of pews, Tessa leading the way. Violet sat between brother and sister and studied her surroundings.

Sun shone through the stained-glass windows on one
wall and reflected color across the polished pews as well
as the heads and shoulders of the people seated in the
front rows. The scenes depicted were robed men and
women, what she recognized as shepherds, the nativity,
the crucifixion. As she looked at each one, she realized
there was an order, beginning with the ten command-

ments, but she didn't know what the loaves of bread or the men on the fishing boat stood for.

The first strains of organ music caught her attention and she straightened to see who was playing the lovely music.

Glancing aside, she caught Ben Charles watching her. Warmth crept up her cheeks.

"Is this different from where you attended church?" he asked.

"Very different." She attempted to look away and let the subject drop, but the lie of omission wouldn't let her keep silent. She looked up into his kind and compassionate eyes. "To be honest, I've never been to church before."

His surprise was evident in his expression. "I hope you enjoy it. If you have any questions, I'll be glad to answer them afterward."

She nodded and averted her gaze just as two rows of burgundy-robed men and women filed in from a side door and stood behind the podium.

The preacher joined them before the seated congregation. "Shall we all rise?"

He prayed, but not as conversationally as Ben Charles did. When he'd finished, he sat and the choir led the congregation in songs. It was obvious Ben Charles and Tessa had sung them many times, because they barely looked at the music book the three of them shared, but Violet followed along with the words.

Ben Charles's nearness beside her as they sang unnerved her. He had a pleasant singing voice, and the barely discernible scents of his woodsy soap and shaving cream pleased her senses. She tried not to be distracted by his hand holding the book or his arm brushing her shoulder, but it was impossible. He was larger than life and because of that his presence took up more space and air than the average person.

The preacher talked about Moses, and Ben Charles turned to the story in the front of his Bible. He held it so Violet could see, too. She listened with fascination as the man spoke of the pharaoh who kept the Israelites in bondage to his will, and how God called on Moses to lead the people to freedom. The man had a gift for storytelling, and Violet sat enthralled as he related how the pharaoh's chariots chased the Israelites and the sea parted to let them escape, then closed behind them, swallowing up the enemies in pursuit.

Occasionally she looked at Ben Charles's Bible to see that the preacher was indeed relating the story as it unfolded there.

After another song the service ended. A few neighbors introduced themselves to Violet, and Ben Charles introduced her to the preacher, whom he called Reverend Densmore.

"You're welcome to join us for lunch," Ben Charles told Violet as they made their way through the path in the snow to the carriage. "But remember it's your day off, and you may do anything you please."

She didn't know anyone else yet, and she had no idea where she'd go, except back to the house alone. "I'd like to join you. Thank you for the invitation."

The dining room of the Conrad Hotel was decorated in warm tones, and a blazing fire burned in a huge stone fireplace. Sounds of glasses and silverware were muted by the massive beams overhead and velvet swag draperies tied back with gold cords.

A waiter brought them menus and Violet studied the meals listed and the prices.

"The roast chicken is always good," Tessa told her. "And the pot roast is tender. It's served with potatoes and carrots in a delicious gravy."

"What do you like?" she asked Ben Charles.

"I almost always get a steak or the trout. And their cook does something special with the fried potatoes that makes them crispy."

When the waiter returned she ordered the trout. They were served steaming bowls of dark onion soup while they waited for their meals.

"Was that story true?" she asked Ben Charles. "About Moses and the pharaoh?"

"I believe the Bible is the inspired Word of God and everything in it is true," he replied. "The men who recorded the happenings were the scholars of their time and wrote it all down as God led them. The Scripture was preserved over time. Scrolls were translated, and eventually type was set and the Bible printed into languages we can all understand."

"It's just kind of hard to imagine a sea opening up and letting six hundred thousand men walk through."

"Able-bodied men, the verses say," Ben Charles agreed. "Plus the children and all the women—probably old men who weren't able-bodied being carried. And their herds and flocks, and the spoils they'd taken from the Egyptians."

"Think of how long it must have taken to get across the sea," Violet said in awe.

"I read about that sea in my studies," Tessa spoke up. "It's known as the Sea of Aquaba now, but it was the Red Sea in the Old Testament. Men have discovered a three-mile-wide land bridge from one side of the sea to the other. Archaeologists suggest a strong wind held back a few feet of water temporarily." She glanced at her brother. "Remember when I showed that to you?"

Ben Charles nodded.

"Then perhaps the whole thing can be explained by natural means," Violet suggested.

Ben Charles smiled. "Archeologists know about that land bridge now, but God knew about it all along. He planned it at creation for such a time as He'd need it to save Moses and his people. I don't believe in coincidence. Even if He used natural means to save His people, God prepared the way supernaturally."

Violet had a lot of information to absorb. "It's all so fascinating."

"The story itself or how God planned ahead to save the Israelites?" Ben Charles asked.

"Both," she said with a smile. "This God of yours seems pretty amazing."

Ben Charles exchanged a glance with his sister. They both smiled at her.

A middle-aged couple stopped to speak with Ben Charles briefly. He introduced them to Violet. "We will see you tomorrow," the gentleman said as they departed.

"What's tomorrow?" Violet asked.

"Guy Chapman's funeral service and burial."

"The ground's not too frozen?" Tessa asked.

"Henry and his helpers were able to open the plot yesterday," he replied.

Violet's mood plummeted.

She finished her tea and folded her hands in her lap. She didn't want to know gruesome details of the burial.

As though he sensed her discomfort, Ben Charles

changed the subject, asking her if she cared for dessert. She was full, as was Tessa, so he paid the bill and they headed for the house.

"I hope snow holds off a day longer," he said as they sat huddled in a row on the seat of the buggy.

The heavy gray sky issued a warning.

"Is Mr. Chapman's family traveling?" Tessa asked.

"Only a son from Iowa, and he's already here," Ben Charles replied. "The rest of his family is close by."

The ride home went smoothly, since Ben Charles had already cleared the road for the horses on their way to church.

"I'll be reading," Tessa said once he assisted them down from the carriage.

He led the horses and buggy to the carriage house.

After hanging her coat and changing out of her good dress, Violet decided to look around the rest of the house. So far she'd only familiarized herself with the kitchen and dining room and the pantries. A formal sitting room at the front of the house was filled with ornate furniture, framed paintings, potted ferns and bric-a-brac. Violet assumed it had been decorated by Ben Charles's mother many years ago. After checking the dirt in which the ferns grew, she got a pitcher and made several trips, watering the thirsty plants.

Across the hall and farther down the hallway she discovered a massive pocket door. Initially she'd assumed this side of the house backed the funeral parlor, but since it didn't she rolled back the door and instead discovered another well-appointed room. This one held more comfortable sofas and chairs, paintings of floral arrangements, several colorful lithographs, a pianoforte and a massive stone fireplace.

On either side of the huge windows at the front were large open shelves displaying vases and busts and wood carvings of horses.

Violet liked the muted wallpaper, the geometric-patterned carpets and the glass bowls of shells and small stones. She'd never seen so many different types of shells and she studied several of them.

Seating herself on a comfortable sofa, she enjoyed the immense space and the care and detail that had gone into every object. The other was a formal room, perhaps for receiving guests, but this one felt welcoming and comfortable. Basking in the tranquility, she breathed deeply and closed her eyes. It had been a long time since she'd had a moment's peace like this.

Nearly half an hour had passed when footsteps alerted her to Ben Charles approaching from the hall-way. He entered the room and spotted her. "You must be chilly. I'll add a log to the fire."

"Now that you mention it, I guess it's a little cool in here. I was enjoying the room so much I really didn't notice."

He opened a hinged box near the stone fireplace and took out a good-size log, which he added to the fire. After he used the poker to arrange it, and added a few sticks, the flames licked around the log, sending their warmth into the room.

"Better?"

"Much. Thank you. I hope it's all right that I came in here."

"This is your home, Violet. That's why I told you to make yourself comfortable."

"No one could be anything but comfortable in this room. Did your mother decorate it?"

He glanced at the wall surrounding the fireplace. "No. Actually about five years ago I refurnished this room to be less formal and more peaceful."

"Well, you achieved that nicely. I admit I haven't been in another home as nice as yours, but I can't imagine anywhere more like a place of refuge."

"That's kind of you to say. Thank you." He brushed his palms together. "I didn't come to disturb you. I wanted to check on the fireplaces and see what was needed this afternoon."

"You're not disturbing me. If this is where you spend your Sunday afternoons, please don't let me displace you."

"I don't want you to feel as though you have no privacy."

"When I need privacy I'll go to my room. Which is another joy to occupy, I mean to assure you."

"If you'd like to make changes, feel free to do so. Is there anything you'd like to add or remove?"

"Perhaps a few shelves for my own books, if it isn't too much trouble."

"It's no trouble. Just show me what you'd like to see."

She sat forward. "I saved a photograph from a magazine. It shows shelves above the windows. If you think the idea is acceptable, I could pay for it myself."

He shook his head. "Show me the clipping and I'll see to it."

"I'll go get it right now." Halfway to the door, she paused. "If that's all right."

He waved her on. When she returned he was seated on one of the sofas, a large book open beside him. He took the picture from her. After a few minutes of discussion he asked her if he could keep the magazine page to show the carpenter. "He's the same fellow who did this room. He'll do a good job for us."

"I have a few framed pictures I'd like to hang in my room if that's all right with you."

"Perfectly all right."

Tessa joined them, carrying a tray loaded with a teapot and three cups. "Time for refreshment, don't you agree?"

She set the tray on a nearby table and served them.

Ben Charles watched Violet's demeanor change, and recognized she was uncomfortable with the role reversal. "We don't want to push ourselves on you, Violet," he said in a gentle tone.

Her dark gaze moved to his, and he read her uncertainty.

"Perhaps if you think of Sunday as a family day, and remember we want you as part of our family, you'll be more comfortable."

A flicker of pain crossed her features, but she quickly hid it. "I'll try."

Chapter Five

The afternoon sun streaming through the front windows enhanced the color of Violet's eyes, which always appeared so dark. In this light they were a rich deep mahogany, flecked with gold and green. The last thing Ben Charles wanted to do was impose on her and scare her off. Apparently she had no one else, and everyone needed a family. His might be small, but he and Tessa had a lot to offer.

"We have a new player to draw into our games?" his sister said as she settled beside Violet. The last word had ended on a higher note, indicating her question.

"I was hoping to make a good impression this first weekend," he replied with good humor. "Not send her packing."

"What games are you referring to?" Violet asked.

Tessa got up and took one of the game boards from the wall.

"I thought those were colorful lithographs," Violet said with surprise.

"They're game boards," Tessa replied. "This one is my favorite."

The game she referred to was 'Round the World with Nellie Bly. Tessa had loved to play this one since she was a child. "She's read Nellie Bly's book a dozen times," Ben Charles told Violet.

"Have you read it?" Tessa asked, her expression animated.

"Indeed I have," Violet answered. "I was twelve when she made headlines. My father and I followed her column in the *New York World* from the moment she left New Jersey, through the Mediterranean, across the Suez Canal and the Indian Ocean, to Japan, all the way until she arrived in New York City. It was the most exciting adventure a girl could imagine."

The pleasure on Tessa's face was worth a hundred Sunday afternoons of playing her game. "I was too young then to remember," she said. "But I read the newspaper accounts in the archives at the library."

Their conversation convinced Ben Charles once and for all that God had answered his prayers and sent Violet. Emotion spread throughout his chest, like a comforting emollient for a previously aching heart. *Thank You, Lord. Your mercies are indeed new every morning.*

"How do you play?" Violet asked.

From a cabinet Tessa gathered the spinner and worn wooden tokens and explained the simple forward and backward movement in the spiral of spaces. "This isn't Ben Charles's favorite game, but he indulges me."

Violet met his eyes, her appreciation and compassion obvious. She gave him a tentative smile that changed the warmth in his chest to something else. Something hotter and more surprising.

Something that didn't resemble appreciation in the least.

"What is your favorite game?" she asked.

"I don't mind a competitive game of croquet," he replied. "Weather permitting."

"I keep telling him there is a parlor croquet set in Mr. Levine's shop."

He grimaced. "If it must be a board game, then I prefer Carrom."

"You fling little disks across the board into pockets." Tessa wrinkled her nose the same way she had since she was five and pointed to one of the larger boards on the wall. "Did your family play games at home?"

"Only checkers," Violet answered.

"Maybe we could read *Around the World in Seventy-Two Days* together," Tessa suggested.

Violet didn't blink an eye. "I would enjoy that."

Ben Charles believed she meant it.

Violet joined the play with enthusiasm, and the two young women pointed out the details of the book at each space on the board. His sister's animation and smile gave him immense satisfaction. The game lasted a couple of hours, until he got hungry. "I'm going to go get us a tray of ham and cheese and bread."

"I can do that," Violet spoke up.

"It's your day off," he reminded her. "We're used to fending for ourselves on Sunday evenings. We can pop corn over the fire later."

It was obvious their routine and customs were new to Violet. He and his sister spent a lot of time alienated from others, but perhaps even in their seclusion they'd been more like a family than anything Violet had experienced.

They shared a simple meal, and later ate popcorn. Tessa played a few pieces on the pianoforte. When she'd finished she said to Violet, "I had a nice time. Thanks for joining the game."

"It was my pleasure."

Tessa kissed Ben Charles's cheek. "Thank you, too. And don't say it was your pleasure."

"It's my pleasure to see you happy."

She briefly pressed her cheek to his. "I'm going upstairs to read before bed. Good night."

Once she was gone, Violet stood and leaned over to gather their dishes on the tray. Without standing, Ben Charles extended his hand and placed it on her wrist. "I'll do that."

She looked at his hand, but he didn't remove it.

He should have.

She was new to their household. He intended for theirs to be a strictly working relationship, but he felt a constant need to assure her she was part of their family. He had no business changing their agreement or making her uncomfortable by letting new feelings get in the way.

She'd only been here a few days.

In those brief moments while her gaze moved from his hand to his face, he went over all the reasons why he needed to keep his distance.

But everything about Violet appealed to him and made him feel protective. He told himself he held only a brotherly concern, like that he felt for Tessa, but the lie didn't convince him.

She didn't pull her arm away. Her curious gaze searched his eyes and moved to his lips. His chest expanded with warmth, and he reminded himself to breathe.

He wanted to kiss Violet Bennett.

Kissing would definitely be inappropriate. She was in his employ.

"Was there something else you wanted?" she asked finally.

He released her wrist finally. "I'll carry that to the kitchen and bank the fire. Run along and get some rest."

His voice was gruffer than he'd intended.

She straightened, wished him a good-night and left the room. Once she was gone, he could breathe more easily. He had a long day ahead tomorrow, and he needed to rest, not stir up his thoughts and reactions to the new cook. He had more fortitude than that.

By midnight he questioned that reasoning.

Chapter Six

Ben Charles and Henry both came to breakfast dressed in black suits and white shirts. Violet couldn't help a second look at Ben Charles's neatly combed hair. He wore a ring with a gold letter on a flat black stone on his little finger. She'd never seen the piece of jewelry before. As she served his coffee, she noted the initial was a cursive *H*.

He smelled good, too—clean with a hint of barely discernible spice. She remembered the warmth of his fingers on her wrist the night before. She hadn't been able to sleep because of that touch. She'd lain awake thinking of the game the three of them had played and the smiles they'd shared. For brief moments during those hours she'd been able to forget she was alone in the world. In those minutes she'd felt accepted and like a part of something valuable.

This morning, seeing him in his funeral clothing ready to perform his duties, she was forced to remember how different the two of them were. She was curious now about the schedule and events, but too cowardly to speak of it.

Tessa surprised her by joining them, dressed in a lovely black dress with pouf sleeves. A sash belted her waist, the tail of the bow streaming down the front of the skirt. Up close, intricate silver-gray embroidery was visible on the bodice. Tessa would be attending the funeral?

As if recognizing Violet's puzzlement, she spoke up. "I help arrange the flowers and chairs in the family room, and I greet family and friends as they arrive." She glanced at her brother. "If a need arises, Ben Charles lets me know and I'm there to handle it."

"You didn't know Guy, but the service is at ten if you care to attend," Ben Charles told her. "Don't worry about our noon meal. There will be food served after the burial. You're welcome to join us."

Just the thought made Violet's heart beat more quickly. She didn't know how people could eat after something like that. "Thank you, but I'll stay here."

"That's fine." Ben Charles finished his second cup of coffee.

"There was a moose on the road this morning," Henry said.

"Male or female?" Ben Charles asked.

"Male. He wasn't inclined to move either."

"Will you check the road again before ten?" Ben Charles asked. "We don't want that animal hindering our guests' arrival." He looked to Violet. "If you go out of doors for any reason, keep an eye out. This time of year the moose can be aggressive. They're hungry and traveling a long way to look for food. They see humans as threats and will attack."

She nodded her understanding.

After they'd gone and she'd washed the dishes, she

wondered if she'd done the right thing by insisting she stay here. Ben Charles hadn't seemed perturbed by her decision, and it wasn't part of her job to attend events at the mortuary.

It was Monday, and as such it was a good day to change bedding, gather the laundry and do some extra cleaning, especially since she didn't have to plan and cook a meal midday.

Upon entering Ben Charles's room, her attention was immediately drawn to an enormous stuffed owl perched on a branch atop a round table in the middle of the room. Its eyes seemed to follow her as she stepped around it, a chill spreading up her spine. The room was functional, with heavy pieces of furniture and a collection of feathers under a piece of glass on a long table. She changed the sheets, then dusted and swept the floor.

Tessa's room was as cheerful as her own, with lacy curtains at the windows and an assortment of bisque dolls on a shelf. On one wall hung an arrangement of four magazine covers, all depicting Nellie Bly in her signature coat and carrying her carpetbag. Violet took a moment to study the colorful images, and she smiled, remembering the girl's enthusiasm.

Quiet and bookish, Tessa was enamored by the adventurous story and the spirit of a world traveler, but when she'd been sent to boarding school, she'd begged to come home. Violet pictured her in this room as a child, mourning the death of her mother. She was fortunate to have Ben Charles.

Violet went about her work, changed her own bedding and still it was barely after nine. After finding the canvas bags for the laundry and packing it all up for

Henry to take to the washhouse, she made herself a pot of tea and sipped a steaming cup.

It took her a few minutes to gather cleaning supplies. She planned to dust and sweep the two drawing rooms before noon. So far she'd kept away from the windows, and she intended to avoid them so she wouldn't see the comings and goings next door.

Stopping beside the pocket door that led to the room they'd used the evening before, she set down her pail and rags in the hall, grasped the indented metal finger hold and slid open the door.

The unexpected sight of a dozen people dressed in black took her aback. Men and women mingled, speaking in low tones. Tessa, who'd been listening to a woman speak, glanced at Violet over the person's shoulder. She gave Violet a soft smile. The woman turned to see who Tessa had looked at, but then distractedly went back to what she'd been saying.

Heart pounding with surprise and embarrassment, Violet tugged the heavy door closed as quietly as she was able. Grabbing her cleaning supplies, she darted into the formal parlor. She stood unmoving for several minutes, absorbing what had just taken place…and what she'd learned.

The lovely room where she'd felt such peace the night before was now being used as a gathering place for mourners. She hadn't noticed another door on the opposite side until her quick glance today. The space had been open to a hallway on the opposite side.

Neither Tessa or Ben Charles had bothered to mention the room's use to her. Should she find withholding that information disturbing—or hadn't either one thought of it? She blocked all thoughts of what was going on next door from her mind.

Violet jerked into action and gave the room a good study before deciding what needed done. She covered all the furniture before dusting the ceiling, wiping the walls and cleaning light fixtures. She wasn't going to get to the other room today, so she'd focus her attention here and do a thorough job.

Finished with the dusting, she pulled off the furniture drapes and carried them out the back door to shake them.

For the second time that day she drew up short.

Fifty yards from the back door stood an enormous moose. Its size—probably six feet high at its shoulders—shocked her. The beast swung its head to look at her as she exited the house. It had begun to snow and the fluffy white flakes showed up against the animal's dark hide. The moose's impressive rack of antlers spread over a foot and a half on either side of its blunt-featured head. The moose stared at her, but didn't move.

She dropped the cloths in the snow and backed up, nearly stumbling in her haste to get safely back inside. Closing the door securely, she went to the long window. The moose had a huge hump across its shoulders and a long hairy beardlike thing hanging under its chin.

The connecting door opened, startling her yet again. She released an involuntary squeak and spun to discover Tessa.

"Are you all right?" the girl asked. "I brought you a late lunch." She set a napkin-covered tray on the table.

"The moose," Violet told her. "It's outside the back door."

Tessa joined her at the window. "He's a big one. I'll

let Ben Charles know, so he can keep an eye out as the guests leave." She glanced at Violet's face. "Did you go outside?"

Violet nodded. "I was going to shake the furniture covers. I left them out there in the snow."

"They're fine. I'll help you with them later."

"What does that thing eat?"

"Roots and shoots. Conifers. They're like giant deer. You've never seen one before?"

"Never."

"Hunters shoot them for their antlers. For the most part the moose are only looking to survive. This one is big and probably eats a lot of food in a day. Today he got a little too close to town, but we're living in his territory, after all."

Violet studied the beast with a different perspective. "Do the hunters eat them?"

"I don't think so. They just shoot them for the trophy."

"Seems like a cruel thing to do."

"I agree." Tessa moved away from the window. "Try the little sandwiches Mrs. Match brought. They're delicious. And I got a slice of cake for you before it was gone."

"Thank you, Tessa. I didn't get around to eating. I've been busy. I'd better think about supper once I've tasted the lunch."

"People will be heading home soon. I'll stay until the last guest is gone and then put away chairs while Ben Charles and Henry see to the grave."

Violet's stomach plummeted. She nodded.

After Tessa had gone, she peered at the food. The thought of eating didn't appeal to her, but she forced herself to taste the sandwich. Again taking control of her thoughts, she moved a chair before the window, carried her plate and sat to observe the moose.

It had moved farther away and was nibbling at twigs poking through the snow. She nibbled at a slice of pickle. She and that moose were getting by the best they knew how. She found the humor in comparing herself to a moose and finished her funeral meal before setting about preparing supper.

It was still early enough to cook a roast, so she browned the meat and set the covered pan in the oven before peeling potatoes and turnips.

She had time later to wash and change before supper. Henry didn't join them that evening. "The sky is threatening snow, so he went on home," Ben Charles explained after he'd prayed. "He looks after his elderly grandfather."

"He never mentioned it," Violet replied.

"News is there's a storm farther north, and it's heading this way. I strung a rope from the back door to the stable before I came in."

"What for?"

"If visibility is poor, I can find my way there and back to feed and water the horses."

"I can help you."

"We'll see what it looks like in the morning. I wouldn't mind the company."

They ate, and the siblings were unusually quiet. Violet assumed they were tired from their long day.

"I liked the biscuits," Tessa told her.

"Klenor," Violet explained. "Sweet cream makes the difference. I made *trivilies* for dessert." She brought a tray with a plate full of the pastries and cups of coffee.

Hot tea for Tessa. The walnut and oatmeal sandwich cookies held a layer of date filling.

"There wasn't anything this tasty at the luncheon today," Ben Charles said. "You go to a lot of work for us."

"I could make these in my sleep," she said. "At the bakery I made hundreds at a time. Even a dozen seems like a lot for us. The extras will be in the pantry."

"Not for long," Ben Charles said, reaching for another.

The dining room was on the side of the house against the funeral home, so there were no windows. Violet was surprised when she returned to the kitchen to hear the wind howling against the door and window. She peered out to discover a flurry of swirling white flakes obscuring the backyard and the stable.

"I grabbed the cloths that were in a heap in the yard," Ben Charles said from behind her.

"Oh, thank you. I'm afraid I dropped it when the moose startled me."

"Henry thinks he's moved on. The animal must have sensed the storm coming and come foraging."

"I never knew a moose was so large!"

"That's why I cautioned you to be alert."

"I'd have run from that fellow even without forewarning."

Tessa helped her with the dishes, while Ben Charles went next door.

That evening Violet selected a book and sat with Tessa in her upstairs getaway. Later the hallway grew chilly, so they decided to move to their rooms where they could stoke their fireplaces.

Alone in her room with the wind battering the window, Violet was thankful for her job and for a warm place to sleep at night. This home was built of brick, and inside they were safe from the elements. She was comfortable here, and the Hammonds treated her well. Church and Ben Charles's prayers were new to her, but he and Tessa set great store by God, and Violet had no evidence they were wrong.

At a tap on her door she stood from her chair, with her shawl wrapped around her, and opened it.

Ben Charles stood in the hallway, holding an armful of logs. "I'm sorry to disturb you. I'm afraid I got busy, but I wanted to make sure you had enough wood to last the night."

She took a step back. "Thank you. I'm keeping quite warm, thank you."

He placed the wood in the bin beside the fireplace and brushed bits of bark from his sleeve, then picked them up and tossed them into the fire. After striding back to the door, he turned momentarily. "Sleep well."

She closed the door behind him and listened to his footsteps move away down the hallway. A feeling of well-being akin to nothing she'd ever experienced washed over her.

She wasn't sure how she knew it, but she belonged here.

Chapter Seven

Ben Charles awoke to the sound of the wind. During the winter months when he wasn't tending to graves or grounds, he had time to work on headstones. He found it immensely satisfying to create monuments that would last through the ages and bless the families of the departed.

In his workshop were stacks of flat cut marble and he had been looking forward to time to work on them.

The tantalizing smells of coffee and bacon drew him to the kitchen, where Violet coached Tessa on cutting circles from a layer of dough. "What are you ladies up to?"

"Violet's teaching me to drop doughnuts." Tessa took two of the circles she'd cut and turned to place them in an enormous skillet of grease.

The resulting popping sounds and the smell made Ben Charles's stomach rumble. "I have an idea where you can drop a couple of those doughnuts." With a grin, he poured himself a cup of coffee.

"I'll fix you a plate," Violet offered.

He stopped her with a raised hand. "I'll get my own. You're busy."

The oven held pans of bacon and a platter of pancakes she'd kept warming.

"I helped make those, too," his sister called.

Ben Charles sat to eat, enjoying Violet and Tessa's chatter as much as the food. "The road must have been too bad for Henry to venture out this morning."

"I can't tell if there's more snow falling or if all that snow in the air is coming from the roof and the trees," Violet replied.

Ben Charles got up for more coffee and stopped at the window. "Looks like a little of both." He filled his cup. "Will you two be all right today if I fill the wood-bins and then go work in my shop?"

"We'll be fine," Tessa answered. "We're making an applesauce cake after these."

He took a doughnut from the plate of finished ones and tasted the warm sugary goodness. "What will you do with extra baked goods we can't eat?"

Violet looked up with a stricken expression. "Is this wasteful?"

"Not at all. I've enjoyed every single treat to come out of your kitchen so far. And it's obviously an excellent learning opportunity for Tessa. She's enjoying herself, and that makes me happy."

"Maybe we can take extras to people in town," Tessa suggested. "Not today, of course, but when the weather permits."

"Good idea." Ben Charles nabbed another doughnut. "Now I'd better go before I eat the entire batch."

"Will you be back at lunch?" Violet asked.

He caught the expectant look on her face, and his stomach dipped unexpectedly. "Indeed, I will."

"What will you be doing today?" Tessa asked.

"I have a couple of more days' work before Ivan Chambers's stone is finished."

"May we bring your lunch and watch you for a while?" She turned to Violet. "I love to watch him work. Will you join me?"

It was plain Violet wanted no part of joining them beyond this side of the house. "Violet probably has other things to do," he said.

Tessa's happy expression faltered. "I don't want to monopolize your time." She waved a flour-encrusted hand. "You go ahead with what you had planned."

Violet's indecision turned to resignation and she set her shoulders. "I'd be pleased to join you. I'm sure it's a fascinating process."

Tessa might have hugged the other young woman if they hadn't both been wrist deep in dough. A smile wreathed her lovely face. "We'll see you around noon."

It had taken a lot of courage for Violet to agree to visit his shop. He admired and appreciated her a little more each day. She was holding back, that was obvious, but whether her reticence was entirely due to her aversion to his work or something else, he wasn't sure. The information she'd volunteered about her past had mostly been about what she'd learned from her father, and he was curious about more.

Ben Charles was a patient man. He could wait.

The closer the hour drew to time for the noon meal, the more Violet's stomach tied in knots. She dreaded walking through that door and discovering anything on the other side. Even though Guy Chapman's funeral was over and, to her knowledge no one else had died, she didn't want to cross that line.

While Tessa timed the applesauce cake in the oven, Violet cleaned a chicken she had roasted earlier and chopped the white meat for sandwiches. She showed the younger girl how to make boiled icing and supervised as she spread a thin layer atop their cake.

Lunches packed and ready, she tidied up in her room before joining Tessa, who held a sketch pad and several pencils. The girl opened the door and gestured for Violet to go first.

Violet's heart thundered. Her ears rang and her breathing grew shallow. She paused to collect herself.

"Are you all right?" Tessa asked.

"Y-yes. I'm fine." She forced her feet into motion and crossed the threshold. Standing in a corridor with two windows like the one in the kitchen, the space was bright and she didn't feel any different. Nothing pressed in or suffocated her.

"All the way along this passage to that door on the far end," Tessa instructed.

Violet didn't look into the rooms off to her right as they passed. A pounding sound grew louder as they approached. She kept her eye on the goal of reaching that door. Tessa reached it first and pushed it open, revealing a huge room lit by windows across the back of the house. The pounding was loud inside the cavernous room.

Against one wall were two short stacks of flat stone. She noticed two massive carts with chains and pulleys, rigged for lifting the stones, and several above-waist-high stations made of logs, holding flat sandbags with works in progress atop them. Ben Charles spotted them and looked up from one, removed plugs from his ears and pushed a pair of goggles upward on his forehead. He wore a canvaslike suit that covered his clothing.

"How far have you gotten?" Tessa asked.

"The family asked for limestone, so this one's going a little faster," he replied. He gestured to another. "That one's taking longer."

The marble stone he spoke of held the outline of letters ready to cut. Only one line of the engraving had been etched, and it read Hayden Langley.

The top of the stone was curved, and there were fine lines showing where a scroll design and a cross would eventually be.

"How do you decide which one to work on?" Violet asked.

"I usually focus on them in the order of burial," he replied. "But I like to work on two or three at a time, so I break up the more tedious work."

"Did you cut all those markers, too?" she asked.

"No, I don't have the equipment to do that. They're cut into sizes at quarries and then shaped at a manufacturer's before coming to me by rail."

"And these are your tools?" she asked.

He straightened an array so she could better see. "Mallets. Straight, toothed and rounded chisels. Rifflers."

The last he'd mentioned looked like files to her.

Tessa walked farther away. "There are finished markers over here."

Violet joined her and studied three finished gravestones. One was a striated stone, arched across the top, with an array of lilies above the woman's name and the dates of her birth and death. Violet was drawn to touch the cold marble, run her fingers over the intricate cuts shaping the flowers.

"Lilies symbolize Christ's resurrection," Ben Charles said from behind her. "Families often choose them because it reminds them of their loved one's hope in eternal life. It's an encouragement to generations to come."

Violet moved to the next stone and admired the vine motif across the top and down the sides and the lamb beneath the name. "What does the lamb mean?"

"Innocence."

Violet noted the dates she'd overlooked before. This stone would identify the grave of a child of only four. She drew back her hand and experienced a deep sense of sorrow and loss.

The last marker had rosettes carved into the shoulders and a dove in flight. Violet glanced at Ben Charles.

"Holy Spirit, purity and love," he clarified without her saying a word.

She couldn't imagine the laborious work that had gone into each detail. "It must take hours and hours and hours of backbreaking work to create a stone meant for a grave," she said, thinking aloud.

"It does."

"Who sees them?"

"Their family. Generations of family."

She nodded and imagined the comfort families represented by these stones would derive. Even a hundred years from now, Ben Charles's work would remain. Incredible, really.

She noticed something she hadn't seen at first. Low on the stone on the section that would be under the earth were three letters: *B.C.H.* His signature. A signature that would endure for centuries. Each finished marker bore the same small identification.

She glanced around. A coal stove burned in the corner, taking the chill from his workshop.

"I'm starved," he said. "I need a minute to wash."

A pump stood at an enormous basin along the outside wall, but she assumed it was frozen. He used water from a pan on the coal stove to wash his hands.

At a scarred worktable they stood and ate their sandwiches and the warm spicy cake. Ben Charles praised their efforts, but Violet compared her temporal travails to his everlasting accomplishments.

"Don't diminish what you do, Violet," he corrected. "Without your contribution I couldn't do my work and Tessa wouldn't be learning. You are a valuable asset, and don't you forget it."

Cheeks warm from his words, Violet removed lids from the Mason jars she'd filled with tea. Once they'd finished, she packed everything away. Tessa made herself at home atop a stack of crates and motioned for Violet to do the same. She did so and Ben Charles handed them each a small ball of clay and instructed them to shape it to the insides of their ears.

Once he returned to his work, Violet was glad for the sound buffer. He worked with small precise and steady movements, making slow progress and pausing often to blow away chips and run his fingers over the indentations.

Violet was captivated. She understood why Tessa enjoyed coming to watch. Time slid away while she appreciated his obvious skill and infinite patience. He often used a brush to clear away debris from the area he focused on, and occasionally he wiped the lenses of his goggles.

He wrapped what looked like sandpaper around a long thin dowel to smooth roughness from the inscription.

She thought about what he'd said. She prepared food that nourished him to do his work. She had taken part of the responsibility of caring for his sister from his shoulders. Perhaps she could make a contribution that would make a difference, even though her work wasn't visible to the eye, nor did it bear her initials in stone.

She could take sizeable comfort from that thought.

Violet grew fascinated with the painstaking care Ben Charles took with each detail, with the strength apparent in his hands, arms and shoulders. He worked as though they weren't there, occasionally glancing over and seeming surprised to find his audience.

Tessa's pencil moved across the paper, and Violet imagined she could hear it, but of course she couldn't. Tessa hadn't had time just now to draw all the sketches arranged around her. She had obviously saved them to work on in increments. She had chosen to work on a richly detailed drawing of Ben Charles's hands, one holding a chisel, the other a mallet. Tessa had somehow captured each crease in his skin, every vein and the inherent masculine strength with her pencil and paper. It didn't take long before watching the artist was as fascinating as watching the craftsman. How many times had they sat like this, brother and sister, together but working apart, silent in their concentration?

Violet could have stayed longer, but after nearly two hours, she told Tessa she was going to plan their supper and make a shopping list. They wouldn't miss her.

Again she avoided looking into the other rooms on her way along the corridor to the kitchen. While her foray to the other side hadn't been unpleasant at all, she felt more at home here. Definitely in her element. No wonder Ben Charles had been out of place and desperate for someone to relieve him of cooking duties. He probably felt as ineffective in here as she did in his workshop.

She had undeniably enjoyed the glimpse into his work. His skills were called into requisition only in times of sadness and sorrow, which to Violet would be extremely uncomfortable. But he seemed focused only on attending families—not merely seeing to the immediate physical concerns, but to honoring their loved ones in posterity.

Her admiration for the man only grew stronger with each passing day and each glimpse into his life.

By five the sky had cleared. Tessa returned, with the news that Ben Charles would be heading out to the barn. "He said if you wanted to help him, to dress warm and meet him out back. Do you have warm boots?"

"Not sufficient for all this snow, I don't suppose."

Tessa headed for the pantry. "I have a pair back here you're welcome to wear."

Bundled for warmth, she joined Ben Charles outdoors and surreptitiously checked the landscape for large animals. The daylight had already begun to fade. Ben Charles went ahead of her, following the rope line, though they didn't need it for visibility, and creating footprints in the snow, which she used. Their breath made white plumes in the frigid air.

Unblemished snow went on forever. The trunks of the heavily laden trees were all that broke up the ocean of white. Ben Charles turned to look back. "You doing all right?"

"I'm good," she replied, though she'd become winded from raising her feet high to plow into his prints in the drifts.

After Ben Charles unbolted a stable door, he stepped inside and glanced around before backing out and gesturing for her to enter ahead of him. The smells of hay, horses and leather that engulfed her sent immediate shafts of memory through her senses and brought the sting of tears to her eyes. For a moment she couldn't breathe.

Pain as sharp as anything physical sliced inside her chest. She saw her father, tall and handsome, dressed for a ride. The scents mingled to create memory images as clear as day. Violet flattened her mittened palm against her chest and tried to breathe.

Ben Charles turned to her, and an expression of alarm crossed his features. He grasped her arm through her coat. "Violet! Are you all right? You're as white as a sheet."

Chapter Eight

She struggled to bring some air into her lungs. Once she was breathing normally, she cast him an apologetic glance. "I'm sorry. For a moment the memories overwhelmed me."

"Don't be sorry. Are they good memories?"

"Oh, they're good. Very good." She swiped a hand across her eyes and blinked away the remaining tears.

He released her arm and took a step back, but kept his gaze on her face. "Can you tell me?"

"I saw my father when he was much younger, as plain as I see you. He looked just like he used to when I was young."

"What was his name?"

Violet paused a moment. She couldn't help a soft smile. "Latham."

He paused. "I've inscribed a lot of names on stones. And I've read a lot more while visiting cemeteries. I don't remember seeing Bennett used as a Scandinavian name."

She dropped her gaze. "No, I guess it's unusual."

She straightened her spine and glanced around. "So there they are."

Ben Charles turned and she followed him. The side of the stable they'd entered into held stalls, where the black horses waited impatiently, snorting and shaking their heads. At the far side stood two fine black hearses adorned with gilded side lamps, the covered buggy and a wagon.

"We'll let the horses into the corral while I clean stalls. You can fill grain buckets. I'll break the ice on the water barrel out back, and you can fill their pails." He rolled back the enormous rear door a few feet.

The Morgans seemed eager to be released and shot out the opening one at a time. Ben Charles set empty buckets outside the stalls and shoveled out the soiled straw.

Violet accomplished her task of filling grain and water, and then joined him in finishing the stalls and spreading fresh straw. Even though she'd pulled on wool mittens, her fingers were soon cold.

It was dark by the time Ben Charles went out and herded the animals back inside. He lit a lantern. Violet remembered which stall each had occupied and stood behind the open gates one at a time, directing. Once they were safely contained, she entered the first stall to acquaint herself.

"That's Clarence. He's the one—"

"You brought when you picked me up at the station," she interrupted.

"I'm impressed."

She spoke softly to the gelding, pulled off her mittens and ran her cold hands over its neck. One by one, she introduced herself to each of the others: Felix, Gaston and Lancelot. "Has Tessa ridden at all?"

"When she was younger. Not for some time."

"Is Lancelot a good match for her?"

"Each has a good temperament, but he's the best choice, I think. We'd best get back. I'm hungry."

Violet wanted to stay longer, but she gave Lancelot a final pat and joined Ben Charles.

"Thank you for helping. The task was accomplished quickly."

She tugged on her mittens. "It was my pleasure. Really."

He picked up the lantern, and shadows swayed with the movement. "I'm not used to having a beautiful woman in my stable."

His eyes showed his good humor and sincerity. Her cheeks warmed at the unexpected compliment. *Beautiful?*

"Was that too forward of me?" he asked.

"I—" She glanced away. "You surprised me is all." She moved away, but paused before reaching the door and glanced up at him. "When the weather clears, I hope it will be all right for me to come and go in my free time."

"Perfectly all right. I told you this is your home, and I meant it."

Her gaze traveled over his shoulder. Though the stable was dark now, she imagined the hearses sitting side by side, as though awaiting their next unfortunate occupants. She shivered.

"We'd better get back in so you can warm up." He handed her the lantern.

She went first this time, stepping in the holes from

their previous steps. The lantern created a circle of golden light around them as they made their way single file to the house.

"My hair is full of dust. I'm going to bathe before supper," he told her. "You can keep a plate warm if the two of you want to go ahead."

"We'll wait for you." She hung her coat and washed her hands at the basin.

Tessa had set places at the kitchen table while they'd been out. "I thought we'd be informal this evening," she said to Violet.

"That sounds perfect." She made the last touches to their meal and set out roasted veal fillets, stewed beets and winter squash. A bowl of rice pudding stayed warm in the oven.

When Ben Charles returned, he prayed and they ate.

"Violet enjoyed seeing the horses," he said to Tessa. "They remind her of her father."

"You are fortunate to have those memories," the younger girl told her.

Violet set down her fork. "Very much so."

"He taught you to ride when you were young?" Tessa asked.

"He taught me everything."

"Like how to bake delicious pastries," Tessa said with a smile.

Ben Charles smiled, too. "You mentioned that when your father got sick, he sold his bakery."

Violet nodded. "That's right."

"And after his death you went to work for the new owner."

"I did."

"Then he closed it? How did it happen that you answered my ad?"

She couldn't continue to lie to this man who'd been so kind and welcomed her into his home. He trusted her.

She got a sick feeling in her stomach. She glanced at Tessa, who was obviously waiting for her reply, as well. "There was a fire," she said. "After that I was out of a job, so I looked for a new one and found your query in the classifieds."

"Was the fire so bad that your employer couldn't rebuild?"

She paused before replying, "I didn't want to wait that long. I was ready to move on anyway."

Ben Charles supposed it had been painful to see someone else in her father's place. Violet didn't seem the type to make rash decisions, so the anguish must have been deep. Her unspoken hurt touched him, and he wished he knew how to help her.

After they'd eaten warm rice pudding, he sat at the table while Violet cleaned up and put on beans to soak. Tessa had excused herself and gone upstairs to read. After a few minutes he noticed Violet hadn't moved. She stood facing away from him, her hands fisted at her sides.

"Violet?"

Slowly she turned to face him. Her dark eyes were wide with emotion he couldn't identify—and hoped wasn't fear.

"What is it?" he asked.

"You've welcomed me into your home. You've trusted me, but I haven't been truthful with you." She swallowed and took a deep breath. "I didn't know where else to go or what to do, and coming here seemed the perfect answer. But I can't lie to you anymore. I will face whatever happens after this, but I cannot keep lying."

A fissure of shock darted through him. Whatever she had to say was more serious than he'd imagined. He didn't like the idea of her being in trouble or distress. She twisted her trembling fingers together. He wanted to close his hands over hers, but he resisted.

"What is it?" Truly concerned now, he stood and led her to a chair and sat adjacent to her.

"Baking was what I knew how to do, so after my father's death, I asked the new owner for a job. He seemed pleased to have me—in fact he was always nice to me. His son worked there, too. Wade."

Ben Charles noted the way she said his name with distaste. Already he didn't like where this was heading.

"Mr. Finney invited me to their house for holidays and sometimes just for supper of an evening. His wife was nice, too. Quiet. I didn't have anyone else, so I joined them whenever he invited me. I didn't catch on for a few months that I was always seated next to Wade or that Mr. Finney sometimes left us alone at the table. But then his comments to both Wade and I became suggestions. Why didn't we attend the Founder's Day picnic together? How about taking the buggy and going for a ride? I had no interest in Wade, and he had none in me. Just the opposite, in fact."

She had Ben Charles's full attention. "What do you mean?"

"He often made rude remarks or criticized something I'd done. His interests, as far as I could tell, were in drinking, smoking, playing cards and coming to work with an occasional black eye or swollen lip. Sometimes his friends came to the bakery, and he left with them— just left the rest of us with his share of the work. Several times I heard him arguing with his father over money." She raised her gaze and held his.

"Go on, Violet."

She straightened on the chair and squared her shoulders. "I stopped accepting Mr. Finney's invitations. He came right out and told me he wanted Wade to marry me and settle down. He said if Wade married a nice girl and had a family, he'd come to his senses. He was determined Wade would take over the bakery one day, and he used the fact that the business meant so much to me to try to get me to comply. If I was Wade's wife, the bakery would still be in my family."

"What a dirty player." A horrible thought made the hair on Ben Charles's neck stand on end. "You didn't marry him!"

"No. No, of course not." She raised her hand in a halting gesture. "I refused to snare Wade, as Mr. Finney wanted, but he didn't give up. Things became tense at the bakery, with the two of them fighting. Then Wade stopped coming to work, except for once or twice a week. I have no idea what was going on at their home or behind the scenes."

Relieved that she'd set his fears to rest, he nodded for her to continue.

"One night he broke the window at the boarding-house where I stayed and yanked me out of bed by my hair."

"Did he hurt you?"

"It hurt when he yanked me to the window to show me the smoke curling up a few blocks away. He'd used kerosene to set a fire at the bakery."

"I guess that's one way to get out of work," Ben Charles said with a wry twist of his lips.

"He gave me money and said if I didn't get out of his life and leave town right then and there, he would tell his father I'd started the fire. He'd used my matches, my apron. And he said there were witnesses. There couldn't have been, of course, but I have no doubt he paid someone to say they'd seen me there."

"What did you do?"

"I left. He told me where he would send my belongings, and sure enough they were waiting for me when I went to Pittsburgh and claimed them. I was afraid there would be a trap, that someone would be waiting, but Wade only wanted me gone. And so I used the money for a room, for food and a traveling suit, and I answered your advertisement."

"And I wired you train fare."

She nodded. "I'm sorry."

"You could have told me this from the beginning."

She tilted her head to the side and shrugged. "I was afraid. You might have turned me in, and the authorities would have come for me."

"What about now?"

The fear in her luminous eyes made him sorry he'd asked. "You might still call the authorities," she answered. "I'm prepared for that."

"I believe you," he said quickly. "What reason would you have to burn down the bakery?"

"Perhaps I despised Wade so much, I eliminated every possibility of being trapped into a marriage to him."

"That's ridiculous. You don't have a devious bone in your body."

"How can you be sure?"

"Did you do it?"

"No."

"That's good enough for me."

"There's something else."

He wasn't in the mood to wait for another divulgence. "What is it?"

"My name isn't Bennett. You were right. That's not a Swedish name. I'm not even a very good liar."

"What is your name?"

"Violet Colleen Kristofferson."

He couldn't help himself. He laughed.

"What is it you find so funny?"

"Not funny. Your combination of Irish and Swedish names is charming."

"I just told you everything you knew about me was a lie. I deceived you in order to get a job in your home. The person you hoped would be a companion to your sister is a liar." She was more than a slightly perturbed. "My life is a shambles, and you're laughing."

"'A merry heart doeth good like a medicine...'"

"What?"

"It's from the book of Proverbs." He composed his features and presumably his thoughts. "I forgive you."

She blinked. They stared at each other. "Just like that?"

"Just like that."

"You aren't shocked or disappointed...or disgusted or angry?"

"I knew you were hiding something. I figured you'd tell me eventually. I'm not particularly disappointed or angry, no."

She looked at her hands in her lap. His reaction

wasn't what she'd anticipated. He was so calm, she didn't feel a sense of relief at having told him. "I don't understand."

"You said you were sorry. I forgave you. Would you feel better if I ranted?"

"Maybe I would."

"Jesus taught if we expect to be forgiven ourselves, then we must forgive. When we repent for our wrong-doings before God, He forgives us. Just like that. We don't earn forgiveness. God isn't angry with us, because He loves us. God sent Jesus to take away the sins of the world by dying on the cross. Jesus cancelled our debt with His own blood. He suffered and died because He loves us so much. He did that for me and for you. The very least I can do is forgive you."

"When you talk about God, Ben Charles, it's as though He's a real person. I can believe He made a plan for those Israelites to escape Egypt."

"He made a plan for all of us. Can I show you some-thing, Violet?"

She nodded.

He left for a few minutes and returned with his worn Bible. "God made provision for us through Jesus." He opened to a page and ran his finger over the words, until he found what he was looking for. "'For the wages of sin is death, but the gift of God is eternal life through Jesus Christ our Lord.'" He looked up. "All we have to do is ask."

Violet listened with keen interest, the words ringing true in her heart.

"Farther on in this book of Romans," Ben Charles continued, "it says if you believe and confess Jesus is the Son of God, that He was raised from the grave, and if you ask Him to come into your life, your sins will be erased and you will join Him in heaven after you die."

"You did this, Ben Charles?"

He nodded. "Many years ago."

"And that's how you can forgive me so easily?"

"That and the fact that you're pretty easy to forgive anyway." He grinned and that charming dimple winked.

"How can I do that? Do I have to tell Reverend Densmore what I've done?"

"No, we can just pray together, the two of us. If it's what you want to do."

"Yes, I do."

"May I hold your hands?"

She offered them to him and he closed his big warm fingers over hers and bowed his head. "Thank You for sending Violet, Lord. Thank You for the provision you made for Tessa and I. Thank You that Violet trusted me enough to tell me the truth."

He glanced up. "Now you just repeat after me, all right?"

She nodded.

He led her through a prayer, telling God she believed Jesus was His son and died for her, asking God to forgive her, asking Him to come into her heart. When they'd finished, the silence of the kitchen wrapped around them. Ben Charles's strong hands were comforting. Violet felt as though a burden had been lifted from her shoulders.

Ben Charles released her and placed his Bible in her hands. "As you read this, it will come alive for you."

Violet absorbed all they talked about, what Ben Charles had read to her from his Bible, the prayers. "Were you my provision?"

Ben Charles's gaze touched her features. "What do you believe?"

"Well...I guess if God is planning ahead for us, He knew what I needed. He showed me your advertisement and directed me here—for this day when I could understand how much He loves me."

His warm smile confirmed Ben Charles agreed.

Chapter Nine

The sun shone brightly for the next several days, matching Violet's new demeanor. She felt like a new person, with the weight of her lie removed and the knowledge of her right standing before God. Ben Charles had been right about the stories in the Bible coming to life for her.

In the evenings she asked questions about what she'd been reading, and he and Tessa helped whenever she didn't understand something.

At church the following Sunday a woman approached her with a smile. "We haven't met. I'm Lenora Grimes. I understand you're in Mr. Hammond's employ."

Violet greeted her. "I'm fortunate to have met him and Tessa, and I enjoy working for them."

"I understand you're an exceptional baker, is that so?"

"I'm a baker, yes."

"She's teaching me," Tessa said, coming up beside Violet. "You haven't truly enjoyed a dessert until you've tasted Violet's cakes and pastries and breads."

"I'd like to extend an invitation to our annual Ladies' Aid Society recital next week. It would be a good time to get acquainted. Mr. Hammond and his sister are welcome, of course."

Her new clothing should be ready in time. She might feel awkward among the other women, but Mrs. Grimes's invitation was kind, and she felt honored to have been invited. "I'd love to come. Thank you."

"I was hoping I could ask you to bake for the event. I spoke with Ben Charles, and he said it was fine with him if you wanted to. The Society will provide all the supplies you need. Will you consider it? Please?"

Baking was the one thing she was confident about. "Yes, of course. Do you have a menu?"

"Perhaps we can plan it together," Lenora suggested. "I'm fascinated to hear your suggestions."

"That suits me just fine."

Lenora reached for her hand and squeezed her fingers. "Oh, thank you, dear."

Violet met the other woman's warm gray eyes. "Thank you for including me."

"Shall we get together this week? I could call on you one afternoon."

"Sundays are my days off."

"Do the three of you have plans for lunch today?"

Violet caught Ben Charles's attention, and he joined them. After a brief discussion it was arranged they would meet Dr. and Mrs. Grimes at the Conrad Hotel shortly.

It turned out Ben Charles was well acquainted with Dr. Grimes. Lenora was friendly and gracious and drew Tessa into the conversation often.

Ben Charles enjoyed eating lunch with their neighbors. The Grimeses lived only a quarter of a mile east on the same road as the Hammonds. The doctor had a small office in town and an assistant who helped out when overnight or extended care was needed.

"Your father was the first patient I ever lost," Allen Grimes told Ben Charles. "I've lost many since, but him…well, I didn't enjoy a good night's sleep for a month afterward."

"We were only first married," Lenora said after hearing his comments. "I wondered how in the world my new husband was going to survive as a physician when losing a patient was so devastating."

Allen had only been practicing a couple of years when Ben Charles's father's heart had weakened.

"When I got out of medical school, I was ready to save the world," he said.

"You have helped a lot of people, though," Tessa piped up. "Ben Charles said you sat with me for two nights when I was small and had a fever. It must be nice helping people recover."

Ben Charles absorbed his sister's remark with interest. It pleased him to see her interacting with the Grimeses, and Violet seemed delighted to have another woman to talk with. She and Lenora discussed frosting and tea cakes as though the fate of the world hung on the correct choices. The animation in Violet's voice and expression blessed him.

Thomas Everett, a young man about Tessa's age, stopped beside their table. He wore his dark blue Sunday suit and a deep red tie. His cheeks were almost the same color, and Ben Charles sympathized with his discomfort. His glance darted to Tessa and then away. He met Ben Charles's gaze and held it. "Mr. Hammond, sir, it's nice to see you."

"You, too, Thomas. How is your father?"

"Just fine, sir. My parents are hosting a birthday celebration for me next Saturday afternoon, and I was hoping you might allow Tessa to join us. My parents and older sister will be chaperones. With your permission I would call for her and bring her back to your home."

"How old will you be on your birthday?" Ben Charles asked.

"Seventeen, sir."

"Seventeen." Ben Charles glanced at Tessa. Her cheeks were pink, but her eyes sparkled, and she gave him a barely perceptible nod and a soft smile. If she wanted to go, he was happy to see her join the other young people. "I'm going to be frank with you, Thomas."

"Please, sir."

His sister might not like what he was going to say, but he wouldn't allow her to be hurt. He didn't care that the Grimeses listened. They were his friends. "Not all of the young people Tessa's age have been kind to her. I'm sure you're aware of that."

"I am, sir, but no one who has ever been rude to Tessa will be invited." He spoke with sincerity. "I give you my word. She will be my guest, and she will be treated with respect in our house."

Ben Charles's throat tightened, and he cleared it. Thomas's blue eyes held his in a steady gaze that held a promise. "I appreciate that, young man." He extended his hand and when Thomas shook it, his palm was damp. "I believe your word is good, and I shall hold you to it."

Thomas grinned and turned to tell Tessa what time he would come for her when Saturday arrived. After he'd walked away and joined his family at another table,

Ben Charles looked from person to person around their table. Allen wore an amused grin, and Lenora Grimes reached over and patted Tessa's hand in her lap. "He's a nice young fellow, dear."

Tessa's cheeks were bright with color, but she and Violet exchanged a delighted look that assured Ben Charles she was pleased.

He'd known this time was coming. Tessa was blooming into a woman. She wouldn't remain with him forever. She would meet a young man, fall in love and start a life separate from his. He'd been praying for her future husband. He couldn't select a man for her, but he had trusted God to do so. He had to trust she would follow her heart while at the same time using wisdom.

The timing for this particular budding relationship couldn't have been better. Tessa already thought the world of Violet, so now she had a confidante. He couldn't wait to talk to Violet about yet another way God's provision had gone before them and cleared a path.

Violet caught his gaze and smiled.

A startling thought occurred to him. He hadn't prayed for a spouse for himself. He had shut off that possibility, but perhaps he hadn't had enough faith— or courage. But it was possible God had overlooked his shortcomings and worked in his behalf regardless. Had God brought someone across the country and right into his home to show him there was still hope for him to find love?

But Violet held strong feelings about his profession. She'd come as far as his workshop, but she found the rest of what he did repugnant. He'd seen it in her face, her body language, her discomfort at even the mention of a person's death. How would they ever be compatible?

Their gathering lingered over dessert, and parted at last.

During the drive home Ben Charles mentioned to Violet that Benjamin Sperry, the carpenter, would be at the house the following morning to build her bookshelves.

"I'll help you this afternoon, and we'll move the furniture away from the areas where he'll be working."

"I'll need to take down the curtains," she told him.

After everyone had changed from their church clothes into more comfortable attire, Ben Charles asked Tessa to join him. Together the three of them moved the bed and bureau, trunks and stacks of books.

He stood from setting down a trunk at the same time Violet turned, and they collided. Ben Charles caught and steadied her with his hands on her upper arms. "I'm sorry."

"No, it was me. I wasn't looking."

They remained standing that way, because he didn't want to release her. The attraction he felt had become more and more evident with each day and every conversation. She had the appearance of delicacy, but her strength was evident. She was kind and capable and gracious. She sincerely enjoyed spending time with Tessa. She took pleasure in ordinary things most people would take for granted.

"When Benjamin arrives in the morning, show him exactly how you want the shelves."

She nodded, her eyes wide and luminous. "Yes. Thank you, Ben Charles."

The sound of his name on her lips unexplainably

touched him. He wanted to pull her close and feel her heartbeat against his. The need was a tangible ache.

So he released her. "I have a few things to do."

He excused himself to go to his shop.

Violet stared at the empty doorway after he'd gone, her heart slowing to its normal rhythm. Things between them had become confusing. He'd made an overwhelming impact on her life. Ben Charles was her employer, but there were so many more layers to their relationship. He was a teacher, instructing by example, showing her who God is. As a mentor he'd opened her eyes and led her in the most important prayer she would ever pray. Those things exemplified who he was as a man. But these other things...

The imprint of his touch remained on her arms. Just when she thought there might be more, he pulled away. But of course Tessa had been in the same room, no doubt puzzling over why her brother stood staring into Violet's eyes.

Yes, Violet was definitely confused.

"Will you join me in my room?" Tessa asked, interrupting her train of thought. "I'd like to show you a few things. If you don't mind." Violet followed and she opened both doors of her armoire. "What shall I wear to Thomas's birthday?"

Removing several dresses, she laid them out on the bed and hung more on the armoire door.

"They're all lovely," Violet assured her. "The blue would look nice with your hair and eyes."

Tessa held it against her and turned to the standing mirror.

"Has Thomas always been kind to you?" Violet asked.

"Always," Tessa answered. "He told me once he was ashamed of the others who said cruel things to me."

Violet perched on the edge of Tessa's bed, careful not to wrinkle a dress. "How do you feel about those others? Have you ever wished your brother did something else?"

Tessa stood behind one of the open doors of the armoire and changed into a peach-colored silk dress. "I believe fear makes them small-minded. People fear death. They fear the unknown." She came out from behind the door and stood in front of the long mirror. "Ben Charles provides a service to people who are going through the worst days of their lives. He makes the transition from having a loved one to being without them easier to bear."

At that moment Violet felt as though Tessa was the older of the two of them. Her wisdom and ability to express it went far beyond her age.

"He is a rock in the midst of a turbulent and confusing time. People rely on him, and he meets their needs with compassion and elegance. When I see that, I'm proud of my family and how we serve our community." She turned. "Not only our community, though. How we serve our fellow man."

Violet's chest ached. Tessa was every bit as kindhearted and straightforward as her brother. Violet felt small and selfish for her inability to overcome her squeamishness and be as accepting and merciful as these two. Both of them took death in stride as life's final transition and were honored to help others through difficult times.

But she had a new tool. God knew all about Violet's aversion and the panic she felt when memories overtook her. She could pray and ask God to help her change her reactions. She didn't want to be one of those small-minded people who let fear get the best of them. She didn't have to join Ben Charles in his work, but she could accept it.

That night, alone in her room, Violet opened the Bible that Ben Charles had loaned her and continued reading where she'd left off. As much as she enjoyed the stories of Moses and King David, Ben Charles had suggested she start in the New Testament and learn about Jesus. After reading the gospels, she understood the meaning of the symbols on the stained-glass windows at church, but even more importantly, she was beginning to understand God's love for her.

Her prayers weren't as good as Ben Charles's yet, but she followed his example and spoke to God with the conviction that He heard her and cared. She asked Him to take away her fear and her aversion to the mortuary.

How long did answers take?

Chapter Ten

At last Marcella Wright put the finishing touches on Violet's dresses, underclothing and coat, and Violet stored everything in her wardrobe and bureau, eager for opportunities to wear her lovely new things.

Tessa was all atwitter on Saturday, reminding Violet she was indeed a young girl. Violet wasn't accomplished at the task, but Tessa showed her how to heat the iron over the flame on a lamp and curl her upswept hair into long ringlets. They went through an assortment of silk flowers and ribbon and put together a small bouquet, which Violet fastened in Tessa's hair.

After endless deliberation she'd chosen the blue dress, and Violet had been right about the color being striking with her complexion and eyes. Tessa opened a lined wood box on her bureau and took out a gold locket. "It was my mother's. I only wear it on special occasions."

Violet took the piece of jewelry and fastened it around the girl's neck. "It's beautiful. And so are you."

The bell chimed, and their eyes met in the mirror with expectation.

Tessa picked up a gaily wrapped gift. "I hope Thomas likes the book I selected."

"He will appreciate that you chose it for him." Violet found a burgundy coat with a fur collar in the armoire and held it out. "This one?"

"Yes. It's pretty and it's warm."

Violet carried the coat downstairs, so Ben Charles could see the full effect of Tessa's dress. He and Thomas stood in the foyer. Thomas was inspecting the plaster cherubs on the ceiling, but at their footsteps he turned his attention to Tessa's approach.

"You are beautiful." Ben Charles gave Tessa a hug and helped her on with her coat. "What time do you expect the party to end?"

"My mother thought one to five was long enough," Thomas replied. "So I will return your sister well before six."

Violet stood just behind Ben Charles so she could watch as the young couple made their way to his buggy and he helped her to the seat. Ben Charles closed the door.

Violet stepped back as he turned. "She's going to have a nice time. He seems like a fine young man."

"I believe you're right." He took his watch from his pocket and snapped it open. "I'll be in my shop if you need anything. Or you're welcome to keep me company."

"I still have a crate of books to unpack and put away on the new shelves. I think I'll get that finished. Then I'll prepare supper so it's ready at six."

He gave a nod and headed for the back of the house.

It took her less than an hour to unpack, sort and place her books on the shelves. The carpenter had built them across the top of the window and along the top of another wall to look as though they'd been there all along. And he'd supplied a short ladder, so she could reach her books without using a chair.

The house was unbelievably quiet. When she stood still and listened she could hear the ringing of Ben Charles's chisel and mallet in the building next door. She pictured him bent over his task, wearing his goggles, his concentration focused on making precise cuts in the stone.

Opening her wardrobe, she planned what she would wear to church the following day and what she would wear to the Ladies' Aid recital midweek. She found the notes she'd made while talking with Mrs. Grimes and sat at the kitchen table to make a shopping list.

A bell rang. She'd learned to discern which one was for this home and which was for Ben Charles's business. That had been the mortuary's bell. A few minutes later it rang again.

Begrudgingly she made her way to the front of the house, opened the door and stepped out into the cold. A woman stood before the double doors next door, shivering. She wore a thin coat and no head covering or gloves. Violet hurried out. "Can I help you?"

She was probably in her late twenties or early thirties, with fair hair. Her eyes were red and her face puffy. As she turned toward Violet, it became clear she was expecting a baby. "Is the undertaker here?"

"He must not have heard the bell. He's in his workshop. Why don't you come inside and I'll find him for you?"

The thin woman looked over her shoulder toward the

horse and wagon sitting several yards away and shook her head. "I'll wait here. I won't leave Joseph alone."

There was no one on the wagon seat, so Violet suspected the worst. Joseph must be lying in the bed of the wagon. "I'll get Mr. Hammond."

She turned and ran back into the house, the soles of her shoes hitting the wood floor as she shot along the hallway to the back and opened the connecting door. The sound of Ben Charles's hammering grew louder and louder, nearly hurting her ears when she threw open the door to his shop and darted in. He didn't look up as she ran forward.

Finally he caught her motion in his peripheral vision and the mallet stilled. "What's wrong? Is it Tessa?"

"No. No, there's a woman out front of the mortuary. I tried to get her to come in, but she wouldn't leave her husband. He's…" She stumbled over the words. "He's in the bed of the wagon."

Ben Charles removed his goggles, unfastened the suit that covered his clothing and stepped out of it. He ruffled dust from his hair with both hands and strode to rinse them in the basin. "Keep her company, if you will please. I'll be right out." He pointed to a door. "That hall leads to the front door."

Violet didn't think; she just reacted, opened the door he indicated and ran along a hallway of polished wood, past an office, past rooms she didn't look into, until she reached a foyer much like the one in the house and threw open the door.

"Mr. Hammond is coming," she said to the woman.

She only nodded, her narrow shoulders hunched forward.

"What's your name?" Violet asked.

"Callie Jefferson."

"Where do you live?"

"My husband…" Her voice caught. "Joseph and I… we have a place to the south." She looked at the wagon. "I don't know what will happen now."

To her relief Ben Charles's boots sounded along the hallway, and he joined them. "Ma'am."

"You the undertaker?"

"Yes, ma'am. Ben Charles Hammond. And your name is?"

"Callie. My Joseph fell from the hay loft. When he didn't come back to the house for lunch, I found him. Broke his neck I think."

"I'm sorry, ma'am. Do you have any family nearby?"

"Joseph's aunt lives in town. He looked out for her. She's up in years."

"If you want to step into the drawing room, I'll put a log on the fire so you can warm up. I'll bring in Joseph."

"I'll help you bring him in out of the cold."

"Let's get you warmed up," Violet suggested in a soft voice.

"I ain't never gonna be warm again!" the woman cried. "My heart is as cold and dead as my husband's. I'm gonna stay with him."

Ben Charles met Violet's eyes with resignation. "I'll get the cart. Violet, find Callie some mittens."

Violet ran for a warmer coat and a pair of mittens for the young woman and grabbed a coat for herself. When she returned, she coaxed Callie to put on the heavier coat.

Ben Charles pushed a narrow waist-high stretcher conveyance with wheels through the open doorway, and Callie followed him to the back of the wagon.

Violet's heart pounded. She had to keep the other woman company. She had to, but everything in her screamed out in protest. This was probably the sort of thing Tessa did to help, and she wasn't here. It was Henry's day off. She was the only person available.

Her legs felt stiff as she followed and joined them. A long form was visible under a tarp, and Violet averted her gaze, keeping her attention focused on Callie's face.

Ben Charles lowered the gate, jumped into the bed and efficiently maneuvered the tarp, then jumped down. His cart came right to the edge and he'd set a brake to keep it from moving. Callie helped him, and he didn't resist. Violet stood behind Callie and made sure she didn't lose her balance.

"I've got him now," Ben Charles told her. "I promise I'll take good care of him. Please let Violet take you into the house, where she'll make you comfortable."

The woman stood trembling in the cold.

"Callie," Violet said gently. "You have to think about your baby. Please come with me."

At last the other woman conceded and let Violet guide her back inside and into the warm comfortable drawing room. Violet led her to a chair near the fireplace. "Your boots are wet. Let's take them off and set them near the fire to dry. I'll get you dry stockings and a pair of slippers."

Callie obediently let Violet remove her boots and wet stockings, and Violet ran upstairs to her own room and returned to put water on to boil before taking the footwear back and helping Callie into them. "When do you expect your baby to be born?"

"One more month," Callie replied in a weak voice.

"I don't know what I'll do now. I can't take care of the ranch by myself."

"You don't have to worry about that today."

"The animals will need feed and water. Our neighbors can see to that. The Cawleys."

"I'll let Mr. Hammond know and he'll see they're looked after." Violet felt completely at a loss. Nothing she said or did could make a difference. This poor woman was suffering, and words were insufficient. Violet didn't have any encouragement to offer anyway.

Callie rested her head against the back of the chair and wept openly, tears streaming down her cheeks, her heartbreak painful to witness. Violet sat with her, a silent companion as half an hour passed. An hour.

At last Ben Charles joined them, carrying a pad and pencil. Callie sat up.

"How are you doing?" he asked.

She shook her head. "I don't know. What will happen next?"

He pulled a chair closer and sat. "I need a little information from you. And whenever you're ready we'll talk about a service and decide where you would like your husband buried. You don't have to decide anything today."

She brushed a limp hand across her eyes. "I won't be able to keep the ranch, so I reckon he'll be buried at the cemetery."

"The ground has frozen over the past few weeks," he told her. "So we won't have a burial until spring."

"Well, of course," she said. "I never even thought of that."

"Joseph's body will rest in our mausoleum over the

winter. It's aboveground and well sealed. He won't be disturbed until you're ready for the burial."

She nodded. "All right."

"Now I need his full name and date of birth, things like that."

Callie told him everything he needed to know.

"I don't have much to pay you," she said. "Not until the stock and land are sold."

"We'll work something out," he assured her.

"We had plans," she told him. "Joseph was going to buy breed stock in the spring. He gave me a cherry tree and planted it because I love cherry pie. He's been making a—" her voice caught "—a cradle for the baby. It wasn't supposed to be like this. Nothing was supposed to be like this."

"His life was cut short too soon," he agreed. He set the paper aside. "Would you like to speak with Reverend Densmore? Or if you're members of the Mount Zion Church, I'd be glad to send for Reverend Knudson."

"We always meant to come join up at the church, but we never got around to it."

"That's all right. If speaking to a preacher would bring you comfort, it doesn't matter if you're a church member or not. All that matters is taking care of you, however that needs to happen."

Callie seemed to think it over. "Maybe later. Maybe tomorrow."

"Whatever you like."

"I didn't want to leave her alone," Violet said. "But if you're going to be here for a few minutes, I'll make tea and bring her something to eat."

Ben Charles straightened his right leg to reach into his pocket and take out his watch. "Tessa should be getting home in a few minutes. Would it be inconvenient for you to serve supper in here this evening?"

Violet glanced around the room she liked so well. "Not at all. I can dish up our meals and bring them in on trays."

Thomas returned Tessa while Violet was steeping tea and arranging trays. Tessa's animated face showed her pleasure. Violet explained that Ben Charles was occupied and thanked Thomas for taking care of Tessa and bringing her home on time. After he'd left, Tessa ran up to change and returned to help Violet.

"I want to hear all about the party," Violet told her.

"I'll tell you both this evening," Tessa assured her. "After the widow has been attended to. Does she have plans for the night? I usually try to find someone to stay with a person who is alone—or I make arrangements for them to stay with a friend."

Violet shared what she knew. "I didn't know what to say, so I just sat there."

"That was what she needed. Comforting someone doesn't always take words. Just sharing human concern and touch is a ministry."

Again Violet looked at Tessa as though she was the older, wiser one.

Tessa introduced herself to Callie and expressed her condolences. Violet helped her move a round table into the center of the chairs before the fireplace, and together they carried trays.

Once everything was adjusted, Ben Charles prayed. "Thank You for Your provision, Lord. Thank You for sending us the people we need to help us through the good times and the difficult times of our lives. I lift up young Mrs. Jefferson to You, Lord. I ask You to be with her every moment of each day while she learns to live without Joseph. Bring her peace and comfort this night, and may Your blessings abound to her. Thank You for this meal, Lord, and it's in Jesus's name we pray."

Amens chorused around the table. Callie's hands shook, so Violet reached to help her with her napkin and spoon.

Violet had prepared a rich dark veal stew, with winter squash, potatoes, cabbage and turnips. With it she served fresh bread with butter, preserves she'd purchased and applesauce.

Callie ate more than Violet thought she would, and she remembered the young woman had told them she'd gone looking for her husband when he didn't come to the house for the noon meal, so she probably hadn't eaten since morning.

She couldn't help thinking about the determination and fortitude it had taken for Callie to get her husband into the wagon and bring him here. She was a slight thing—and with child—so the act amazed her.

Violet studied the frail-looking woman in a new light.

Strong people did what they had to do.

Chapter Eleven

Violet hadn't wanted to leave the safety and blissful comfort of the house to assist Ben Charles today, but she'd done it. Henry hadn't been here. Tessa had been gone. She'd been the only person who could sit with Callie Jefferson. She'd felt inadequate and unprepared to comfort the woman, but there hadn't really been a choice.

Did that make her a strong person, too?

Not really. She wasn't the one left widowed and carrying a baby and not knowing what was to become of her life. But thinking back over the past months, she realized she'd been in a similar position after her father's death, after Wade had threatened she'd go to jail and chased her off. Maybe she was stronger than she thought.

"I'd like for you to stay with us tonight," Ben Charles said to Callie. "Tomorrow I'll go talk with your neighbors and see if they can put you up for few days, so you won't be alone."

A pang of appreciation and deep admiration cut into Violet's chest with a sensation akin to pain. Tessa didn't appear at all surprised at his unplanned invitation, and Violet suspected they had offered shelter to grieving family members more than once.

He glanced at Violet. "Will you light a fire in the bedroom beside yours, please?"

"Yes, of course." Tessa gathered the dishes, so Violet stood beside Callie. "Let's go get you settled for the night."

Upstairs in the bedroom Ben Charles had indicated, she started a fire in the fireplace and turned down the sheets. "The water closet is just down the hall. There's a stove to heat water, and if you'd like a bath, I'll start it for you."

"Right inside the house? I've heard about necessaries indoors, but I've never seen one."

"Why don't I get water ready. A nice warm bath might relax you."

"You're very kind, Miss Violet."

Violet heated water and poured it into the tub, then laid out toweling, one of her own nightdresses and stockings before leading Callie to the bathing room.

She stood outside the door, feeling helpless as soft sounds of weeping echoed in the tiled room beyond. Tears formed in her own eyes at Callie's misery. She understood what it felt like to be alone and faced with an uncertain future. She knew exactly how devastating the loss of a loved one was. She blotted her eyes on her sleeve.

"Are you all right?" Tessa asked from several feet away.

Violet moved away from the door. "It's not me," she whispered.

"Mrs. Jefferson?"

Violet nodded.

"I'm sorry I wasn't here when she arrived."

"Don't be silly. You deserve to have a good time. I'm excited to hear all about the party."

"Come to the library after Mrs. Jefferson has gone to bed."

An hour later Violet sat in one of the comfortable chairs at the front end of the hall while the girl jumped up and down from her chair, animatedly sharing the events of the afternoon.

Ben Charles had joined them and now listened to his sister with a relaxed expression.

"Thomas's family was so kind to me." Her lovely face glowed. "It wasn't at all like it was in school. No one mentioned where I live or what the family does. No one was standoffish. I participated in the games. Thomas brought me so much punch, my teeth were having boat races."

Violet laughed softly. "It sounds perfect."

"It was. He's such a gentleman. He's handsome, too, don't you think?"

"I do." The contrast in atmosphere between Callie's room and being out here was like night and day. While the other woman mourned her beloved husband, Tessa was discovering a budding first attraction, with all the innocence and anticipation that came with it. Tessa deserved this happiness.

"I'm pleased you enjoyed yourself." Ben Charles stood and gave his sister a peck on the cheek. "I'll leave the two of you to discuss Thomas's finer points."

He left quietly, heading for the back stairs. Violet turned her attention back to Tessa.

Later she heated water and washed dishes in the

kitchen, glad to perform a mundane chore and step away from the high emotions of the day. She used the peaceful time to pray for Callie, and while she was at it, she prayed for Tessa and Ben Charles.

"Was there any coffee left?" Ben Charles descended the rear stairs.

"I'll make some more," she offered.

"I would appreciate it. I'll be working late, and I wouldn't mind a fresh pot." He stoked the stove, then took a seat at the table while she filled the pot and measured grounds. "Thank you for taking care of Mrs. Jefferson today, Violet. It's hard when there's no family."

"You don't have to thank me."

"It's not part of your job."

It may not be part of her job, but it had been the right thing to do. Human kindness was always the right thing to do. "She's a remarkable woman."

"No more remarkable than you."

"I don't have the strength to do what she did."

"I think you do. You sell yourself short."

The coffee boiled, and a few drops hissed on the surface of the stove. She dried and put away the remaining dishes, then poured his coffee.

"Tessa had a nice time at the party. She seems happy."

"That's all I want for her."

"You've done a good job raising her. As well as any parent and better than most."

"I wasn't always sure I was doing the right thing. A girl needs a woman's guidance, and Mrs. Gable filled in a lot, bless her heart. When she left I wasn't sure how we'd get by, but then God sent you."

"I'm glad to be here for her."

"I hope it's not too much pressure for me to say that. I'm only assuming you'll want to stay."

Violet read his hesitancy. "I want to stay."

"Good. Because I want you here."

She didn't know what to say to that. Her cheeks burned.

He set down his cup and stood. She thought he was finished and heading next door, but instead of turning away, he crossed the distance between them. "I don't want to make any mistakes with you, Violet."

This close, he was so tall and his eyes intense, but she didn't step back. "What do you mean?"

"You came here to work, and you do an excellent job. I asked you to look after Tessa, and you've done more than that. You've become her friend. I won't do anything to spoil that. Tessa is everything to me."

"I understand. I'm content here. Truly."

"Do you…?" His hesitancy was out of character. She waited. "Do you sense something between the two of us?"

She was too surprised to answer.

"I'm saying this wrong. And maybe the timing is bad." He ran a hand through his hair, and it stood out in charming tufts. "I feel something for you. It's unexpected and it's uncomfortable—but it's good. I wasn't open to these feelings, because I know your aversion to my work, and I've been down that road in the past. But the feelings are there, and I can't look away from them. Denial would be cowardly."

"The last thing you are is cowardly, Ben Charles."

"My concern is that after I share this with you, it will change everything. I don't want to do something to change how comfortable you are here. If our working relationship is spoiled, you might want to leave. So I'm conflicted. I want to see if there is a hope of something between the two of us, but I don't want me asking to change everything that's good if it's all wrong."

"I understand what you're saying."

He let his arms fall slack at his sides. "All right."

She collected her thoughts. It had been an emotionally exhausting day. "This job is important to me. Tessa is important to me. But the rest of it—what you do—frightens me. I'm sorry I fall into that category of small-minded people who—"

"You don't."

"Maybe I do. Just going out there to that wagon today took every bit of fortitude I possess. And even then I couldn't look. I can't look, Ben Charles. You said you can't become cowardly, but I am."

He rested a hand along her upper arm. "You're not a coward."

"You don't understand."

"I do understand, Violet."

She shook her head. "Tessa has more maturity and acceptance in her little finger than I do in my whole body."

"She's been around this her whole life."

"I am not like you. I can't deny I have feelings for you, though. I just don't know what to do with them."

"Here's the thing, Violet. If I kiss you and you don't like it—if it's the worst thing you could imagine—you say so and we go back to where we were before. But promise you won't leave."

Her heartbeat skittered, and she forgot to breathe for a moment. *Kiss her!* "I won't leave."

He raised his other hand to cup her jaw, and his palm

was warm against her skin. His eyes held a promise she intended to make him keep. And in that moment she was impatient to know everything there was to know about him—and to feel his lips against hers.

She raised on tiptoe to meet him as he lowered his face and kissed her. Her head felt light and her heart pounded erratically, but she wouldn't have missed this moment for anything. He threaded his fingers into her hair, and her scalp tingled.

He cupped her face in both hands and drew away long enough to whisper in a gruff tone, "Say again you won't leave."

"I won't leave," she promised. "And that kiss definitely wasn't the worst thing I could imagine." She let her lips curve into a smile. "In fact, I wouldn't mind if you did it again."

She didn't have to ask twice. The second kiss was less tentative, yet every bit as tender. Ben Charles's kisses were definitely worth repeating.

When he ended the kiss and took half a step back, she felt bereft without his warmth. "You don't know how long I've wanted to do that," he said.

"How long?"

"Probably since that first day when you showed up without proper boots and leaned across the snow to touch Clarence's neck."

"The horse."

"Yes. The look on your face was as though you'd found a friend in a strange land. You've still never looked at me the way you looked at him."

She had to laugh then. "And you wanted to kiss me."

"Well, I noticed how pretty you are, and if I noticed that I must have thought of kissing you."

She wanted to belong here. She wanted to belong with this man, but she had no idea how to overcome their differences. How to overcome her *fear*. Because no matter what he said, she was a coward.

Chapter Twelve

"No one will come," Callie said for the third time since Violet had helped her dress. She'd spent another night with them, and Ben Charles had taken her home to get clothing and to speak with the neighbors, who were looking after the stock.

The scheduled service, which would be held at the funeral home, was only minutes away. "Mr. Hammond said some of the men from Carson Springs will be here," Violet assured her.

"I don't think I can do this." The other woman slumped onto a chair.

"Do you feel all right?" Violet took her hand.

"No, I feel sick through and through. My heart's a big hard rock in my chest." She grasped Violet's hand hard. "Stay with me, Violet. Will you stay right with me, please?"

"Well, I—I don't know. I don't usually—"

"Please," Callie begged. "Please stay close. I don't know how I'm going to bear this."

Violet didn't know how she would bear it either, but she couldn't say so. Callie needed her. She would feel the same if it was her, and she would need a friend. "Yes. Yes, of course I'll stay with you."

More tears flowed down the other woman's cheeks. "Thank you."

Violet started talking to herself right then and there. She could do this. She would do this. She would set aside her debilitating fear and be a friend.

Ben Charles couldn't have been more surprised to see Violet in a black dress, similar to his sister's, as the three women entered the drawing room. Callie Jefferson supported herself on Violet's arm, and trembled visibly. Violet, on the other hand, looked cool and calm. Tessa led them to chairs, where they waited while he went out of the room to greet townspeople and direct them along the hallway to the small chapel, where Joseph's body lay. Reverend Densmore and his wife had arrived early, and the reverend spoke to Callie.

Once Ben Charles thought everyone who would be coming had arrived, he went into the drawing room. "It's time."

He offered Callie his arm, and she leaned upon him, trembling. Violet supported her on the other side, and they approached the chapel.

He glanced at Callie's face, then at Violet's, and didn't know which one was more visibly shaken. The color had drained from Violet's complexion and her lips were white. He feared she would be the one to faint or be sick, but she stoically walked forward.

He led Callie to the pine box supported on a skirted riser, where she could say her final goodbyes to her husband. Afterward he and Violet helped her to a wooden folding chair, and Reverend Densmore came forward to speak.

The reverend was good at conducting funeral services, always sharing encouragement for the departed's loved ones. Today he spoke of how Joseph Jefferson had left behind earthly things and gone to sit at the right hand of Jesus.

Callie seemed to take strength from his words. She clung to Violet's hand until Ben Charles wondered how Violet kept from crying out. But Violet remained unmoved, handing Callie a fresh handkerchief, comfortingly rubbing the back of her hand.

Tessa moved to the pianoforte behind a palm plant, where she played a hymn and sang along in her lovely unwavering contralto voice. His sister was such a help, he sometimes wondered how he would ever get by without her. When the song ended, the reverend prayed.

Once it was time for Ben Charles and Henry to put the lid on the casket, he asked Callie if she wanted another moment. She shook her head, and the two men covered the pine box.

Townspeople and a few ranchers offered Callie their condolences. She hadn't wanted a meal, so the service ended.

The Jeffersons' neighbors, Mr. and Mrs. Cawley, waited for Callie to gather her things. She was going home with them for the time being. Callie hugged Violet and thanked her again and again.

Violet returned the hug and followed them out of doors. Ben Charles and Henry lifted the casket to the cart, so they could move it to the mausoleum. There would be a burial service in the spring.

Returning from the cemetery nearly an hour later,

Ben Charles caught sight of a lone figure standing in front of the house. Violet. Unmoving.

"Henry, will you take the hearse to the stable, please?" He jumped down and strode across the snow-cleared drive to where she stood. "Violet?"

Her lips were blue from the cold. She didn't respond. "Violet?"

Finally she turned her head to look at him.

"What are you doing out here?" He grabbed both of her hands and chafed them between his to warm her fingers. "Your hands are freezing."

"They're dead," she said.

He glanced across the road and back. "Who is dead?"

"All of them. All of them."

"Come inside." When she didn't respond to his urging, he swooped her up in his arms and carried her into the house. He took her into the drawing room, stoked the fire and brought her a blanket. "Tessa!" he shouted up the stairs and shrugged out of his coat.

"I'm up here."

"Violet's been out front all this time. Will you make her tea?"

"What?" She darted down the stairs. "What was she doing out there?"

"Just standing."

"I'm so sorry. I thought she'd gone to the kitchen. Is she all right?"

"We need to get her warm. I'm not sure what's wrong."

Back at the chair where he'd settled Violet, he knelt at her feet and took her hand. At her detached behavior a shudder of unease moved through him. "Violet, will you talk to me?"

"They all died, Ben Charles."

"Who were they?"

"I didn't know them. Mothers and fathers. Children. Mama. Mama died, too." She turned her dark gold-flecked gaze on him, and he knew she was speaking to him now, telling him something he wasn't sure he wanted to know, but she needed to say it.

"Why don't you tell me everything," he coaxed in a low tone.

"We were riding the train back from Pennsylvania, where my mother's sister lived. One minute Mama was reading to me. The next moment the sounds of metal were so loud we couldn't hear each other scream." She blinked and relayed the story as though it had happened to someone else. "We were tossed about. The screams and cries were as terrifying as the confusion."

"You were in a train accident."

She nodded. "It seemed an eternity, those minutes, even though the whole thing happened suddenly. And then everything was still."

The hair on Ben Charles's neck stood up at the telling.

"It was so quiet," she said barely above a whisper. "Moaning. A baby cried, but it was far away. I think I cried, too. My mama didn't answer me. She was lying across my legs and something heavy was on top of her. I couldn't move."

The realization of what she was revealing sunk in, and he struggled to comprehend. She'd been in a rail-car accident in which her mother and others had died, and she'd been trapped.

"How long?" he asked. "How long were you trapped?"

"Hours."

He wanted to cry for her. He wanted to hold her. He wanted to take away the nightmare of that day and all the days she'd lived with the memories since. He brushed his thumb across the back of her hand. "How old were you?"

"Six."

All he had were words and words seemed so ineffectual. Too ineffectual for an experience as traumatic as the one she'd suffered.

"Even though the accident was a blur at the time, the nightmares are as clear as the day it happened. Detail by detail. The waiting. I've had nightmares all these years."

He nodded his understanding.

"When my father passed away I asked for a quick graveside service."

"Nothing wrong with that. Everyone grieves differently."

"Today brought it all back—all the images and sensations I'd tried to keep buried."

"But you pushed through that for Callie's sake. You were a rock for her, Violet."

"How do you do it, Ben Charles? How do you watch people suffer like she's suffering? I thought the other side of it—death—was the worst, but that's not even half the horror. It's the living, hurting people who are in the most pain—who cause the most pain."

"Those people are going to hurt if I'm there or not," he said. "It's a fact of life, people die. Each one of us comes into the world and each one goes out. Wives and husbands and sons and daughters, we all lose loved ones. It's part of life. If I can make a difference for them when the time comes, then I feel as though I've made a contribution to the bigger picture. I may only have one or two days with them, but in that time I want to make the experience as easy to bear as I can."

"You do. I've seen that you do."

"These bodies of ours are merely vessels we live in while we're here on earth. They help us do the work that needs to be done. Once we die, our spirits move on to eternal reward, and what remains is nothing to fear. Joseph isn't in that shell you saw today. That's his earthly vessel. If he knew Jesus as his Lord and Savior, he's in glory, seated at the right hand of God."

Violet's gaze shifted to Tessa, and Ben Charles realized his sister had been sitting behind him this whole time. She came forward to give Violet the cup and saucer she'd been holding. He let go of Violet's hand so she could take it.

Violet sipped her tea. "You could never have anticipated what an inappropriate cook you were hiring."

"I don't believe that," he disagreed.

Her gaze touched on his chin, his eyes and lips. "What do you believe?"

"I think you know."

She appeared to think about her answer only a moment. "You believe in God's provision."

He nodded. "It's harder to believe you came here by mere coincidence than it is to believe God directed you to us for new understanding and healing. God saw your need and created a plan for the day when you would trust Him to take away this pain. The Bible says He heals the brokenhearted and binds up their wounds."

"When you prayed for Guy Chapman's family that day weeks ago, I wondered if it was too late for me, but I was hesitant to ask."

"Ask what, Violet?"

"If it was too late for me to have peace and comfort about my mother's death."

"It's never too late to pray," he said softly. "I've been praying for you all along, without knowing the specific problem. I asked God to let you trust me enough to tell me."

"I trust you."

"And I've prayed for the truth to be revealed about all things, including what happened back in Ohio."

"You've prayed for me?"

"Yes, of course."

"Will you pray now?"

Ben Charles turned and reached for Tessa's hand, drawing her down to the floor beside him.

Chapter Thirteen

"Lord, when one of your children is hurting, we all hurt. Violet has lived with the painful memories of that day when her mother died for too many years." Ben Charles stopped and got up, returning with a Bible from one of the shelves. Opening it, he flipped to the passage he wanted. "'O death, where is thy sting? O grave, where is thy victory? The sting of death is sin; and the strength of sin is the law. But thanks be to God, which giveth us the victory through our Lord Jesus Christ.'"

He closed the Bible and took both women's hands again. "Thank You, Lord, there is no fear in Your perfect love. Thank You for making provision for Violet. I ask that You show her Your perfect love and grant her the peace that comes with knowing You and abiding in Your will. Deliver her now from the pain of the past and bring her into the peace and prosperity You've promised. Those whose sins are forgiven have no fear of death, and You've given each of us the victory through Your son, Jesus."

Tessa's soft voice continued the prayer. "Thank You, Jesus, for bringing Violet into our home and our lives.

Your mercies are new every morning, and I pray that each day You open her eyes more and more to Your love, Your endless mercy and abounding grace."

As they said their amens together, tears poured down Violet's cheeks. Warmth flowed over her and through her, and a sense of calm and peace rested on her with a new assurance. What had happened in her childhood was a terrible experience. She would never completely forget. But she didn't have to let the memory control her life and blacken her future.

She might never be as completely at ease dealing with death as these two were, but she wasn't going to be bound to the past any longer. As though a weight had been lifted from her shoulders, she took a deep breath and straightened her shoulders. *Thank You, Lord.*

That night she rested well, and when she woke, Callie was on her mind. She prayed for her and made a mental note to check on her later in the week. She had a lot of baking to do for the Ladies' Aid Society event.

For two days she baked and frosted and filled pastries with a light heart, humming to herself, sometimes praying and always being grateful.

The evening of the event she'd laid out her clothing when there was a knock. She pulled on her dressing gown and opened the door to discover Ben Charles. He wore a suit and tie and a brilliant white shirt. His appearance and smile took her breath away. He'd become dear to her, so dear she ached for words and actions to let him know. Her heart was full. He held out a small box. "I got you something."

Surprised, she hesitated momentarily before reaching for it. She couldn't remember the last time she'd received a gift. It had probably been something from her mother when she was a girl. Her heart sped up. "Why did you get me a gift?"

"No reason except I thought you'd like this."

She removed the green ribbon from the box and lifted the lid. Inside lay a pair of silver-and-pearl hair combs. Violet tucked the lid under the box so she had a free hand to take one out. "These are lovely." She lifted her gaze to his. "I don't know what to say."

"You could say you like them, if you do."

"Of course I do. I've never had anything so exquisite. I'm just surprised."

"I'll let you finish getting ready."

"Thank you." Words were inadequate for what was in her heart.

"You're welcome." He smiled before turning away.

Violet carried the box to the bureau and set it down. She took out the combs and held them, ran a finger over the smooth pearls. It was an extravagant gift. What was she to make of it? She redid her hair, sweeping up the sides and securing them with the combs. She turned her head in the lamplight to see how they looked against her dark hair. The effect was striking.

After donning her new rose-red dress with the embroidered sateen yoke and sleeves, fitted forearms and fur collar, she tugged on kid-leather boots and the matching hat and went in search of Tessa. The girl exclaimed over Violet's dress and hair—noticed the combs—and together they descended the stairs to the foyer, where their coats had been hung on hooks.

Ben Charles joined them from the drawing room, and his eyes lit up. "I have the pleasure of the company of the two prettiest girls in all of Colorado. One for each arm."

Tessa laughed and reached on tiptoe to kiss his cheek. "Help me on with my coat."

He did, and all the while his eyes were on Violet. She waited and turned her back to slip her arms into the sleeves when it was her turn. The appreciative look on his face touched her. His gaze went from her hair to her eyes and lips, and he gave her a private smile.

Violet's heart fluttered.

He had taken her across town earlier that afternoon to deliver and help arrange all the pastries at the Walsinger Estate, where the recital was to be held. Now Ben Charles ushered them into the buggy and urged Clarence into a trot.

The rooms in Sebird and Dollie Walsinger's home were large enough to entertain numerous guests comfortably. Ben Charles told her Sebird owned stock in the railroad, and had started three of the businesses in Carson Springs, including the bank and the newspaper. He and Dollie were down-to-earth and friendly, however, and Violet's concerns about not fitting in were put to rest.

Chairs had been arranged in an enormous music room decorated with velvet drapes, paintings, potted ferns, even a baby grand piano and two elaborately carved and gilded organs. Violet hadn't imagined the event would be this grand or anticipated the number of people who would be sampling her pastries.

"Violet, there you are." Lenora Grimes joined them, dressed in a russet gown that bared her shoulders. She wore three strands of pearls and matching earbobs swung when she spoke. "I've been telling everyone they're in for a treat this evening. I confess I tasted one of each. What do you call the balls filled with dates and rolled in coconut?"

"My father simply called them delights."

"How fitting. The *kringla* twists melt in the mouth, and those cookies with the clove…?"

"Pepper *kakor,*" Violet told her.

"You've outdone yourself. I can't thank you enough." Lenora turned to Ben Charles. "Does she cook *everything* that well?"

"Indeed she does." He gave Lenora a crooked smile. "We've never eaten so well."

"What beautiful hair combs, Violet," Lenora complimented.

Violet's cheeks warmed. "Thank you. They were a gift."

Lenora's gaze moved from Violet to Ben Charles and she smiled. After she moved away, Violet glanced at him, and he winked at her.

Soon they were asked to take seats, and the president of the Ladies' Aid Society spoke to them about where the funds that were raised would be going this year. The group sponsored several charities and a children's hospital.

The musicians were accomplished, playing pieces on harpsichord, organ and violin. Lastly the singers performed, and Violet found it amazing so many talented people lived in or near Carson Springs.

"I've never heard music or voices so beautiful," she whispered to Ben Charles.

The entire evening was enchanting. Later, when it was time for refreshments, her baked confections were praised as highly as the performances.

"Wherever did you come by these lily-shaped cookies?" a woman asked Lenora.

"Those were made by none other than Miss Violet Bennett," the woman answered.

"It's Kristofferson," Violet corrected. "Violet Kristofferson. Those are calla lilies."

"It must have taken you hours to make all of these," the woman said in amazement.

"Once you've shaped as many as I have, they don't take that long."

"Where did you learn to do this?"

Violet explained to her and eventually numerous people knew how her Swedish father had taught her his specialties in his pastry shop. Ben Charles kept her punch cup filled, and she chatted with everyone who approached her.

Thomas Everett's family had attended the recital, so Tessa had yet another opportunity to spend time with the young man. Ben Charles observed the two as they smiled awkwardly at each other over cups of punch. He made a point of speaking to Thomas's parents and thanking them for seeing that Tessa had a nice time at the birthday party.

As he watched Violet talk to the townspeople who greeted her and praised her pastries, he took pride in seeing her happy and interacting with others. He was grateful to Lenora for giving her this opportunity to not only meet people, but to feel confident and accomplished.

He'd been attracted to her all along, as he'd told her, but he hadn't been comfortable with his growing feelings. It had seemed wrong to bring her so far to work for him and then change the stakes.

He no longer thought that way. If she felt about him the way he felt toward her, they had something they could make work.

She'd worn a red dress with fur trim, and the color

was striking on her. Her near-black hair was the perfect contrast for her ivory skin, and the pearls on her hair combs stood out. When he stood close enough, he could smell her fragrant hair. He imagined it would be soft and silky to the touch.

It wasn't only her beauty that appealed to him. Every day he recognized another quality he admired. He wanted what the Grimeses had. He wanted Violet as his bride and to have her at his side for the rest of their lives. He wanted to have children with her and watch them grow up. He wanted the sign on the mortuary to again one day read Hammond and Son.

His chest swelled at the imagined thought of calling her his wife.

This was nothing like his experience with Madeline so long ago. Violet hadn't come to him out of a morbid curiosity about his occupation. She'd had a genuine fear that she'd carried since her childhood, and that he believed she would overcome with the Lord's help. She was compassionate and kind. Generous and sincere. Only one thing stood in the way.

They hadn't discussed it further, but if she had been blamed for starting the bakery fire back in Ohio, the truth would have to be told so her name could be cleared. He'd been thinking about the matter for a while, but now the time had come. Tomorrow he would send telegrams to officials to get an idea of what needed to be done.

Again he would place his confidence in God for a good outcome.

Chapter Fourteen

It was snowing again. Ben Charles had said he'd be back before dark and had ridden into town.

The previous day Violet had helped Callie move her things into Carson Springs. She had sold the ranch, and Ben Charles had been the first person she'd paid. She had paid for a headstone, as well. They had taken her clothing and personal items to a two-story house on a shaded street where Joseph Jefferson's aunt lived. The elderly woman needed someone to look after her, and Callie needed a home for herself and the baby, which would arrive soon. The arrangement pleased Violet, and Callie was close enough she could call on her.

One of Callie's new neighbors had given Violet a chicken in return for her date-delight recipe, and now the pieces were frying to a golden crisp on top of the stove while she stirred slaw and kept rolls warm.

The kitchen door opened and a flurry of cold air and snowflakes swirled in around Ben Charles's ankles.

"You're just in time for supp—"

He tossed his hat toward the rack, but it missed and sailed to the floor. "Violet!"

His face was red from the cold and his hair disheveled. "Yes?"

"Sit down."

"I'm putting supper on the table."

He grabbed a pot holder and moved the heavy skillet of chicken off the flame. "Supper can wait."

Her heart sank at the urgency in his voice. She dried her hands. "What's wrong?"

He pointed to a chair. "Sit."

She obeyed.

He shrugged out of his coat after taking a folded piece of paper from the pocket.

"What's that?"

"Telegrams from the Ohio State Police, the local police office and a couple of shop owners near the Finneys' bakery."

Violet's heart leaped into her throat. She flattened her palm against her chest. What had he done? "Am I under arrest?"

"No, you're not under arrest."

"Tell me!"

"There was no crime committed. There wasn't even a *fire!*"

She blinked in consternation. "What?"

"Obviously Wade Finney made up that story about setting a fire with your apron to get rid of you. And it worked. But there was no fire. The bakery is still standing right where you left it."

"But I saw the smoke. I heard people running toward it."

"Seems there was a report of a trash barrel smoking in the alley, but it was thought to be cinders caught fire. Wade didn't start a fire and he didn't accuse you of anything. He made you think he'd done it, and once you'd gone he was off the hook from marrying you. According to one of the shopkeepers who responded, he's still raising a ruckus in town, and his father is at his wit's end."

The news took a minute to settle in her mind and turn to sharp anger. "Why, that no-account, low-down, good for nothing..."

"Person who drove you to Colorado," he finished for her.

The flash of resentment she felt was minute compared to the flood of relief. She blinked and stared at him. "I haven't been accused of anything?"

"Not a thing."

Her mind turned over a dozen thoughts at once, making sense of them. "What would you have done if your findings had been different?"

"I'd have gone to Ohio or hired a lawyer or done whatever needed to be done to clear your name. We couldn't just leave the concern hanging over our heads forever."

"Why didn't you tell me you'd been contacting people in Ohio?"

"I wanted to have all the facts first."

"Not because you didn't trust I'd told you the truth."

"No, of course not. I knew you told me the truth. I wanted to find out if the police had a case against you or if they were searching for you, and if so I needed to prove you innocent. We couldn't have moved forward with that uncertainty hanging over our heads. Don't you see? Now you're truly free because you know the truth."

Ben Charles was right of course. She'd been foolish to ignore the problem or think she could hide from it forever. Violet had been released from her imagined chains of bondage. "You sought the truth just to prove me innocent?"

"I sought the truth to give you the freedom to make a decision."

"What kind of decision?"

He looked down at his rumpled shirt and ran a hand through his hair before meeting her eyes. "This wasn't how I planned it at all."

"Ben Charles?" A ripple of unease passed through her.

He strode forward and pulled her to her feet and into his embrace. Lowering his head, he kissed her soundly. She forgot about their discussion and lost herself in the warm tenderness of his affection. Yes, this man had become dear to her. She dropped the towel she'd forgotten she was holding and raised both hands to bracket his face.

He separated them only enough to whisper, "I love you, Violet."

Joy spread through her heart and worked its way to her limbs. "I probably smell like chicken."

"I like chicken."

"I love you, too," she told him with more assuredness than she'd ever felt about anything. "You have changed my life and changed my heart. I can't take my next breath without thinking of you and wanting to be with you."

He grabbed her wrists and lowered himself to his knees, where he looked up at her. "Be my wife. I didn't know how much was missing from my life until you came here and showed me. I thought I was content, but I was only telling myself that to keep the loneliness at bay. I might have gone on that way forever if you hadn't chipped away the barriers around my heart with your tenderness. Marry me, Violet and I'll spend all my days making you happy and showing you how much I love you."

Overwhelming love and joy brought tears to her eyes. She couldn't speak around the swelling emotion in her throat.

"Stand up," she managed, and he obeyed. She flattened her palms against his chest and felt the steady life-affirming beat of his heart. "You have a heart big enough to hold enough love for a lifetime. I've seen how you love, and I will be the most fortunate woman who ever lived to have you love me like that, Ben Charles."

"Did you say yes?" he asked.

"I'm saying it now. Yes. Yes. Yes. I'll be your wife."

He kissed her again, a kiss filled with promises and hope. A kiss that held their future and encompassed their love. She was free to give in to her feelings, to show him her love this way, to tell him as often as she liked. *Thank You, Lord.*

On a sunny Saturday afternoon several weeks later Violet and Ben Charles stood before Reverend Densmore at the front of the Carson Springs First Christian Church. Tessa finished playing a hymn on the organ and their friends gathered behind them. As the last strains died away, Tessa stood and came to Violet's side.

Reverend Densmore read a few verses from his Bible and led the couple through their vows. When it came time for Ben Charles to put the ring on her finger, Violet gazed with surprise at the exquisite diamond-and-emerald band.

"It was my mother's," he whispered.

Violet turned quickly to seek Tessa's approval, and the girl smiled through her tears and nodded. Violet was honored to have something that meant so much to them both. She felt cherished that Ben Charles loved her so deeply. Her gift of embroidered handkerchiefs she'd given him didn't seem nearly enough, but he'd assured her he treasured them.

"By the power vested in me by God and the state of Colorado, I now pronounce you man and wife." The reverend closed his Bible.

She raised on tiptoe for a kiss to reaffirm their sacred vows and seal this commitment before God. Ben Charles's eyes shone.

They turned and the congregation enveloped them with congratulations. Callie Jefferson gently handed a flannel-wrapped bundle into Violet's arms.

Violet nestled the baby girl and raised her close to brush her lips across her downy forehead and inhale her scent. "Thank you for coming to our wedding, Annalie."

Ben Charles's large hand dwarfed the infant's head as he smoothed her feathery hair. "How is your little blessing, Mrs. Jefferson?"

"She's a comfort, I assure you. I thank God for her every day. I pray for a baby as pretty and healthy for you two very soon."

"Thank you," Ben Charles said. "We will appreciate every blessing that comes our way." He kissed Violet's forehead.

She handed the baby back to Callie and took her new husband's hand. Neighbors offered them wishes and filed out the door.

"I've been waiting to eat cake all day," Tessa said,

motioning them forward. The Walsingers had graciously offered their home for a reception.

"Not every bride makes her own wedding cake," Ben Charles teased.

"Not every bride bakes like Violet," Tessa answered with a laugh. She donned her coat and dashed out of doors.

Ben Charles took Violet's wrist and pulled her into the deserted coatroom. "I love you, Mrs. Hammond."

"I adore you, Mr. Hammond."

He kissed her and she thanked God for her many blessings this side of heaven. What had seemed impossible only a short time ago had become a reality. She had a husband, a sister, even friends. And she believed without a doubt that the all-encompassing love of God would sustain them for a lifetime.

* * * * *

Dear Reader,

What better way to spend a cold winter day or night than curled up with a book—and maybe a cup of hot chocolate? Some stories are simply more fun to write than others. Violet and Ben Charles's story was one of those, a story with two people meant for each other but fearful to risk their hearts. It's unusual for me to create a character who is not a person of faith, so writing from Violet's perspective was a challenge—but a challenge I enjoyed.

There's nothing I like better than creating story people who are so different from each other that it seems there's no way they will ever work things out to be together. So we have Ben Charles, a man comfortable in his profession as the undertaker and confident in his belief in God. Violet, on the other hand, is fearful of anything pertaining to death and has little knowledge of God…so I introduced them to each other—and let them make their own discoveries.

If you enjoy their story as much as I enjoyed writing it, drop me a line at SaintJohn@aol.com. I'd love to hear from you.

And don't forget the marshmallows!

Cheryl St. John

Questions for Discussion

1. Violet arrives in Colorado with only a few dresses, but two crates of books. The first time I ever moved, I cluelessly packed all my books in large boxes—boxes my poor husband could barely budge. We laugh about it now. Have you moved books with you from place to place?

2. Violet learned her baking skills from her father and has fond memories of her mother cooking. Do you have memories of being in the kitchen with a parent or grandparent? What did you take away from that time?

3. Even though Violet is put off by Ben Charles's occupation, she admires his confidence and appreciates his love for his sister. Can you see how his example leads her to trust him and provides opportunities for him to share about his faith?

4. Ben Charles believes God provides for us before we ever call on Him. One of his examples is the Israelites' escape from Egypt. Can you see ways God has made advance provision for you?

5. Violet's tragic past is a dark cloud over her life. We can't change our pasts, but we can place our confidence in God to guide us forward into the fullness of His joy. If there is anything holding you back from being all God wants you to be, maybe this is a good time to trust Him. Is there someone who will pray with you?

THE RANCHER'S
SWEETHEART

Debra Ullrick

To my wonderful husband, Rick,
whom I love so dearly.

Thanks for putting up with me for thirty-eight years
and for loving me for me. Your unconditional love
has taught me so much and has helped me weather
many a storm and trial. Thank you for always being
there for me, for supporting me and for being so
understanding when I'm up against a deadline.
You're my hero, and you always will be.
I love you so very much!

For I am fearfully and wonderfully made.
—*Psalms* 139:14

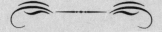

Chapter One

Kremmling, Colorado
1898

People froze to death in these kinds of blizzard conditions.

When Sunny Weston had started out from her family's ranch this morning for the five-hour ride that had now turned to seven, the sun had been shining. Now blinding snow swirled around her and her two horses, making it nearly impossible to see where she was going. She squinted, barely able to make out the aspen trees just a mere ten yards in front of her. Right now all she could do was hope and pray that she'd make it to her uncle's ranch alive.

If there was ever a time to pray, that time was now. "Lord, help me to get there safely. Sending a few angels to watch over me and guide me wouldn't hurt none neither. Thank You, Lord."

Her fingers stung and the wet gloves weren't helping any. Snow pelted into her face and eyes, stinging everything else with a head-numbing chill. Her beaver cowboy hat and knit wool scarf did a fair job of keeping the icy needles off her but not from the exposed parts. She wanted to dip her head to keep the ice pellets from hitting her face, but couldn't because she needed to see where she was going.

The farther she went, the more she struggled to get her bearings. She had no choice now but to depend on familiar landmarks to show her the way. When the fenced cemetery that held generations of Westons came into view, she felt some relief knowing she was heading in the right direction.

As she passed the tombstones, something sharp like barbed wire scraped painfully across her heart. They reminded her of her parents' graves back at their ranch.

Her ranch now.

She still hadn't gotten used to calling it *her* ranch and probably never would. But it was true nonetheless because three years ago her ma had died, then her pa passed away two months back. Her heart ached something awful, and she suspected it always would. The back of her eyes stung, but there'd be no tears today. She had to be strong. Had to press on. All the other choices in life had been buried right alongside her folks.

Aunt Minnie and Uncle Emmett were probably worried sick about her by now. Her uncle had wanted to send someone to fetch her, but she assured him she didn't need anyone. Now she hoped her foolish pride didn't have her regretting that decision.

She heaved a heavy sigh knowing she would have never had to leave her home in the first place if her family hadn't lost most of their livestock last year to the worst, deadliest blizzard this part of the county had ever seen. Down here in the lower part of the county they didn't get hit as hard as her family had living higher up the mountain and all. Uncle Emmett had only lost a few head of cattle and had offered to help her pa, but Pa was a proud man who convinced her uncle they'd be just fine.

And they were, too.

For a short while anyway.

For a short time that now seemed like a blink they were able to keep the ranch going on what little livestock had been spared. Then things had taken a turn for the worse when Pa had gotten sick and she'd been forced to sell the few remaining head of cattle to buy his medication and to pay for supplies in order to survive.

But Pa hadn't survived. Fresh pain assaulted her heart again. All her efforts to keep him and the ranch alive had failed. Uncle Emmett had taken the news real hard that his only brother was gone. Like her he'd hoped Pa would beat that Rocky Mountain spotted fever. They'd all been praying for just that, but whatever the good Lord's reasons were, He obviously had other plans. Plans she would never understand as long as she lived.

Her thoughts spun back to the day Uncle Emmett had asked what her plans were now that her folks were gone. He'd offered for her to come live with them, but she'd told him she wanted to find a way to make her and Pa's dream of building up the ranch again come true. Her uncle had said he understood and had even offered to lend her the money to do just that, but respectfully she'd turned down his offer.

Pa taught her to never go into debt. To pay for everything and to owe no man nothing as the Bible said. Her neighbors thought she should take the money or sell the place. But they didn't know how it was, being unbelievers and all. Plus they didn't know how determined she could be.

In that determination and desperation she'd come up with a plan to ask her uncle for a job instead. It'd been real hard to do and just as hard for him to say yes. After all, he and Aunt Minnie were the only kin she had left, and they struggled with the idea of her working for them. Said she was family and family helped one another. She assured them they were helping by giving her work. They did a heap of talking trying to convince her into letting them provide her with a home instead. Well, she had a home. And it was up to her alone now to keep it. Working for her uncle would help with the money she needed to get it going again.

She couldn't wait to get to the Flying W to see the aunt and uncle who had always made her feel as if she were someone real special. She only wished it was under better circumstances.

Because the snow swirled like a menacing fog around the horses, she could barely see the pack animal next to her. She huddled closer to her ride. In the very next minute, Rascal, her more sure-footed horse of the two, dropped forward, plunging head-down into the deep snow and nearly toppling her with him, but she grabbed the saddle horn and hung on.

When he got his footing back, he and Rowdy continued to struggle forward, plugging through the sixteen inches of freshly fallen snow. She knew their hooves had to be filled with hard-packed snow by now, making it even more difficult for them to walk.

That thought no more slipped through her mind, when both of her horses stopped, unwilling or unable to continue. She nudged the heels of her boots into Rascal's side and tugged on Rowdy's lead rope attached to her saddle horn. Both fought hard against her—not turning, not moving, just giving up—but she refused to give up. Giving up was never a consideration before, and it wasn't going to be one now. "C'mon, boys. We've only got a little bit farther to go. I promise once we get there you'll be rewarded with a nice warm barn, some good mountain hay and a huge scoop of wild oats."

Rascal let out a long whinny, shimmying Sunny's body in the saddle. She knew it wasn't in response to her promises. She strained against the thick snowfall to see what caused Rascal to get so excited. In the distance a hazy shadow of a horse and rider came into view. She pressed her eyes shut to clear her vision, and when she opened them again, the rider was still there. Uncle Emmett must've decided to come meet her after all even though she'd told him not to. "Thank You, Lord." She raised her hand to greet him, but no greeting came back to her. How odd.

The rider drew closer. One look at the cowboy and Sunny realized the man on the horse was too stout to be her uncle. With a quick turn she yanked her loaded Winchester lever-action .30-30 rifle out of the scabbard, ready to use it if necessary. She'd never killed anyone before, but after her pa had died, she'd wounded a man. She'd had to, to protect herself, and this time would be no different if the stranger made any troublesome moves.

"Miss Weston." The man's voice floated along on the snowflakes drifting toward her. The closer he got, his bundled image got clearer. He sat tall in the saddle, wearing a brown sheepskin coat, brown cowboy hat and woolies chaps.

Right about now she wished she had a pair of those leather woolies chaps with the long hair still on them. They would've kept her half-frozen legs warm. Unlike the two pair of woolen underdrawers, split woolen skirt and long woolen coat she had on.

Sunny warily eyed the cowboy when he reined his horse within a few feet of hers.

"Your uncle Emmett will be relieved to know you're safe. He sent me to escort you home."

So, the cowboy knew Uncle Emmett. That settled her heart enough for her to lower the gun. Sitting taller in the saddle, she squared her shoulders and lifted her chin, a move that let cold flakes drift far too close to her nearly exposed skin. "Thank you just the same, but I don't need no escort. Besides, who might you be?" she asked.

He chuckled, a nice, deep sound, and his lips turned upward in an amused grin. "That's what your uncle Emmett said you'd say. And I might be Jedidiah Cooper, at your service." He touched the brim of his hat and gave a brief nod. His blue eyes twinkled with humor.

Indignation lit into her at the thought that he might think she was incapable of doing something like this on her own. Who needed a man to be "at your service"? Certainly not her.

"Foreman of the Flying W ranch," he continued.

Her uncle's ranch. She pursed her lips together but made no reply.

"And now, miss, if you will allow me, I'd like to escort you home."

"I done said I don't—"

"I know, I know." He raised his hand. "You already said you don't need an escort. No disrespect, ma'am, but I don't work for you. I work for your uncle. And he sent me to fetch you. And fetch you I will."

Too cold and tired to argue, she placed her rifle back in its scabbard, coaxed her horses forward and slogged past him. Thankfully Rascal and Rowdy willingly moved forward. "Then you'd best get to it. You coming?" she hollered over her shoulder.

Jed stared at the cowgirl's back as it disappeared into the blinding snow. Her uncle had warned him about her, and he wasn't kidding. Spirited. Uh-huh. Independent. Right again. Sassy. Sure enough. But then again, Emmett said not to let that tough exterior fool him, that she was a real sweetheart.

Tough exterior? Tough something, but there wasn't much exterior to her.

From what he could tell, the woman wasn't any bigger than a flea on a cow. Still, Jed couldn't wait to get a glimpse of that sweet side. In all fairness to Miss Weston, she was allowed to be a bit cranky since she'd been out riding in this weather for hours. He knew he would be.

Even in her cantankerous state, judging by the view of her eyes, which was all he could see in their brief encounter, there was no mistaking she was a pretty little thing. A pretty little thing he needed to guard his behavior around because earlier that morning her uncle had held a meeting, warning the hired hands if he caught any of them trying to woo her or anything of that nature, he would fire them instantly. When Emmett had finished talking to them, he'd taken Jed aside and asked him to keep an eye on Sunny for him, to make sure the men left her alone and all. The last time Jed had been thrown together with a woman like that was at the last ranch he'd worked on.

At only seventeen Louisa had thought herself to be in love with Jed. One day she had caught him off guard and kissed him, and her father had come into the barn at that exact moment. Jed had taken a beating that day and had been sent away.

The sad part was, he didn't even know what he'd said or done that had encouraged Louisa where the two of them were concerned. But, according to her, he had.

Well, he might be thrown together with Miss Weston, but he would be mindful of how he behaved around her. He would be friendly, but not too friendly; polite, but not too polite. After all, he couldn't afford to lose this job. It paid better than any other around. Because of Emmett's generous wages, it would only be a matter of time before Jed had enough money saved to buy his own spread.

Realizing Sunny was yards ahead of him, he tapped his horse's sides and trudged through the snow until he pulled up alongside her.

She glanced over at him but didn't say a word. Frost covered her eyebrows, ice and snow covered her shoulders, and her leather gloves were wet. The woman had to be freezing from her long ride down the mountain. Twenty miles, to be exact. Twenty miles of trudging through thick forest, sagebrush, badger holes, rough terrain with no trails, and adverse weather conditions to boot. One thing was clear—she wasn't made of anything soft.

Another thing even clearer was, he wouldn't be any kind of man if he didn't offer her his gloves. He prided himself on being a gentleman, and wasn't about to go and ruin that reputation just because she was as welcoming as a porcupine. He peeled his elkskin chopper mittens off and handed them to her. "Here. Put these on."

She glanced at his wool-lined mitts. "I can't take those. You need them."

"Not as much as you do. Besides, we're almost there and my hands aren't cold. Take them." He stretched them even farther toward her, hoping she would give in and take them before frostbite set in.

Her eyes never strayed from them as they rode forward, one rocking step at a time.

Jed couldn't stand it any longer. He stopped their horses and without her permission removed her gloves, revealing beet-red fingers and colder-than-icicles hands. As fast as his large fingers would allow, he slid her tiny hands into his sheepskin-cuffed mittens, knowing the wool lining would warm them quickly.

At first she moved to protest, but when her hands were sunk deep into the mittens, she let out a long sigh. "Thank you. I must admit, that feels nice." She glanced at his hands and concern replaced the relief he'd seen in her eyes just moments before. "You sure about this?"

Oh, he was sure, all right. "Yes, ma'am, I am. Now let's get going."

Off they went, trekking their way through the blue spruce pine and aspen trees. Round about ten minutes later the long L-shaped log cabin came into view. Minnie, Sunny's aunt, stood at the window peering out. When she spotted them, the curtain dropped into place. By the time they pulled their horses up to the hitching post in front of the house, the door to the mudroom flew open. "Oh, Sunny. Thank God you're all right. Come. Get inside here where it's warm."

Jed hopped off his horse and went around to the side of Sunny's horse to help her down.

"I don't need no help. Thank you."

"I know. But let me help anyway."

She shook her head and rolled her brown eyes at him. A glance toward her aunt must have convinced her to let him, though. When her feet met the ground, he released her, towering over her by at least ten inches or better.

"You coming?" Minnie's voice rose above the wind.

"You'd better hurry." Jed yanked his head her aunt's direction. "They've been waiting since early morning."

Instead of going toward the door, Sunny walked to the front of her steeds. "I'll be in as soon as I unload my things and take care of my horses."

Minnie rubbed her arms. "Let the boys take care of that, child. You come inside where it's warm."

Jed reached for the reins. "I'll take care of things for you. Go ahead and go on inside." Jed gazed down at her, hoping she'd take him up on his offer. Being half-frozen and all, she needed to get inside as soon as possible.

Instead of agreeing to let him, she cupped her hands over her mouth and hollered over the wind that had picked up even more now, "Don't wait for me, Aunt Min. I'll only be a few minutes."

Mrs. Weston's shoulders rose and dropped. "All right. If you're sure."

"I'm sure. Thank you." The door closed, and Miss Weston faced him for all of two seconds before retrieving the reins from his hands.

Emmett had said she was stubborn. This went beyond stubborn.

"I promised Rascal and Rowdy hay, oats and a warm barn. I aim to keep that promise as soon as I get this here packsaddle unloaded."

Jed wanted to argue. Oh, how he wanted to argue. But from the little he'd seen and from what her uncle had told him about her, he just shook his head and walked over to her packhorse and got to work helping her unload her belongings into a corner of the large mudroom. When they finished, the two of them leaned into the wind as they headed to the barn. Once again she refused his help with her horses. Hard as it was, he left her to it while he tended to his own.

While she brushed her horses down, he went ahead and hauled water into all the stalls.

"Where do you want me to put my boys?" Her voice was as soft and smooth as a rose petal now that it wasn't being drowned out by a blizzard.

"In here." He led her to the stall he'd readied for her horses earlier that day.

Hay already filled the manger, but she kept that promise of hers and gave her horses a nice helping of oats, too. Both geldings dove their mouths into the fare, greedily munching their oats. A sound he enjoyed. Something about it always seemed so soothing.

"See you boys tomorrow." She patted their necks and closed the gate on them. "Hoo wee. Sure glad that's done. I can't wait to get inside." She rubbed her hands over her arms. Then all he could see was the top of her cowboy hat. "Thanks for getting their water and for helping me unload my things."

"You're welcome."

She raised her face and gazed up at him with those

big brown eyes. Some of that sweetness showed up really pretty in them.

They stood there for a moment.

"Well, I'll see you tomorrow." She opened the barn door and headed toward the house before he even had a chance to open it for her.

Jed caught up to her, amazed at how fast those short legs of hers could move.

She glanced over at him as she crunched through the snow. "I don't need no escort for sure now. Never did need one."

"I got that." He couldn't help but chuckle. "I'm not escorting you. I'm going home."

"Oh. You live near the house?"

"No. I live *in* the house."

"You do?" She yanked her head his direction and tripped at the same time.

His arm shot out to steady her and neither one of them lost stride when he did. "Uh-huh. Sure do."

"Oh."

She probably thought it strange the hired help lived with the boss and his wife, so he'd just go on ahead and explain why. "When I was first hired on, there wasn't a bunkhouse. It was just me and your uncle doing all the work at the time. When he started expanding, we built the bunkhouse for the extra men he'd hired. I went to pack my things to move out to it, but Emmett insisted I stay right where I was. Which is the room they added onto the side of the house when I first arrived here."

"Oh, I see."

Did she? Did she really know how it was between her relatives and him? Every time he'd heard she'd visited over the past three summers, he'd been at cow camp. So how could she know?

They arrived at the front door. Jed reached around her and opened it, then moved out of the way for her to enter first. She stepped inside the small mudroom far enough to let him in. He shut the door, grateful to be out of the wind and bitter winter weather. He would never tell Sunny, but his hands tingled from the cold.

They removed their outer wraps and wiped the snow from their boots and once again he opened the door for her to step inside the cabin.

She turned to thank him, and his breath hitched. He'd only been able to see swatches of her face earlier. Now he had a full view of it. Her uncle had mentioned she was an attractive woman, but he didn't mention just how beautiful she really was, with those big brown eyes, slightly rounded face, high cheekbones, bowed lips, and white and fairly even teeth.

He swallowed hard. *Attractive* didn't begin to describe her. He felt mesmerized by her beauty. His feet remained glued to the spot. When he realized he was staring, he forced himself to look away.

He needed to talk to Emmett about having someone else to watch over her. Jed no longer trusted himself to keep his distance.

Or to keep romantic inclinations far from his mind, which had just taken a trip in that direction.

That wasn't good.

No, siree.

That wasn't good at all.

Chapter Two

"Precious!" Aunt Minnie's voice broke through the howling wind's barrier as it buffeted the outside of the house.

Sunny's attention yanked from Jedidiah to Aunt Minnie. At fifty-one years old her aunt didn't look a day over thirty. Not one gray hair anywhere in those buttercup tresses. In fact the only gray thing on her aunt was her deep-set eyes. "Aunt Minnie, I sure have missed you." Sunny gave her aunt a big hug.

"It's so nice to see you again. It feels like it's been forever since I saw you last. August 29, to be exact." She looped their arms and all but dragged Sunny into their living room, which was twice the size of the one at her family's ranch house.

"I wish I could've come more often, but with Pa sick, I didn't want to leave him alone."

"We meant to get up there to your place, too, but it just seems like time's gotten away from us lately."

"I know what you mean." They both smiled.

Heat from the open rock fireplace drifted around Sunny. Worn out from her long day of travel, all she wanted to do was sit, remove her boots and stick her feet as close those hot flames as possible without catching her woolen stockings on fire. Her toes were close to being numb, same as the rest of her body.

"Sit here, precious." Her aunt scooted one of the four rocking chairs in front of the fireplace closer to the roaring blaze. "Take off them wet boots so your feet can warm up. I'll go get you something hot to drink." Before Sunny could object to being waited on, Aunt Minnie was halfway into the kitchen.

She turned and stared at the flames. Their dancing settled her nerves, and she gave a short prayer of thanks that God had seen her safely through the blizzard.

"Jed, you get on over there, too. I'll bring you and Sunny something warm to sip. Dinner's on the stove. As soon as your uncle gets in here, we'll eat."

Sunny shifted in her chair, wanting to see their faces instead of having her back to them. The other way just somehow seemed rude.

"Where's he at?" Wrinkles lined Jedidiah's handsome face.

"He went to the woodshed to get more wood. I think he's afraid we'll get snowed in and not have enough. You know how he is." Her aunt sighed.

Sunny glanced at the overflowing wood box.

"I'll go help him." Jedidiah turned and headed toward the back door.

"Oh, no, you don't." Aunt Minnie grabbed him by the shoulders and gave him a light shove toward the fire. "You just get your hide right over there and sit yourself down."

Uncertainty tumbled across his face like an uprooted sagebrush in a windstorm.

"Go on now. Do as I say." She pushed him in Sunny's direction again.

Their eyes connected and he lifted one shoulder.

Sunny shrugged back at him. She faced the fireplace and tugged on the strings holding the legs of her split skirt closed.

Jedidiah pulled one of the rockers closer to the fire and sat down next to her. Lye soap and leather brushed up her nose when he did.

Still leaned over undoing her fastenings, she glanced over at him only to find him staring at the bottom of her legs. His attention slid from there to her eyes.

"I've never seen anything like that before." He nodded to her strings.

"It helps keep the snow out. My pa taught me that."

"Interesting."

She finished untying and pulled her boots off.

Jedidiah already had his off and was settled all cozy-like into his chair.

Tiny red sparks flew like exploding fireworks as the flames licked the sap in the pine logs. Not caring if the sparks hit her feet, she sat back in her chair and raised them toward the blazing fire. Warmth seeped through her stockings and she sighed deep and long.

"Feels that good, huh?"

Without looking at him, she replied, "Sure does. My feet are freezing."

"I'm sure they are. How long you been out in that storm anyway?"

"About an hour into my ride down here the snow hit. Wasn't bad when I left."

"That's Kremmling for you."

They laughed together. Anyone who lived in Kremmling, Colorado, knew that to be true. Sunshine one minute, snow the next.

She glanced over her shoulder to make sure her aunt couldn't hear what she was about to say. She leaned toward him and whispered, "Aunt Minnie always order you about like that?"

His firm masculine lips and the corners of his eyes curled upward. "Uh-huh. All the time. Truth is, she treats me more like a son than a hired hand."

Sunny leaned back in her chair. "Aunt Min always wanted a whole houseful of children. She lost several babies, you know?"

He shook his head. "No. I didn't know. That's too bad. She would have been a great mother. Your aunt and uncle are wonderful, God-fearing folks."

"They sure are. I only wish we could've visited them more often. But every time we'd tried to, something would go wrong. If it wasn't the cows taking sick or tearing down fences, it was something else. Then my ma took sick and wasn't well enough to travel anymore."

"How long was she sick?"

"Five years."

"Five years?" His rich honey eyebrows rose. "What was wrong with her?"

"She had emphysema and died back in '95. Can't believe she's been gone three years already."

"And your pa?"

"He died the beginning of November." A long, slow breath slid from her lungs and she swallowed hard to fight back the heart-wrenching emotions swelling up in her. She hadn't talked much about her folks with anyone. While it felt kind of nice, it was strange at the same time. After all, Jed was a complete stranger to her.

"Sorry to hear about your loss. If you don't mind me asking, how did he die?"

"From Rocky Mountain spotted fever. Got it from a tick, you know?"

He nodded slowly. "Uh-huh. I know. Knew a few who died from it myself."

"Of course you'd know that." Her eyes darted upward. "Anyone who lives in this neck of the woods long enough would. How long you lived here anyways?"

"Here at your uncle's place three years now. I was born and raised in Colorado."

"Whereabouts?"

"Denver."

"How'd you end up here?"

"I met your uncle at a stockyard down in Denver. We hit it off, and he asked me if I'd be interested in coming to work for him. Best decision I ever made, too."

"Your kin still live there?"

His bluebird-colored eyes clouded over, and he shifted slightly in the chair.

"Here you go." Aunt Minnie stepped up beside Jedidiah and handed each of them a cup of steaming brew.

"Thank you," they said at the same time, and both sat up straighter in their chairs to accept the mugs.

Aunt Minnie sat in the rocking chair on the other side of Sunny and crossed her legs toward her niece. "How was your trip down here, precious?"

"Long."

The three of them shared a laugh.

"Did you run into any trouble?"

She never got to answer that question because the back door flew open, and Uncle Emmett stepped inside with his arms loaded with firewood.

Jedidiah leaped out of his chair and rushed to help.

"Hello, Uncle Emmett." The love she felt for her pa's only brother flowed through her voice. Uncle Emmett resembled Pa in looks and in personality. Seeing him sent a fresh round of grief forking into her heart. But she wasn't much one for crying in front of people. The tears she'd already shed over her pa and ma were enough to flood the Colorado River banks. A slight exaggeration but it sure felt like it at times, and she wasn't about to let them start flowing now. They might never stop.

The need to feel her uncle's arms around her about now pressed in on her. She started to rise, but her aunt stopped her. "Oh, no, you don't. You just sit there, young lady. He'll come to greet you in a minute. Won't you, sweetie pie?" Aunt Minnie looked over at her husband.

"Yes, ma'am. I sure will." He winked at his wife.

Sunny always envied the closeness her aunt and uncle had. Same with her ma and pa. Someday she hoped to have a marriage just like both of theirs. That is, if she could ever get over her fear of being used again.

Her attention drifted to Jedidiah and to his hair that was the color of summer wheat, his wide-girthed back as he stacked the wood he took from Uncle's arms, his stout legs, narrow waist and slightly bowed legs. She had to admit he'd caught her attention from the moment she'd laid eyes on him. If he was near as fine a person on the inside as he was on the outside, then he'd make a fine husband. Husband? What was she doing thinking about him like that and getting all moon-eyed over some man she didn't even know? Hadn't she learned anything from her last episode with a man?

Still, he must be a good man or her aunt and uncle wouldn't have him living under their roof and be treating him like a son. Didn't matter to her none, though. Her main concern right now was getting her family's ranch up and running again. Marriage would have to wait. That is, if she even married. She wasn't sure she could ever trust another man, especially after the last one who'd wanted to court her. Good thing she'd overheard that slimy snake Duke Graham telling her pa's workers he didn't care anything about her, he just wanted to get his hands on her ranch.

Well, he hadn't. And she wouldn't be fooled like that again. Even with someone as tempting as Jedidiah Cooper.

Jed wished Emmett hadn't asked him to keep his eyes on Sunny. Oh, he wanted to keep his eyes on her, all right, and that was the problem. He'd never been so attracted or drawn to a woman before. Especially one he'd just met. Perhaps it stemmed from all the great things he'd heard about her from Emmett and Minnie since he'd arrived here three years ago. He felt as if he knew her as well as they did, and once again that was a problem.

He wasn't sure how he was going to handle spending so much time around the spirited cowgirl and keep from falling for her. She was a refreshing switch from the women he'd known back in Denver. They wanted to be coddled and kept; Sunny clearly could take care of herself. That intrigued him more than he wanted to admit, or more than it should.

Emmett's warning about no one wooing his niece hammered into Jed's head about the time his heart took a trip he really shouldn't have been taking. *God, help me to honor my boss. Show me how to be friendly to*

Sunny, how to keep an eye on her and how to not lose my heart to her.

"Something wrong?" Emmett's voice broke into his unyielding thoughts.

Jed looked at the man he respected. Icicles clung to his moustache and beard, and concerned green eyes gazed back at him.

"No, sir." He swallowed back the lie. Everything wasn't all right, but he would make sure it would be. Even if it took every bit of willpower and energy he possessed. Which where Sunny was concerned didn't seem like much at the moment. How could someone he had just met get to him so quickly?

Emmett frowned, then nodded. After his arms were empty of wood, he hung up his coat and hat and headed toward Sunny. His niece rose and threw her arms around him. The top of her head barely reached the man's barrel chest.

"Brrr. You're cold." She shivered but didn't move away.

"You let her go, you ornery old bear." Minnie popped him playfully on the arm.

"Oh. So you wanna get rough, do you?" Emmett swung around, grabbed Minnie around the waist and buried his wet, partially icicled moustache and beard into her face. She squealed and wriggled, but Jed knew she loved the attention.

Jed wondered what it would be like to have a wife like that—one who loved him unconditionally, no matter what he looked or smelled like after a hard day's work.

When he got his own spread, then and only then would he consider finding a wife. His father's words ran through his mind. *Why can't you be more like your brothers, boy? Just look at Daniel and all he's accomplished. He's a big-time lawyer back East with a beautiful wife and a growing family, and he can support them in the style they deserve. Same with Sebastian. He lives right up the street in a mansion bigger than ours, even, and he's part owner of one of the largest railroad companies in these here parts.* His father went on and on about his older brother and his younger one, as well. Jed had heard it all a million times.

Being the middle brother, Jed was often overlooked. Every time his father gave him that lecture, Jed felt smaller and smaller and less significant in his father's eyes. His father had a way of making him feel like that.

Well, Jed was no city boy. Working in an office would kill him. Ranching was in his heart. He just hoped when he bought his own ranch and built it up to as fine a spread as what Emmett had here that maybe, just maybe, his father would be as proud of him as he was of his brothers. Just why that mattered to Jed exactly, he didn't know or understand, but gaining his father's approval meant more to him than anything else.

"Dinner's getting cold." Minnie's giggling drew Jed's attention away from his miserable thoughts.

Emmett stopped tickling Minnie but his arms still held her as he glanced over at the stove. "So it is." He kissed her.

Having witnessed their playfulness and affection often, Jed was used to it by now. How did their niece feel about it? He shifted his focus onto Sunny, who gazed at them with a smile of contentment on her face.

She sure was a pretty little thing.

As if she sensed him looking at her, her attention

drifted to him, but quickly he looked away before she could capture his gaze. He would not let Emmett down. The man who'd been nothing but kind to him deserved no less.

"Let's eat, woman. I'm starved. What about you, Jed?" Emmett let his wife go, waiting for Jed's answer.

"Uh-huh. Sure am." His belly had been rumbling for some time now.

Within minutes they were sitting at the table. Roasted beef and rich brown-gravy aromas lingered in the air.

"Aren't the ranch hands joining us?" Sunny asked.

"No. They take their meals in the bunkhouse now. Sam Marsh does the cooking for them," Minnie informed Sunny.

"You remember Sam, don't you, Sunshine?" Uncle Emmett forked a thick slice of roast beef and set it on his plate.

"Sure do. How's his leg doing?"

"Not bad. He's slow getting around. But he likes keeping the bunkhouse clean and doing the cooking. Truth is, I think he enjoys it more than ranch work. That way, he never has to get out in the cold other than for supplies now and again. It's the perfect job for him."

"It sure was nice of you to give him a job, Uncle Emmett. And me, too." Love and gratefulness overcame her sweet face.

Emmett set his fork down and rested his hand on top of hers. "You know you don't have to do this, Sunshine. I told you I'd help you."

"I know you did. And I appreciate that. But it's something I need to do for myself. Everyone out here thinks because I'm a woman and because I'm small that I can't make the ranch work, but I know I can."

"I have no doubt about that, Sunshine. You are definitely your pa's daughter." Pride mixed with melancholy filled his words. He cleared his throat, lifted his hand from hers and reached for the mashed potatoes, plopping a huge dollop onto his plate and topping it off with a pool of rich brown gravy.

Sunny's eyes glistened and her dark lashes settled against her rosy cheeks.

"I'm sure sorry we couldn't make it to Bobby's funeral. If that blizzard hadn't come in, we would have, but the storm never let up for days. Then there was so much snow there was no way we could make it up the mountain."

"That's okay, Uncle Emmett. I understand and I'm sure Pa did, too."

The room grew quiet for several long minutes until the sound of Sunny clearing her voice broke the silence. "You never answered me earlier, Jedidiah, about whether or not you had kinfolk in Denver." Her brown eyes touched on his. Gone was the sheen of tears.

"Jedidiah?" Minnie glanced at him, then Sunny. "Don't know anyone who calls Jed that."

Neither did he. Only thing was, it didn't sound condescending at all coming from her, but more musical than anything. Even respectful. He liked that. "Only one who does is my father. Everyone else calls me Jed."

She smiled a smile befitting her name. "Jed it is, then. If that's all right with you?"

"Uh-huh. Sure is," he answered, dropping his gaze to where he was cutting his meat. Lands, she was easy on the eyes.

During dinner he had a hard time keeping his attention off Sunny. She was definitely one beautiful woman, from what he could tell, both inside and out. Any man would have trouble not staring at her. No wonder Emmett had warned his men beforehand about wooing her. The man had reason to be concerned.

When dinner was over, Jed was glad because he would no longer be sitting across from Sunny and trying to keep his mind off her.

He and Emmett headed to the rocking chairs in front of the flickering fire.

The ladies served them peach cobbler with sweetened whipped cream drizzled over it, then joined them by the hearth. Orange, red and blue flames sent a glow about the shadowy room. The wind whistled and howled outside, swirling the snow and splattering it against the window. If it weren't for the chinking in between the logs keeping the wind out, the room would be freezing cold, of that he was certain.

Warmth, excellent company and a full belly relaxed Jed.

Must have Sunny, too, because her mouth stretched into a wide yawn. "Sorry," she said with sleepy eyes. "I know it's early and I hope you don't mind, but I'm ready to head to bed now."

"No one minds, precious. And even if they did, they'll just have to deal with their disappointment, won't you, fellas?" Aunt Minnie looked at Jed and then her husband.

"Yes. Yes, we will." Emmett nodded, his face filled with amusement.

Jed just smiled.

When Sunny rose, he and Emmett did, too. "What time do we start in the morning?" she asked.

"We—" Emmett looked over at Jed "—start about

seven. You—" he pointed to her "—need to catch up on your rest."

With no warning she planted her fists on her hips. "Now, Uncle Emmett, I came here to work, not sleep. Remember? So I'll be ready before seven, and you'd better have a nice long list of chores for me to do by then." No disrespect filled her words, only a determination. The same one filling her brown eyes.

"See what I told you, Jed?" With the two women sandwiched between them, Emmett peered over the top of Sunny's head at him.

"Uh-huh. She is a stubborn little thing," Jed agreed, amused by the display.

"Stubborn? You told him I was stubborn?" Her head yanked Emmett's direction and those wide eyes of hers were even wider.

"Sure did, Sunshine. Amongst other things." Emmett smiled.

"Other things? Like what?" Her small calloused hands knotted at her tiny waist.

"Let's see. I told him you were stubborn, ornery, willful, determined and at times sassy. That your heart was bigger than this here ranch and that under all that toughness is a real sweetheart. But mostly I told him that you are one fine rancher."

Her hands slipped from her sides, her eyes softened with wonder and her lips curled upward. "I can live with that. You're forgiven." She stepped around her aunt and kissed Emmett's cheek.

"Yes, I am." He laughed and everyone joined him.

"Well, I'll see you all bright and early. Now, where do you want me to sleep, Aunt Min?"

"I'll show you to your room." She looped her arm

with Sunny's and led her past the kitchen toward the other end of the house where the family's bedrooms were, on the opposite end of the house from where Jed's was.

It had been a long day, so right about now sleep sounded good to him, too. "Think I'll turn in early myself." He faced Emmett. "We've got a long day ahead of us tomorrow."

"That we do. But it won't be quite as long with Sunny around."

Jed glanced in the direction where Minnie and Sunny had gone, making sure they were out of earshot. "She really that good a hand?"

"She really is. Don't let her size fool you. Just wait until you see what all that niece of mine can do." Pride filled out Emmett's barrel chest even farther.

Jed couldn't wait to see just what the lady could do. Tomorrow couldn't come soon enough.

Chapter Three

With the sun nowhere near to rising yet, Sunny didn't want to sit around doing nothing until it did. So she decided to make herself useful. Dressed for the outdoors, she quietly opened the mudroom door and stepped outside. Mid-January's bitter cold stung her cheeks and the crisp, frigid air frosted the inside of her nostrils.

She pulled the red-and-white bandanna from around her neck and covered her mouth and nose, then yanked the collar of her coat upward to where it touched the back of her tall-crowned cowboy hat. She was grateful for her ankle-length thick woolen coat along with the leather chaps that covered the top of her winter boots and kept the cold from biting into her legs.

Her eyes traveled over her uncle's ranch. White, white and more white. Well, with the exception of the red barn, outbuildings and wooden structures, and the animals who were mooing and nickering for her to come and feed them. The last time Sunny had visited her relatives, she'd helped with the chores, so she knew the basic routine. She'd start in the barn first.

Because the wind had blown so hard during the night

most of the freshly fallen snow didn't cover the hard-packed layers already there, making the ground under her feet slick. She focused on keeping her feet underneath her. The last thing she needed was to end up stranded out here.

Most of the four- to five-foot drifts were piled high against the barn door or the buildings. She jerked up the shovel that rested against the barn and moved the snow away from the door before abandoning the shovel and stepping inside. Wasn't much warmer inside than it was outside. Horse, hay and leather scents seeped through her bandanna. All scents she loved. She smiled as they filled the world around her.

She used a metal bucket and dumped grain into the built-in boxes inside the stall where her horses were. "Morning, Rascal. Morning, Rowdy." She patted each neck in turn, and their eyes blinked with tenderness and love for her in response to her gentle touch.

Horses from the other stalls whinnied, so she went down the line and fed the rest of them first grain, then hay. She broke the layer of ice in the water buckets and the water tank in the corral.

When those chores were finished, she milked the Jersey cows and put the milk in the ranch house mud-room, along with the eggs she'd gathered after feeding the chickens.

With at least an hour to go before sunlight, Sunny decided to hook up the two draft-horse teams her uncle used. She'd never told anyone how she'd always been intimidated by their massive size. A lot of healthy respect went a long way in knowing they could trample her. Tethered to the metal ring in front of the four-foot-high grain boxes, crunching their oats and stomping a foot now and again, while they finished eating their grain, Sunny went and gathered their harnesses.

While they ate, as she had so many times before, she stood on the harnessing platform, which made putting the harnesses on them much easier.

Though they were much, much higher than her, she showed no fear as she led them outside and past the tongue of the sled. She backed the draft horses up to the tongue and completed hooking them up, huffing and puffing and straining the whole time she did it. Doing them alone took the wind right out of her. She and Pa used to do this together. It was definitely a whole heap easier with two people.

Standing on her tiptoes, she draped the lines through the rack at the front of the sled. A feeling of being watched came over her. She squinted, peering into the wooded area, then the outbuildings, the corrals, and ending at the barn. There Jed stood in the doorway. Goose bumps rose on her arms, and chills raced up her spine, and neither one had anything to do with the cold. Many a good-looking cowboy had crossed her path but none as fine as Jed. Before she allowed her mind to wander in a direction it had no business wandering, she reminded herself why she was here. With that settled in her mind, she greeted him with a pleasant smile. "Morning, Jed. How long you been standing there?"

He smiled in return, and her mind went right back to where it was just seconds before. *Oh, horseflies. Help me out here, will You, Lord?*

"Long enough." Jed headed toward the front of the wagon where Sunny stood.

Her uncle wasn't kidding when he said just wait and

see what his niece could do. The sun wasn't even up yet and that niece of his had all the chores done except for feeding the cows. "You sure handled those boys well, which ain't easy with them two. Usually Samson and Goliath sidestep when you back them up to the tongue."

She tilted her head back and gazed up at him. All he could see was the puzzlement in her eyes. "I didn't have a bit of trouble with them."

"So I noticed. You're lucky. You got them on one of their good days. Emmett is thinking about replacing them."

"I hope not. I'll take them if he does."

"You may want to rethink that. Wait until you're around them a few times."

"Fair enough. Well, I'd best hook up the other team now."

"I'll help."

Together they readied the other team. When they finished, knowing Boomer and Tucker's gentle nature and that they wouldn't take off, Jed tied them to a hitching post while Sunny climbed onto the bed of the other sled and grabbed the lines. She braced her knees against the rack, pulled back on the left line and turned the horses around, and stopped the sled right in front of him. "Hop on." Her eyes smiled and he assumed under that bandanna her mouth did, as well.

He stood there for a moment, admiring the ease with which she'd handled the rowdiest team Emmett had, then climbed aboard and stood beside her. His five-foot-eleven frame towered over her.

"You want to take over, or do you mind if I do it?" She held out the lines to him.

A smile curled inside him. Made him feel good that

she asked him and that she respected him as a boss.
"No. You go right on ahead. I'll stand here and enjoy
the ride for a change."

She gave a quick nod, then with a slap of the lines,
she guided the team like an expert out to the lower
meadow and lined them right up alongside the haystack,
impressing Jed even more. It had taken Cody, one of his
other ranch hands, three tries to get that maneuver accomplished without taking out half the haystack.

"Whoa, boys." She pulled back on the lines, bringing
the horses to a stop. "Will these two stand here without
being tethered to a rock or something?" She gazed up
at him with those big brown eyes of hers.

"For a few minutes they will. If they're standing in
one place too long, they get pretty restless." *Restless*
wasn't quite accurate. Those two got downright bel-
ligerent.

Sunny gave a quick nod, then wrapped the lines
around the side of the rack closest to the hay pile. She
snatched one of the metal hay forks off the bed of the
sled and climbed up the wooden rack. She made her
way up the mound as if she were climbing a ladder instead of loose hay.

Jed shook his head, wondering how someone so
small could climb up with such ease while holding a
metal pitchfork in her hand no less.

After he got over his initial shock, he joined her at
the top. The two of them worked at knocking the snow
and ice off the top layer, huffing and puffing as they
did. Once they had it removed, they worked in layers,
loading the loose hay onto the bed of the sled.

Three-quarters of the way through, Jed heard voices.
He looked toward the opposite end of the haystack.

Here came Matt, George and Cody driving Boomer and Tucker, the pair of matching dapple grays Jed and Sunny had readied earlier. Cody guided them until they were alongside the stack.

Didn't take long before the three hired hands made their way to them. They stood below gazing up at Sunny with curious stares on their faces.

Jed opened his mouth to introduce her to them, but George started talking before he had a chance. "Hey, thanks for doing the chores, boss."

"I didn't. Sunny did." He yanked a thumb her direction.

George looked over at Sunny. "So you're Sunny, huh?"

Sunny stopped forking the hay and dipped her head George's direction. "Sure am. And you are?"

"George Elder." George raised his hat and that wild lock of his blond hair fell across his forehead. He raked the strand back into place and replaced his hat.

"Nice to meet you, George. I'd come down and shake your hand but I ain't climbing up this here thing twice in one day."

"How'd an itty-bitty thing such as yourself get up there anyways?" George asked, clearly puzzled.

"Same way anyone else does. Put one foot in front of the other and climb."

Jed chuckled under his breath at that one, and his gaze went to the three cowboys. Something told him they'd just met their match.

"Ah, c'mon, tell the truth now. You ain't any bigger than a tick, so how'd you really get up there? Did the boss man here help you?" An insinuating smirk ran across George's face.

One Jed didn't like at all. He narrowed his eyes at George, hoping he would get the message.

"Ah, who told?" Sunny yanked her hat off and slapped it across her knee. When she did her bandanna fell from across her nose down to her neck. "I've done been found out." White puffs floated from her mouth as she exhaled. "Yup. That's it. Jed picked me up and tossed me up here 'cause you know there's no way someone who ain't 'any bigger than a tick' could get up here all by themselves." She shoved her hat back onto her head, slid down the stack and quick as a wink climbed up on top of it again.

Jed looked over at George. His mouth hung open wider than a canyon, and so did Cody's and Matt's.

"First time I've seen you speechless, George."

"I would've never believed it if I hadn't seen it with my own eyes." George stood there shaking his head.

"Well, maybe you didn't really see it, George. Maybe your eyes was playing tricks on you." The serious smile curling those full lips of hers belied the mirth in her eyes.

Stunned Jed into silence. Neither he nor George said anything for a moment.

Sunny, well, she went back to tossing hay onto the sled as if nothing was amiss. It was. Not only had the men never had a woman sass back to them but they'd never been outwitted either. That was, until now.

Jed finally cleared his throat. "By the way, Sunny. That's Cody Bower." He pointed to the tallest one of the men. At six foot three, Cody had four inches on Jed.

Sunny looked down at him, and Cody raised his hat to her. The copper color in his hair magnified under the bright sunshine. "Nice to meet you, ma'am." He tugged his hat back onto his head until his ears stuck out like a monkey's. Jed had never understood why he did that.

"Nice to meet you, too, Cody."

"And that's Matt Duncan." Jed pointed to Matt.

Sunny's attention drifted toward Matt—the only teenager of the bunch. Matt removed his hat but all you could see was the top of his molasses hair. "Ma'am," he drawled, never looking up.

"Pleasure to meet you, Matt. Judging by your accent, you must be from the South."

"Yes, ma'am. I am."

"Whereabouts in the South are you from, Matt?"

"Chattanooga, Tennessee, ma'am." Matt still hadn't looked up at Sunny yet. Jed felt sorry for the shy boy. The only relative he'd had was an uncle who had moved them out West to start a new life. Shortly after hiring on to the Flying W Ranch, his uncle had keeled over, died of a heart attack. Emmett had kept the boy on and gave him a job. The Westons had a way of taking in strays. And Jed wasn't talking about animals either.

"Oh, I've heard of that place." Sunny smiled and her face beamed. "A fur trader from Tennessee came through our ranch several years ago. Told us all about Tennessee. How green it is. How friendly the people are there. You must be right proud of your home state."

Matt's head rose toward Sunny. "Yes, ma'am. I am." Homesickness drifted through his voice and across his face. Jed knew Matt missed his family something awful.

"Well, someday I'd love to hear more about it."

"Yes, ma'am." Daylight filled his eyes, replacing the darkness in them from moments ago.

Without even knowing it, Sunny had said the right

thing. Jed knew it helped Matt to talk about Tennessee, to remember his folks.

"Hear you have a ranch up the mountain a ways. I'd love to see it someday," Matt said with a half smile.

"Hey, there you go, Sunny," Cody piped in. "Matt's a hard worker. A great hand. Knows all there is to know about ranching. You and Matt could get hitched. Then you'd have a man to help you to get that place of yours up and running again. Course, he ain't much taller than you so not sure how that would work." Cody guffawed.

Matt blushed and ducked his head.

George stood there with not only his mouth wide as a canyon again but his eyes, too.

Sunny whipped her head in Cody's direction. Fire flashed from her eyes.

Before the scene got ugly, Jed spoke up. "Don't you men have work to do?"

Cody yanked his gaze to Jed's.

Jed narrowed his eyes, sending Cody a warning glare. The young man was always spouting off without thinking and his mouth had gotten him into more trouble than he was worth.

Cody's pale complexion turned the same shade of red as the bandanna around his neck. He nodded, and without saying another word, he headed back toward the direction he'd come from, looking back once, then twice, then three times.

George and Matt excused themselves and followed him.

Jed turned toward Sunny, not sure what to say or if he should say anything at all.

"I get so sick and tired of being teased 'cause I'm

small." Sunny sighed, driving her fork into the hay with more force than what was needed.

"You get teased a lot about that, do you?" Jed stabbed his hay fork into the mound and tossed a large heap onto the almost-filled sled.

"Yup. Get mighty fed up with it, too." She stopped forking hay and looked over at him. "But I'd rather be teased about that than—" She stopped, her eyes snagged on his. In a flash she scooted down the stack and onto the sled, stabbing her pitchfork into the dried grass. Without a glance his way she positioned herself on top of the hay behind the rack, braced her feet against the boards and picked up the lines.

Jed let out a short breath before joining her. He braced his legs alongside hers, careful to keep enough distance between them. "What were you about to say?"

"Nothing. I don't want to talk about it. Forget I said anything."

He wanted to argue. Instead he nodded. He knew enough not to pry information out of the cowboys, and from what he'd seen, she was tougher than any cowboy he'd ever worked with.

Chapter Four

"What next?" Sunny asked Jed after they finished feeding the cows. She was relieved the other hands were still feeding cows up on the upper meadow. She'd barely started this job and it was happening already. If only she'd been born a boy. She sighed, dreading the inevitable—the constant teasing from the men about her size or her tomboyishness or even worse...that it was her fault her family's ranch had failed.

That's what Pa's hired hands had told her the day her pa had to let them go. It wasn't true of course, but still, it hurt nonetheless knowing people believed that. Well, she could no more control their flapping tongues or what they believed about her than she could the weather that had all but destroyed their ranch. So she was just going to keep going, keep walking and keep working and trust that someday, somehow, she would make this all work out.

"We need to check the water hole." The words had no more left Jed's mouth than Sunny noticed her uncle galloping toward them.

"Whoa." Sunny pulled back on the lines, stopping

the horses right when her uncle reached them. "What's wrong, Uncle Emmett?"

"I need you to come with me, Jed. I got a cow upside down."

"I can help." Sunny handed the lines over to Jed.

Uncle Emmett's green eyes met hers. "I'd rather Jed help me this time, Sunshine."

Oh. Sunny's shoulders drooped. She knew why he wanted Jed. Even though her uncle said he believed in her abilities, his actions just now spoke something very different.

What did it take to prove to people she was just as capable of handling whatever problems came up on a ranch as any man?

After all, she'd been doing it her whole life.

She sighed, realizing the only person who truly believed in her was her pa, and he was gone. *Oh, Pa. I miss you so much.* It had only been a little over two months since his death, and while she'd cried buckets of tears, she hadn't really had a chance to fully mourn the loss of him yet. She'd been too busy taking care of business and arranging things with her neighbor, who agreed that in exchange for watching over her place while she was gone he could use the outbuildings and meadows.

Thinking about the ranch she loved so dearly, determination rose up inside of her. She wouldn't let her uncle's decision bother her none. Instead she'd work even harder to prove to him and anyone else she was more than capable. Nothing or no one would stop her from bringing her homestead back to the greatness it once was. She was here to do a job, a fine one at that. "What else needs done, then?"

"You think you can handle putting the team up by yourself?"

Sunny pressed her shoulders back, careful to hold the frustration inside her from showing on the outside. "Of course I can."

"She sure can, Emmett. She had them all hitched and ready to go by the time I got down to the barn this morning."

That surprised even Uncle Emmett. His raised eyebrows showed it. "By yourself?"

"Yup."

Pride replaced his surprise. "Good job, Sunshine. I'm proud of you." That meant a lot coming from him. It truly did.

"Me, too," Jed added. "It isn't easy handling these two." He pointed to Samson and Goliath.

"Well, we gotta get going, Sunshine. When you finish putting the team up, grab your horse and a pick, then head on out to the water hole to make sure the cows have water. You remember where it is, don't you?"

"Yup. Sure do."

"On second thought, wait until one of the other guys gets back before you go, all right? I don't want you out there by yourself in case you slip and fall."

Once again Sunny struggled to not let her frustration show and to make sure she kept her tone even when she spoke. "I've done it many a time by myself, Uncle Emmett."

"I know you have, Sunshine, but just help your uncle out here a bit. I don't want something to happen to you, too."

Sunny's heart softened the instant she noticed the sadness that had drifted across her uncle's face. She knew he was worried about losing her like he had her pa. Uncle Emmett loved his brother, and Pa had loved him, too. She didn't want to be the cause of any more pain for her uncle so she nodded. "I'll wait until the men come back, Uncle Emmett."

"Thank you, Sunshine. I appreciate that."

"Hey. You're the boss." She winked at him to lighten the mood.

He shook his finger at her. "Yes, I am. And don't you forget it." He gave a wink back at her. "Well, we better run. That cow doesn't have long before she'll be dead. If she ain't already. See you later, Sunshine."

Jed jumped down from the sled, swung up on the back of Uncle Emmett's stocky horse, and off they went.

Sunny gave a quick slap of the lines and braced herself as the sled jerked forward.

Every now and again the sled runners scraped over a rock hidden beneath the snowy surface. Each step the horses took made their necks sway and the tack rattle in harmony. She loved that sound. It was soothing to a body, downright peaceful. The flaxen manes of both horses fanned out and some strands stuck straight up in the air. These stocky animals sure were beautiful. God had done a right fine job on them.

Overhead an eagle screeched. Sunny searched the blue sky until she spotted the bird with its six-foot-plus wingspan gliding through the air. She watched it for the longest time, her heart soaring with it. The scripture in Isaiah 40:31 came to mind. "'But they that wait upon the Lord shall renew their strength; they shall mount up with wings as eagles; they shall run, and not be weary; and they shall walk, and not faint.'" She quoted it out loud from memory as she watched that eagle soaring high above.

That Scripture ministered right where she needed it to—deep in her weary heart. But she vowed right then that she would not grow tired and she'd depend on the Lord's strength to do whatever it took for her to make the family's ranch, her ranch, a success.

In the distance her uncle's log cabin came into view. She fixed her eyes on the pine- and aspen-tree-covered mountain above her uncle's homestead. A scene similar to her own spread. Like the blanket of snow around her, a hankering for home spread over her.

Oh, how she loved riding through wooded areas, listening to the forest floor crunching under her horse's hooves and drawing in the fresh scent of blue spruce pine trees and clean air. Every now and again she had been fortunate enough to come across a black bear hidden high up in a tree, or a bobcat climbing the rocks in the distance, or a cuddly-faced pine marten draped across a jagged hollow tree stump, or her favorite of them all—a six-point bull elk. She closed her eyes, imagining the lyrical sound of the elk's bugle during mating season. It was like sweet music to Sunny's ears. One time she'd even come across a cow moose. Sure was an ugly thing. She didn't stick around to study it too long knowing how dangerous they could be and all.

She opened her eyes and movement north of her uncle's house drew her away from her thoughts. Her uncle's hired hands were coming down the road driving the dappled gray team. Within minutes they'd be coming right alongside her.

All of a sudden a loud boom burst through the quietness.

Her team shied sideways, then bolted forward into a dead run.

The reins very nearly jerked from her hands, and Sunny's heart raced right along with the panicked horses. "Whoa! Whoa, Samson! Whoa, Goliath!"

Her body struggled to stay upright as the sled bounced over the uneven snow-packed terrain.

Chunks of hard-packed snow flew from the horses' hooves high into the air, some came very close to hitting her.

With all her might she tugged hard on the lines but the horses never stopped. They plowed over the snowy terrain as if it was race day. "Whoa, boys. Whoa." She drew back even harder, her arms aching from the strain.

Just when she thought her arms would give out, she spotted a snowdrift ahead. Shooting up a quick prayer, using both arms and all her strength she pulled back hard on the right line only, forcing the team into the snowbank and into a jolting stop.

The animals trembled and snorted. With each short breath the horses took, their sides expanded rapidly and steam rolled out in long white puffs from their flared nostrils. "Easy, Samson. Easy Goliath." She drew out their names making sure to keep her voice even and smooth even though her insides were shaking like a willow bush in a turbulent wind. "Everything's all right, boys," she said, trying to reassure herself as much as she was them.

"Are you all right?"

Sunny swung her head toward the sound of Jed's frantic voice. He and her uncle, along with the other hired hands, were hurrying toward her at a pace slow enough as to not frighten the horses further.

"I'm fine," she said loud enough for them to hear, but not loud enough to startle the horses.

Before her uncle had a chance to dismount, Jedidiah flew off the back of Uncle Emmett's horse and strode to her side. "You sure?" His hands spread around her waist, and he hoisted her off the sled. His hands stayed right where he'd placed them even after her feet touched the ground. Fear and concern wrinkled the corners of his eyes. She hated thinking she'd been the cause of that worry.

"You all right, Sunshine?" A tremor ran through Uncle Emmett's voice.

Quicker than a heartbeat Jedidiah's hands dropped from her sides, and he backed away as if she'd suddenly sprouted porcupine quills or something. The look on his face didn't give anything away as to why he'd acted like that.

"I'm fine." She dusted the clumps of snow off her chaps and coat.

"What happened?" The same concern and fear she'd seen in Jedidiah's eyes was now settled in her uncle's.

She wanted to pull him into a hug to comfort him, but she didn't know if it would embarrass him in front of the others or not. She knew how funny men were about those things. Sure, at the house he didn't hold anything back when it came to showing Aunt Minnie her affection, but out here in front of all his men, she wasn't sure, so she just held back and instead answered his question. "There was a loud bang and the next thing I knew the team took off. Thank God Pa taught me what to do when that happens."

The wrinkles on Uncle Emmett's forehead let up. "He did a fine job of it, too, Sunshine." He smiled down at her, then yanked her into a hug before releasing her and turning his attention onto Cody, George and Matt.

Guess hugging in front of the men was all right after all.

"Sorry, Mr. Weston. Cody here wasn't thinking." George yanked a thumb toward the tall cowboy. "He spotted a coyote and took a shot at it."

Raw anger flooded over her uncle's face. He tugged his hat up and down twice. "Well, you just better thank the good Lord that my girl here knew how to handle those horses."

All three of the hands looked at her with awe. Made her feel high as the cloudless sky.

Despite the fact that her insides were still shaking from her ordeal, she smiled, realizing these men had just witnessed her handling that runaway team all by herself. With a little bit of luck maybe, just maybe, they'd see that size didn't make one lick of difference. And maybe, just maybe, she'd earned their respect as a fellow ranch hand now. She sure did hope so, but only time and a lot of hard work would tell.

Jed was thankful it had only taken a few minutes to right that cow. When he had seen Samson and Goliath thundering through the snow and Sunny trying to control them, he thought his heart had stopped beating.

He silently cheered Emmett on when he gave Cody a good tongue-lashing for his carelessness. Something Jed wanted to do himself. That boy sure needed some horse sense whipped into him. Even then Jed wasn't sure it would make any difference. That kid just didn't think. Shooting at a coyote with Samson and Goliath nearby proved that. Cody had to have seen them. His carelessness could have kill... No, Jed couldn't even say the word.

Thoughts of harm or something even worse coming to that pretty gal twisted Jed's gut into a tight knot.

He liked her.

A lot.

The woman had spunk. Something he loved in a woman. But he'd keep his feelings to himself. He'd never go against Emmett's wishes. He only hoped his holding on to her longer than necessary hadn't given Emmett cause for alarm.

They all headed back to the barn and unharnessed the horses and put them up. Before they went to make sure the cows had water, they stood outside the barn, talking about who was going to do what.

"You sure did a fine job of handling those horses today," Matt drawled, looking down at the ground and scraping the toe of his boot across the snow.

"Thank you, Matt."

"Aw, c'mon. That was plumb luck and you know it." Cody's auburn brows danced with mirth, only Jed noticed Sunny wasn't smiling.

"Luck had nothing to do with it," Jed defended her.

"That's right." Her chin rose and defiance scribbled across her face.

"Ah, come on, armrest." Cody laid his forearm on Sunny's shoulder.

"Who you calling armrest?" Sunny's voice lowered to a growl.

Jed stepped forward to remove Cody's arm from Sunny's shoulder but never got the chance. She flicked his arm off and took two steps sideways, looking as if she might well punch the obnoxious cowboy in the gut if he tried that again.

"You." Cody guffawed. "You make a pretty good one, too. Yessiree, your shoulder is just the right height and makes for a right nice resting post."

Jed heard the humor in Cody's voice, but he knew how Sunny hated to be teased. He also knew if he said something, she'd tell him she could take care of herself. So he decided to wait and see what happened. If Cody got too out of line, though, he didn't care if Sunny could defend herself or not, Jed would say something and put a stop to it.

"Admit it, short stack. It was just a lucky break." The man had the nerve to wink at her, and Jed had the horrible thought that he might have to pull her off Cody to keep her from pulverizing him.

"Luck had nothing to do with it. My pa taught me how to handle horses since I was no bigger than a newborn calf."

"Well, you ain't any bigger than a three-day-old heifer now." That taunt came from George. His glinting smirk showed he was just teasing Sunny, but Jed fully understood what she meant when she'd told him she got sick of it. Again he wanted to say something, but something inside him told him to wait, that he'd embarrass her if he intervened.

Sunny's gaze shot to George, then back onto Cody. Her eyes narrowed and she raised her chin up another notch. "You don't have to have brawn to know what to do; you just have to have horse sense. Something you obviously don't have or you would've never fired that shot."

"She got you there, Cody," George said with a punch to Cody's skinny arm.

"Didn't neither." Cody slugged George back. "Been shootin' coyotes since the day I got here."

Jed had heard enough. This was his chance to say something, to stand up for her without appearing as though he was defending her. "Yes, but you've never done it with Samson and Goliath nearby. You know how flighty those two geldings are. Sunny did a great job of handling them. And driving them into that snowbank was sheer genius." Jed smiled down at Sunny, not even bothering to keep his admiration for her from showing. Of course she was the only one who could see it.

When he and Emmett had topped the hill and seen the runaway team and Sunny pulling back on one line, forcing the horses into the bank, he'd been surprised someone as tiny as her could handle such a large team.

"I still think it was luck." Cody turned to walk away.

"Where you going?" Jed stopped him.

"To fix the fence."

"George and Matt can do that. I want you to come with me and Sunny. So get your horse ready." Jed hated to do that to Sunny, but the boy had a hard time taking orders and tended to go off on his own and do what he pleased. Which was sometimes nothing. Besides, Jed was the boss, not Cody. Cody needed to respect that. If he let him go this time, he would keep doing it, like he had before. It had taken some time before Jed had finally broken him of that, so he couldn't allow it to start up again.

Cody glanced at Sunny, then back at Jed. A quick nod and he grabbed his halter and lead rope and strode toward the corral where the horses were. Matt and George did the same.

"Thank you for standing up for me, but you don't have to do that."

So she had caught on to what he was doing. "I meant every word."

"I know you did. Thank you." She smiled up at him, and his heart did a little smiling of its own.

Careful, Jed. Remember Emmett's warning. "Well, we better go get our horses ready."

Minutes later the three of them headed toward the river. Cody remained quiet the whole way.

Down at the river Sunny slid from her horse, grabbed the pick tied to her saddle and started chipping away at the ice, making steps for the cows to walk down to the one spot where the creek water ran rapidly, leaving a small pool.

Jed noticed Cody standing there, staring at her. He walked up alongside the boy. "Admit it. She's pretty impressive, isn't she?"

Cody looked at him. "She's off-limits. Remember, boss?" With those words Cody grabbed the metal pole with the thin flat side on one end and started chopping ice as far away from Sunny as possible.

Right then and there Jed realized Cody's problem. The poor boy had feelings for Sunny. Jed had his work cut out for him. Trying to keep a young buck from going after a wide-eyed doe wouldn't be easy. Keeping himself from going after her was going to be a challenge, as well.

Chapter Five

The temperature dropped far below freezing, owing to the continued snowpack and clear night skies. Taking a bath in a barrel of hot water had helped ward off the cold, but standing here in her nippy bedroom, Sunny shook with a chill. She glanced at her pa's long-handled underwear, then at her door. She always felt sneaky wearing those things. Women just didn't do that. Well, most women didn't, but this one did. As far as she was concerned there was no sense freezing when there were garments to keep a body warm. Whether they were made for a male or a female didn't matter to her none. But other people sure seemed to mind. She slipped them on and covered them with her petticoats as fast as she could in case her aunt came in.

The rest of her garments—a brown woolen skirt, tan high-neck blouse and brown woolen vest—went on a bit slower. Sheepskin-lined slippers won over her boots for the same reason.

She ran her ma's brush through her long wet hair, braided it and wrapped it into a bun at the bottom of her neck. Dressed and ready, she headed out into the living room.

Aunt Minnie stood at the stove holding a lid in one hand and stirring something steaming hot with the other.

After a long day of being outside in January's bitter cold, a hot meal sure sounded good. "What can I do to help, Aunt Minnie?"

"You can holler at the men. They're in your uncle's office."

"Will do." Sunny's skirt swished back and forth like a horse tail as she made her way to her uncle's office and knocked on the door. "Uncle Emmett, dinner's ready."

"Thank you, Sunshine. We'll be right there," he said from the other side of the door.

Instead of waiting for them, Sunny headed back into the kitchen. She pulled the buttered rolls out of the oven, and when she turned around, she caught sight of Jed's look of approval. But just barely.

A quick glance at her uncle and Jed looked everywhere else but at her. He did that often, and she wondered why. Truth be known, it bothered her that he was so intent on not looking at her, but she refused to dwell on it. He was a man, and she had long ago given up trying to figure them out.

Within minutes, they all sat down to fresh home-made noodles and beef soup, cheese and buttered rolls. Just like last evening, during the entire meal, Jed barely looked at her. His actions befuddled her. He was nice to her during the day, but in the evenings, sitting with her aunt and uncle, he barely spoke to or looked at her. Maybe he was shy like Matt. Around her relatives, at least.

Oh, well. One look at the dessert her aunt handed to her and, not caring how unladylike it was, she took a large bite. The chocolate cake with sweetened cream drizzled over it melted in her mouth. "Aunt Minnie, you outdone yourself on this here cake."

"You sure did, wife of mine." Uncle Emmett reached over and squeezed her aunt's hand.

Their eyes held and never moved even when Jed added, "I'll third that." Jed forked a bite every bit again as big as the one she'd just taken. And of all things, the man winked mischievously at her when he did. That meant only one thing…. He'd noticed the huge bite she'd taken.

Heat rushed to her cheeks, and she looked down at her plate. This time the bite she took was much, much smaller. She looked up at Jed and a grin shifted his lips. Feeling somewhat ornery, she forked another huge piece and shoved it into her mouth, not even caring that some of it stuck to her lips. A deep chuckle came from Jed. He forked an even bigger bite. Then she did, then he did, until the cake was gone and chocolate and cream covered their lips.

Sunny glanced at her aunt and uncle. They were so engrossed with each other that they didn't notice the fun between her and Jed. It felt right nice feeling like a kid again.

Everyone finished their dessert. Jed and Uncle Emmett retired to the rocking chairs, Sunny and Aunt Minnie cleared the table and did the dishes and then joined them around the fireplace.

"I meant to ask you earlier, precious, how was your first day on the job? My, that sounds strange. You shouldn't be working for us."

"Yes, I should." Sunny smiled. "And it was, um, interesting."

"Oh. How so?" Aunt Minnie asked.

She told about the runaway team, the guys teasing her about being short, which everyone laughed at but her. She tried to find the humor in it. Truly she did. But after hearing short jokes most of her life, she'd grown to detest them. Mostly the ones when they said she couldn't do something because she was so small. A lot of the times they weren't joking and she knew it. Well, she might be little, something she'd inherited from her mother's side of the family, but she was strong. She had to be.

"Anyone up for a game of dominoes?" Uncle Emmett asked.

"Sure am." She and Jed answered at the same time.

"Great. You wanna join us, sugar?" Uncle Emmett asked Aunt Minnie.

"No. You go on ahead. I don't feel like it tonight. I'll just sit here by the fire, where it's nice and warm, while you're over there, wishing you were here, warming your feet like me," she drew out dramatically and winked at him.

"Well, I have news for you, woman. I'm bringing the table over here," Uncle Emmett said, and he and Jed went to get it.

Sunny never tired of watching the fun interaction between her aunt and uncle. Once again it reminded her of her own parents. Sunny's heart took a sad turn thinking about them. She sure did miss her ma and pa.

"You all right, precious?" Aunt Minnie laid her warm hand on Sunny's arm.

Sunny glanced down at it. How many times had her own mother done that very same thing?

"You thinking about your ma, honey?"

Sunny nodded. "How'd you know?"

"It's been ten years since I've seen my own mama. Sometimes I miss her so bad I can hardly stand it. Someday I hope to go back to Scandinavia for a visit. Emmett says it's too far to travel, but do you know what my mama would say to that?"

Sunny shook her head.

"There's no road too far where love takes you. She's right, you know."

"Who's right?" Uncle Emmett set his side of the bulky table behind the rocking chairs.

"We were talking about my mama."

"What brought that up?" Uncle Emmett opened the drawer, pulled out a box of dominoes and set them on the table.

"Nothing." Tears filled her aunt's voice. "Excuse me." She pushed herself off the rocker and headed to her bedroom. Uncle Emmett excused himself and followed her.

"I didn't mean to upset her." Sunny stared at her lap, feeling slimier than uncooked liver for making her aunt so sad.

"You didn't." Jed stepped between the two rockers, sat down and looked at her. "Every now and again, she gets like this."

"I understand. Sometimes just thinking about my ma gets to me, too." Sunny peered over at him. "Is your ma alive? If so, does she live around here?" She'd asked about his kin before but each time they'd been interrupted before he'd had a chance to answer.

Once again his eyes clouded over with hurt or frustration or both, she wasn't sure.

He drew in a long breath. "Yes, they live in Denver."

"Denver ain't that far. You're lucky you can still go and see your parents. There's no railroad or any road that can take me to where mine are at." Her eyes fell to her lap again and she struggled to not cry in front of Jed. Crying in front of people was something she'd never been comfortable with.

Jed could tell Sunny was hurting and trying not to show it. He wished he could pull her into his arms and comfort her, make all her hurt go away, but holding her wasn't an option. Sunny thought he was lucky. Well, he wasn't, but she didn't know that. If her parents were anything like Minnie and Emmett, he could see why she'd think that.

But neither one of his parents were.

Mother ignored him, always had. Her devotion and love was spent on her first- and last-born sons. Neither of which he was.

Being the middle son Jed had always pretty much been left out. He wasn't anything like either one of his brothers. They were both rich and successful like his parents.

Oh, he could be successful, too, if he wanted to sit around all day long in his father's office doing paperwork and being criticized and compared to Daniel and Sebastian. Nothing could induce him to endure either one of those things.

Cooped up in an office would kill him, of that he was certain. He loved the outdoors. Loved ranching. He just hoped when he bought his own spread, with his own money, that his father would finally be proud of him, too.

"You ready to play dominoes?" Sunny asked, more chipper than he knew she felt. Her eyes said it all, that's how he knew.

"Sure."

They stood. Jed turned her chair around, waited until she was seated, then grabbed his and placed it on the opposite side of the table from her.

Once the dominoes were sorted, they started to play. Sunny concentrated hard each time it was her turn.

After one of her turns, out of the blue she asked, "What were you and Uncle Emmett talking about so seriously earlier?"

Jed frowned. "What are you talking about? When?"

"When I fetched you two for dinner. I heard Uncle Emmett say he was concerned."

"Oh. That." Jed looked up from his dominoes and his eyes snagged on hers. "He spotted mountain-lion tracks up on the north ridge. He's concerned about them killing more of his yearlings."

"More?"

"Uh-huh. He found a dead one this morning."

She set her domino down and looked him square in the eye. "After we get done feeding tomorrow, how about you and I track and shoot it before it gets any more of Uncle Emmett's cattle?"

Jed's eyebrows reached for the ceiling. "That's no job for a lady. As little as you are, that mountain lion might mistake you for his next meal." The instant his teasing words left his mouth, he realized what he'd just said and done, and his gaze flew to hers. "Sunny…"

Her lips pursed and her big eyes were narrowed into thin slats.

He held up his hand. "I'm sorry. I wasn't thinking."

"That's right. You weren't." She shot upward and even with her standing and him still sitting, her face was barely inches above his. "Well, let me tell you something, Jedidiah Cooper. Don't let my size fool you. I aim to prove to you and everyone else here that I'm more than able to hunt down that mountain lion. I've been hunting for years. And I'm quite good at it, too. Now if you'll excuse me. I'm going to bed. I have a mountain lion to catch in the morning." She spun around and stormed toward her bedroom.

He hadn't meant to make her mad and felt terrible that he had. But she'd caught him off guard. He'd had no clue that the woman hunted. Hopefully she wasn't foolish enough to go hunting that thing alone just to prove a point to everyone.

Uncertainty cut deep into his belly. As stubborn and determined as she was, she just might. Whatever Jed did, he needed to make sure he was up before her tomorrow morning and that she didn't go hunting alone. That was never a wise thing to do, especially when going after something as dangerous as a hungry predator.

The next morning Sunny dressed in her pa's woolen pants. She didn't want her bulky woolen skirt and undergarments hindering her today while she hunted down that mountain lion. She'd show Jedidiah just how capable she was. Course, he had no way of knowing she'd shot a few in her lifetime already. Still it angered her that he thought she couldn't. No, that wasn't true. It didn't anger her, it hurt her. His comments last night hurt her even more. She'd thought he was different, but she was wrong. He was just like everyone else. That's all right. When the time came, it would make leaving here that much easier.

She headed into the kitchen. Aunt Minnie wasn't up yet, no one was. Course it was only four-thirty. Mornings had always been special to her. Quiet and peaceful-like. She stoked the fire in the woodstove and fireplace, and extended her hands toward the heat of the burning pine. When her fingers finally got warm, she sat in her chair and picked up the Bible on the nearby round table.

Finished with her daily reading, she put a pot of coffee on, fried up a mess of bacon and scrambled a dozen eggs.

"You're up early."

Sunny's heart slammed into her ribs, and she whirled toward the sound of Jed's voice. "You scared me."

"So I noticed." He chuckled. Pulling out a chair, he shifted it around, straddled the seat with his long legs and rested his arms on the back of it, facing her.

"You're up early." Sunny turned back to scrambling the eggs.

"Funny. I just said the same thing to you."

"You did, didn't you?"

"Uh-huh. Do you always get up this early?"

She shifted until she could see his face but kept scrambling away at the eggs. "No. But I've always been an early riser. My pa used to say I got up so early that the rooster waited on me to let him know when it was time to wake everyone else up."

Jed chuckled again, then the noise in the kitchen went quiet for several seconds, and the only sound was the scraping of the spoon in the skillet.

"Sunny, about last night. I really am sorry for teasing you."

Sunny looked at his face and saw true remorse there. Maybe he wasn't like everyone else after all. No one else had ever apologized. "Apology accepted." She shook her finger at him. "Just don't let it happen again." She sent him a sassy, playful smile.

"I won't. I won't. Trust me." He laughed and she joined him.

"I thought I heard voices in here." Aunt Minnie walked into the kitchen, adjusting her hairpins as she did. "Are those your pa's pants?"

Sunny glanced down at the brown pants in question, then over at Jedidiah, whose eyes were taking in the length of them. "Yup. Thought they'd be a whole lot warmer and easier to work in than my skirt today."

"What's so special about today?" Aunt Minnie glanced into the pan of eggs, then raised the cloth off the bacon. "Looks like you have breakfast all ready, precious. Thank you."

"You're welcome." Sunny dumped the eggs into the bowl she had ready for them. Hoping her aunt would forget her question, she turned to place them on the table, but paused. Jed was now standing in front of the fireplace with his back to her. Why had he left in such a hurry? She shrugged and set the eggs on the table.

Uncle Emmett walked into the room. "Morning."

Everyone said *morning* back.

"Breakfast is ready, sweetie pie. Sunny made it."

Uncle Emmett kissed Sunny on the cheek and whispered in her ear, "Your aunt had a restless night. She's pretty worn out this morning. So thank you for helping her." He went and sat down at the table.

Sunny insisted her aunt join him while she laid the food on the table.

Grace was said and they started to eat.

"You weren't planning on going by yourself today, were you?" Jed asked, biting off a chunk of bacon and chewing it.

"Going where by yourself?" Uncle Emmett stopped buttering his roll and looked over at Sunny.

"Sunny's going after that mountain lion today." Jed scooped up a forkful of eggs and continued as if nothing was amiss.

Sunny kicked Jedidiah under the table.

"Ow-w." He leaned down, narrowing his eyes at her, and, judging by his movement, rubbing his shin.

"No need for you to do that, Sunshine. The boys and me'll go."

Sunny shot a glaring look at Jedidiah before turning in her chair and facing her uncle. "I'd like to go along, too. You know Pa took me hunting with him all the time and taught me to shoot real good." She gave him that pleading look, the one he couldn't refuse, but it was important to her to be the one to take down the animal.

His eyes softened.

She had him. He'd always been a sucker for both her and her pa.

"All right, Sunshine. You can come with us."

Sunny jumped up and threw her arms around her uncle's neck and kissed his cheek. She raced to the door and slid her foot into one of her snow boots.

"Hold on there, girl. We ain't leaving yet. We haven't even eaten."

"Oh. Right." She yanked her boot off and raced back to the table and started gobbling her food down.

"Slow down, girl. You'll make yourself sick."

Sunny raised her eyes up from her plate and glanced at her uncle, then over at Jed.

One of his brows quirked and amusement danced in his eyes.

Heat rushed into Sunny's cheeks, knowing her cheeks were puffed out with an overload of food. Again.

"A little anxious, are we?" Jedidiah asked before he laughed and everyone at the table joined him.

She smiled the best she could with a mouthful of scrambled eggs. She chewed fast and swallowed. "Yup. I am." She shoved the last of her food in her mouth. "You ready?"

"Guess so." Jed picked up his coffee cup, gulped what was left in a few swallows and stood.

"Wait for me, you two." Emmett stood, holding his coffee cup and gulping its contents, too. He kissed Aunt Minnie and followed them to the mudroom where they all dressed for the cold and grabbed their rifles before heading outside.

Chapter Six

Three days went by and they still hadn't been able to go after that lion. One thing after another kept going wrong. Broken sled boards, broken harnesses and an unusual amount of broken barbed-wire fence all conspired to keep them off the mountain. The mangled fence was probably due to the yearlings trying to get away from the lion. Last night it had snowed again, making tracking the animal easier.

Today they would try again. Jed hoped so anyway. That animal had to be caught, and soon.

Bitter cold sucked the air out of Jed's lungs the instant he stepped outside.

"Brrr." Sunny pulled her bandanna over her mouth and drew the collar of her coat closer around her neck, and Jed did the same, hoping it would help as a barrier against the cold. "It's even colder today than yesterday." Sunny wiggled and shifted about like a worm, trying to get warm no doubt.

"That's for sure," Emmett added as he stomped through the snow beside them. "I think we'll forget tracking that lion again today, Sunshine. It's just too cold for you to go traipsing about the woods."

"The cold never stopped me before."

He shook his head and chuckled. "See what I mean, Jed?"

"Sure do." Jed laughed but secretly he admired the woman. She had nerves of steel and a spine to match.

"Tell you what. I'll do the chores around here. You and Jed go feed on the upper meadow today and the boys can feed on the lower. If it's warmed up any after we've finished, we'll go track that lion then. Fair enough?" Emmett asked.

Sunny's eyes went from the color of molasses to rich brown honey. "Fair enough."

"If you don't give Jed here too hard a time, I'll even let you have first shot at it."

"Me?" She pointed to herself. "Give someone a hard time?"

"Yes, Sunshine. You. You put the *S* in *sassy*."

"Uncle Emmett!"

He winked at her and grinned.

Down at the barn they leaned their rifles against the wall and fed the team. Minutes later, they had them readied.

"I'll drive today."

"Don't trust me, huh?" Sunny's eyes held only mischief.

"Nope." He winked at her and immediately realized he shouldn't have done that now or earlier. Both were done in fun, but he couldn't afford to give her or Emmett the wrong idea.

They jumped on the sled, and Jed unwrapped the

lines. On the way to the haystack, he asked, "You done much hunting?"

"Enough."

"Just what does 'enough' mean? Are you any good at it?"

"Yup."

"Think you can kill that mountain lion?"

"Yup."

"You seem pretty confident."

"Yup."

Jed laughed. "Is that all you can say?"

"Yup."

Even though her mouth and nose were covered with a blue-and-white bandanna with little squirrelly design things on it, he knew she was smiling by the crinkles around her eyes.

"Did you have mountain lions on your ranch?"

The crinkles disappeared. "A few. Had a few bobcats and lynxes, too."

"What's your place like anyway?"

She turned toward him, draping her arm over the rack and leaning her side against it. "It's wonderful. Our barn and corrals are every inch again as big as Uncle Emmett's. Our house isn't as large, though. Pa wanted to add on to it, but Ma said it was a waste of money, having to buy fixings and furnishings to fill it and all. So Pa used the money he'd set aside for it to build up the herd."

"I heard what happened to your livestock last winter. I'm sorry about that."

"Sure did change things." The brightness in her eyes dimmed.

"What are your plans with the place now? You going to sell?"

"Sell?" She shook her head hard and fast. "Absolutely not. I'm hoping to earn enough money to buy a few head of bred cows so I can build up the place again."

"How you going to do that alone?"

Her eyes narrowed, and she shifted away from him and faced the team. "I did a right fine job of taking care of things for my pa when he took sick." She glanced back at him as if waiting for his snide response.

He had none and only nodded, impressed by every inch of her heart and soul. "I heard you did. You're really blessed to have your own place, you know that?"

"I do."

"I hope to buy my own spread someday." In a way they had that in common. Both wanted to build up their own place and he believed her reasons were much the same as his. To prove to others they could, but most of all because they loved ranching. Only thing was, she owned a place already. He didn't. But…it wouldn't be long until he did. He smiled slightly and mentally went through the calculations again of his savings and how much a place would cost.

"Got anyplace particular in mind?" she asked, breaking into his thoughts.

"Uh-huh. Thinking about buying a place up the Troublesome around Gunsight Pass."

"Never been there before."

"You haven't?"

"Nope. We were always too busy to go anywhere. We rarely even got to visit Uncle Emmett and Aunt Minnie except for a few times in the summer. We spent a lot more time with them when I was younger. Before we increased our herd. After that, it seemed like it got harder and harder to get away. Sure did miss seeing them as much."

"They're pretty special. Your uncle's a great man."

"He sure is. He looks a lot like my pa, you know?"

"No. I didn't know that. I never had the pleasure of meeting your father."

"You would have liked him. And I know he would have liked you, too." Her confidence in that warmed Jed through and through. "There's a picture on our mantel with my pa, Uncle Emmett and Grandpappy. Their pa. The resemblance is amazing."

They pulled up alongside the haystack. "I don't look anything like my father." He said it low enough that he barely heard himself speak. As soon as he did, he wished he hadn't. He didn't want to talk about his father. It hurt too much. "Well, we're here. We'd better get this thing loaded."

Sunny looked over at him with understanding in her eyes. He hadn't fooled her. Not saying anything showed she understood and even respected his wishes by not bringing it up. His admiration for her increased.

They loaded the wagon, fed the cows and headed back down to the barn. As they removed the tack from the draft horses, Sunny raised Samson's hoof. "Jed, look here. He's thrown a shoe."

Jed ran his hand over Samson's rump as he walked close behind the large animal. Bent over, Sunny rested his hoof on her leather chaps above her knees.

"I'll just have to fix it. Do you want to help?"

Sunny lowered the hoof slowly and stood. Her mouth quirked off to one side and her eyelids settled on her cheeks. "That's one thing I can't do."

Jed could tell by the way she said it just how hard that was for her to admit.

"The reason you can't do it wouldn't be because you barely come up to Samson's knee, could it?" Cody stepped up to them. "Oh, pardon me. My mistake. You ain't Sunny. You must be her twin brother." His gaze slid to the men's trousers she wore.

Her eyes slatted as a scowl came to her face, and Jed wanted to punch the younger cowboy for taking her admission and stabbing her with it. "I do not barely come up to his knee."

"I know. That's what I said."

"Huh?" She cocked her head to the side, then rolled her eyes. "That's not what I meant." Frustration bit through her words. "I meant I'm taller than that."

"Not by much," George chimed in jokingly from behind Cody.

Jed knew Cody and George were just teasing her, but he knew how much their teasing flustered Sunny so he stepped in to intervene. "George. Cody. That's enough. I don't want you talking to—"

"It's all right, Jed. Thank you, but I can handle these two myself."

She stepped right up to them and pointed her finger at them. "Listen here. I might be little, but—"

"Wait. Just a minute, Sunny," Cody interrupted her. He picked her up underneath her arms and held her eye level to his six-foot-three frame. Her legs dangled in the air. "There, now I can see you."

Jed braced himself, waiting for her to blow like a fired cannon.

"Thank you, Cody." She bent her head back and

looked up at the sky. "I always wondered what the view was like from up here in the clouds."

Jed knew his chin had to be touching his neckerchief.

"So what's it like being the first one to know when it rains?" Sunny continued. "Are you sure your name isn't stretch? Or high tower? Or beanpole? I'm sure it's really beanpole and you just won't fess up to it. *Beanpole* definitely suits you better with them long, skinny legs of yours."

Less than a second went by and Sunny was back on her feet.

Cody whirled and stormed off, mumbling, "I ain't that tall. Ain't that skinny neither."

Jed threw back his head and laughed. George joined him and so did Matt, who'd stood silently in the background the whole time.

"Ain't funny," Cody tossed over his shoulder.

"How does it feel, Cody, to be teased about your height?" Jed called to the cowboy's retreating back.

"You sure got him a good one," shy Matt said as he and George turned to leave.

"She's a sassy one," Jed heard George tell Matt.

Jed looked over at Sunny. "You really are sensitive about your height, aren't you?"

"You would be, too, if you'd been made fun of all your life for it. Grows old real fast."

"Just how tall are you anyway?"

"Five foot."

"Five foot what?"

"That's it. Five foot. There is no 'what.' Sure wish the good Lord would've given me a few more inches at least. Then people wouldn't tease me so much or mistake me for a child or for a boy just because I wear pants to keep my legs warm."

Jed kept himself from looking at Sunny's womanly curves hidden under all that heavy outside winter garb.

He followed her gaze as it slid to his legs. "Where'd you get them woolies chaps from? I'd sure like to get me a pair someday."

"I made them."

Her eyes widened. "You did?"

"Mmm-hmm."

"Do you think you could make me a pair of them?"

Again warmth touched his heart. He'd never heard her ask for anyone's help, and now she'd asked for his twice in less than thirty minutes. He smiled, wholly aware of the trust she was placing in him. "Sure can. In fact I have two more hides just like the one this was made out of in the bunkhouse storage room."

"What would you charge to make me a pair?"

"Nothing."

She tilted her head and frowned. "I don't need charity, Jedidiah."

Jedidiah? That wasn't good. It was his turn to frown. "What do you mean? I'm not giving them to you out of charity. Just as a friendly gesture."

"Oh." She sighed. "Sorry, Jed. Guess I'm too sensitive for my own good."

He wondered what had brought that on. Had she lived off people's charity? If so, had she been picked on for that, too?

Sunny hadn't meant to snap at Jedidiah. It was just that it always came back around to the same thing. After she'd had to accept charity gifts from her neighbors when her pa had taken sick, it made her feel as though she'd failed him. Pa had said she hadn't, but she couldn't help feeling as if she had. Jed didn't know about none of that, though, and it was a gift and not charity. "If you're sure about this, then I'd be right honored to accept your gift."

"Thank you, Sunny."

"Why are you thanking me?"

"For allowing me to be a blessing in your life."

That he was. A blessing that had nothing to do with his gift offering. She liked him. Liked being around him. Liked that he never teased her. Well, except for that one time, but he'd apologized for that. Something no one else had ever done. Jed even took up for her when no one other than her pa ever had.

"You ready to go track that lion?"

Sunny looked up at him to see if he was serious. "Sure am!"

"Well, let's get to it, then."

"Will the men be going with us?" *Please say no.*

"Uh-huh. The sooner we get rid of the lion, the better. Emmett's already lost three yearlings to it."

Three yearlings was a huge loss. Jed was right. The sooner they got it, the better. "Do you want me to run and get Uncle Emmett?"

"If you wouldn't mind, that'd be great. I'll get the horses ready. Which one of yours do you want? The bay or the paint?"

"Rowdy, the paint. He's not easily spooked."

"From what I've witnessed, handling a spooked horse wouldn't be an issue for you anyway."

Jed's words of confidence made Sunny feel as if she'd suddenly grown an extra foot or two. "Thank you, Jed."

"For what?"

"For saying what you did. It means a lot to me."

"It's the truth."

Sunny stared into his eyes.

Eyes the color of a bluebird.

Eyes filled with warmth and honesty.

Eyes she could see herself waking up to every morning.

Sunny blinked. What was she thinking? Here she barely knew the man and she was thinking about waking up next to him?

Don't lose sight of why you're here, Sunny. It ain't to get no husband. Keeping your promise to Pa comes before you ever think about marrying.

"I'll go get my uncle now. I think I saw him heading to the house earlier." Sunny whirled, rushed to the cabin and stuck her head inside the front door.

Her uncle stood with his back to the fire, warming his hands.

"Uncle Emmett, it's warmed up a bit. We're ready to track that mountain lion now." Excitement rushed through her voice.

"That's good. But why don't you go on without me? I have some paperwork that needs my attention."

"You sure?"

"I'm sure, Sunshine. Be careful."

"I will." She closed the door and ran back to the barn.

She wished her uncle were going, but she understood how much paperwork was involved in running a ranch of this size.

Jed stood outside the barn. He had the horses saddled and bridled and their snowshoes and rifles mounted on their saddles.

"Can't believe you got these two ready that quick."

"During calving season I learned to saddle a horse real fast."

"I know that one." They shared a chuckle. "That's one of the few things I don't much care for about ranching."

"Calving season?" His brows disappeared under the brim of his black cowboy hat.

"No. No." She waved her gloved hand. "I love calving season. Well, the first few weeks of it anyway." She grinned. "I don't like having to saddle a horse in the middle of the night and head out in a heavy wet snowstorm or freezing cold to bring a cow in so I can pull its calf. Seems to me they always calve during the worst storms."

"Sure does, doesn't it?" They chuckled over that one, too, knowing just how true that was. "It never fails. We could have ten days of nice sunny spring weather and very few calves are born those days. But let a spring storm come in, or a bitter-cold night, and them cows popped babies out like there was no tomorrow."

"That's for sure. Seems like that's when the breach calves come, too."

Cody, George and Matt stepped out of the barn, leading their horses.

"So, you're really going with us, huh?" Cody asked, his disapproval obvious.

"Why is that so hard for you to believe?" Jed answered for her.

"Because she's a girl. She has no business tracking down a mountain lion. It's dangerous."

"What does my being a woman—" she stressed the word *woman* because she hated being called a girl "—have to do with anything? What should matter is if I can shoot this thing." She patted her rifle resting in its scabbard. "And how accurate my aim is. Let me assure you, Cody." She looked right at him, dead center of his eyes. "It's accurate."

"We'll see." Cody mounted his horse and headed toward the direction where the mountain lion had last been seen.

They all mounted and followed him.

"That man is going to find himself in trouble one day. If it isn't for spouting off his mouth, it will be for that big head of his." Jed's head slowly shifted back and forth. "Let's just hope it isn't today." His attention slid to Sunny. He stared at her and wrinkles lined his forehead. "You know, the more I think about it, the more I think Cody needs to stay behind and do something else." Jed nudged his horse into a trot.

Sunny caught up with Jed and stopped him. "Please, Jed. Don't. Cody'll blame me for his not getting to go along. I already get enough flap jaw from him. I don't want him hating me, too. Just let me prove to him that I'm not helpless."

Uncertainty flitted through his eyes. "He's never hunted down a mountain lion before. I'm not sure I trust him helping us."

"Please, Jed?"

His chest rose and fell. He gave a quick nod. "But only because I believe in you."

Sunny's chest expanded farther than Jed's had. Only, hers was from pride. Jed believing in her and saying it, meant a whole lot to her. "Thank you." She gave him her biggest smile, and when he gave her one back, her heart hopped in her chest, and it wasn't from excitement neither. It took a lot to scare her, but that did. A lot.

* * *

They made their way to where the mountain lion was spotted last. Evidence of the animal's presence was visible. Another yearling half-eaten and buried to be consumed later. With winter so bad this year, food was scarce for the animals. If only they could trap the animal and transport it somewhere else. But anyplace where the lion would have an abundant supply of food besides the rancher's cattle would take days to get to.

Time no one had to spare.

And the weather made that feat impossible anyway. Jed blew out a long breath. As much as he hated killing any animal, he knew it had to be done before too many more cattle went up missing.

Its hide, thick and light, would make a good vest or small jacket for someone. Someone like Sunny.

"Over here," the object of his last thought spoke in a hushed tone.

The men headed over to where Sunny was crouched down. "It's a female."

"How can you tell?" Cody asked with sarcasm.

What was wrong with Cody? Sunny had done nothing to warrant his behavior.

Sunny remained squatted but shifted to where they could see the print. "Male toe prints aren't teardrop-shaped like these here are."

She was right. Jed's admiration for her slid upward a few more notches. He'd never met a woman like her before.

"Looks like it headed toward the Kids Pond."

"I think you're right. Well, let's go find out." Jed nodded to his men and to Sunny.

They mounted their horses, and Cody took off ahead

of them. That boy was looking for trouble, and Jed wished he hadn't let Sunny talk him into letting Cody come.

With the fresh snow it was easy to see the lion's prints. When the snow went from a foot to two feet, too deep for their horses, they stopped and tethered them to a rope they strung between two trees. "Who wants to volunteer to stay back with the horses?" Jed asked, not wanting to leave the horses defenseless if the lion chose to come back around. Mountain lions were known to wait until a person was cornered with no way of escape. Or it might back itself into a cave knowing that when the person stepped inside, it had the advantage over them, and would attack.

"I'll stay." Sunny surprised Jed by volunteering. He knew how badly she wanted to hunt that animal and why.

"Scared?" Cody taunted her.

"Nope." She just smiled at him.

"Prove it. You go, and I'll stay." He crossed his arms over his lanky chest.

Sunny yanked her rifle out of its scabbard. "Sure will. See you later. Have fun, Cody." With those words she headed off in the direction of the tracks.

Jed had to keep himself from laughing. He, Matt and George hurried to catch up with her. They followed the tracks higher and higher up the mountain, traipsing through the thick trees, fighting branches and large trunks from felled timber. Near a rock dwelling the hair rose on the back of Jed's neck and arms. From past experience that meant only one thing—the lion was nearby.

Sunny stopped, squatted down and pointed upward. "There it is," she whispered.

They joined her and followed her pointing finger.

"Good job, Sunny."

George raised his rifle.

Jed grabbed the barrel and lowered it. "Emmett said Sunny could get the first shot."

George looked at her.

"It's okay, Jed. Let George nail it."

"You sure?"

"Yup." She smiled, and his admiration toward her went up yet another notch.

George braced his rifle against his shoulder and pulled the trigger hammer back, then the trigger.

Bam!

The mountain lion sprung upward. Before anyone could get their rifles aimed, it fled out of sight. Heart racing faster than the wind, Jed, along with everyone else, tossed their rifle straps over their shoulders and charged after it.

"It's circling around to the where the horses are," Sunny said from beside Jed.

"Yes, I know. We need to hurry and hope and pray that Cody is paying attention."

Amazed at how fast Sunny's short legs moved, especially since she had to pick them up and set them down because of the snowshoes, Jed had trouble keeping up with her.

Within yards of the horses Sunny suddenly stopped, slipped her rifle from around her shoulder, aimed and fired.

Cody jumped up and whirled. The mountain lion lay only feet from him.

They rushed to the motionless animal. Jed pressed his boot on it and moved it, making sure the animal was in fact dead.

Cody stared at the large cat, his face white as the snow around him. "I—I didn't even hear it or see it." His gaze went to Jed, George and Matt, but not to Sunny. "Thank you, whoever shot it."

"Sunny did," Jed informed him, his foot still on the carcass.

Cody's wide eyes flew to Sunny. He gawked at her, and his cheeks turned the same red color as his neckerchief. He ducked his head, headed to his horse, untied him and swung himself in the saddle. With one last look at them and the lion, he fled down the mountain.

"I didn't mean to embarrass him." Remorse shrouded Sunny's face as she looked up at Jed, then at George and Matt. "But that lion would have killed Cody if I hadn't seen her and shot her when I did."

"No need to apologize. You saved Cody's life. The man should have been paying attention." Jed shifted his focus from her onto the men. "Let's get this thing loaded and get out of here."

All the way down the mountain Jed thought about Sunny. He may have only known her a short while, but without a doubt, he knew he wanted that sweet, gutsy woman for his wife. But he also knew that wasn't ever going to happen.

Chapter Seven

For almost a week now, Cody had avoided Sunny. Wouldn't even look at her. Jed seemed somewhat distant, too. Oh, he was nice to her and all, but the easy friendship they had shared somehow didn't feel the same anymore.

What had she done that was so wrong? To Jed? And to Cody? Was it because she'd shot that mountain lion? If so, would the two of them have rather that she let that lion kill Cody? It wasn't as if she was trying to show off or anything. When she'd seen it, it was within seconds of pouncing on Cody. She didn't have time to ask them if one of them wanted to shoot it. If she had... She shuddered to think of what would have happened. That lion would've had Cody by his neck in an instant.

Thinking of Cody, Sunny set her sights on the bunkhouse where she'd seen him head moments ago. She stormed away from the water trough over to the bunkhouse and banged on the door.

"Who is it?" She recognized Cody's voice. Rather than give him a chance to ignore her again, she said nothing, hoping he would just come and answer the door.

She banged on it again.

"All right, all right. I'm coming."

Footsteps pounded inside. Sunny took a step back when they neared.

The door swung open. Cody frowned and started to close the door, but Sunny put herself in its way. "We need to talk."

"I have nothing to say to you." No anger, no feeling at all came through his voice.

"Well, I have something to say to you." She pushed past him, relieved to see it was just the two of them. The smell of leather and wet wool filled the air.

Cody peered outside before closing the door and facing her. "Fine. Say what you have to say, then you need to leave." Cody crossed his arms over his chest and leaned against the door. He stared down at her, his face a sheet of blank emotion.

"Look. I'm sorry I embarrassed you the other day. What did you expect me to do? Just let that mountain lion kill you?" She shook her head. "I don't understand you, Cody. One minute you're teasing me, the next you're angry with me. Why do you dislike me so much?"

"I don't dislike you." He shoved off from the door and stood so close to her she could smell his citrus soap. His green eyes peered into hers. "I do, however, have a problem with working with you. I just don't believe women are capable of doing man's work. Ranching can be dangerous. Especially for someone as tiny as you are. You're gonna end up hurting yourself or someone else. I've seen it happen one too many times."

Sunny couldn't believe her ears. For days now Cody had seen what she could do. She'd even saved his life.

What more would it take to convince him and others like him that she was capable of doing ranch work—all of it?

The door swung open, and Jed stood in the doorway. "What's going on in here?" Jed looked at Sunny, then at Cody. His face was as hard as flint and his eyes didn't look any kinder.

"Nothing's going on in here, boss. Sunny was just leaving."

"I was? We aren't through with this yet." She turned her attention onto Jed. "Did you need something, Jed?"

"Emmett sent me to fetch you."

"How'd you know she was here?" Cody asked with a frown.

"Emmett and I saw her come in here."

Cody's face paled, and his hand darted upward. "We was just talking, boss. Nothing else." Those words shot out of Cody faster than a fired bullet.

Sunny fixed her eyes on the man, wondering what was the matter with him. Cody looked downright nervous. But why? She thought about it a moment. No. Surely Jed didn't think there was something going on between her and Cody. Did he? Well, she'd set them thoughts to rights this instant. "If you must know, I came here to apologize to Cody."

"For what?" Suspicion she didn't like one whit poured over Jed's face.

Just who was he to act like that? Resentment pooled inside her. "That's none of your business, Jedidiah." She brushed past him and laid her hand on the door latch.

Jed reached for her arm and stopped her. "It is my business when it comes to Emmett's niece and his hired hands."

Sunny whirled and yanked her arm from his grasp. "What's that suppose to mean?"

"Emmett asked me to keep an eye on you."

Her eyes flung open like an unlatched barn door caught by the wind as understanding smacked into her. "He what?" So that's why Jed was so friendly to her. Not because he liked her, but because he was just doing his job. That hurt more than she wanted it to, right in the middle of her heart. But she wouldn't let him know that and give him power over her like Duke had had at one time. "Fine. You've done your job. I'm leaving now." With that she yanked the door open, stormed around the side of the bunkhouse and strode up through the trees.

Through a haze of angry tears her uncle's hunting and fishing cabin came into view. She hadn't realized she'd walked that far, but she was glad to see it. She'd always loved this place. It held fond memories for her.

At the snow-covered porch, she brushed the white powder off the tree stump her uncle had cut into the shape of a chair, tucked her full-length woolen coat underneath her and sat down.

Without wanting them to, Jed's words scrolled through her mind, hurting her with the same force they had just minutes ago. A fresh round of tears came. She hated that she'd gotten close enough to the man that she was now shedding tears over him. What a fool she'd been thinking Jed liked her when all along he was just doing his job. Well, what did she care anyway? She was here to do a job, too.

His handsome face and the curve of his lips when he smiled fell into her mind. She squeezed her eyes to blot them out, but all she saw was the blue of his eyes and the crinkles that fanned from the corners of them when he was tickled about something. Her heart reached out to those images, embracing them and pulling them to herself, pulling *him* to herself. When she realized what was happening, she shook her mind free of the silly schoolgirl notions filling her brain. Notions she would never give in to because she knew all too well the heartache those thoughts led to.

"Remember what Emmett said," Jed warned Cody. A snake of jealousy had wound through him when he'd opened the door and seen Cody and Sunny standing so close together. Here he was warning Cody, when what he really needed to do was to warn himself.

"Seems to me like you need to remember that more than me, Jed." Stunned by Cody's perception, he opened his mouth to say something, but Cody beat him to it. "No disrespect, boss, but I've seen the way you look at her. And I don't blame you. She's quite a looker."

"The only way you've seen me look at her is with respect. Something you ought to try for a change." Jed spun around and closed the door behind him.

Out of earshot, he mumbled to himself, "Can't a man look at a woman with admiration without everyone seeing more into it than what was there?" Who was Jed kidding? He was attracted to Sunny. "Yes, I am. But I also know she's off-limits, so it doesn't matter." Jed continued carrying a conversation with himself. One he wasn't winning, so he turned his mind onto following Sunny's tracks up into the trees.

Judging by her footprints he'd say she headed toward the hunting cabin near the springhouse and wild strawberry patch, and that's exactly where he found her. "Sunny." He spoke her name softly, not wanting to startle her.

Her gaze swung his way and she crossed her arms over her chest. "If you come up here to keep an eye on me, no need to. You can go back and tell Uncle Emmett I'm just fine."

Jed stepped onto the porch, cleaned off one of the chairs similar to Sunny's and sat down beside her. "I shouldn't have told you that. I can see I've hurt your feelings, Sunny. I'm sorry."

She thumbed her cowboy hat up and looked at him. "So that's the reason you've been spending so much time around me, huh? 'Cause Uncle Emmett told you to." The hurt was right on the surface of her lovely face. "I thought you were my friend. And here all this time you've just been doing your job. What a fool I was to think you cared about me as a friend."

"I do care about you, Sunny. And you are my friend. When I said Emmett wanted me to keep an eye on you, that didn't mean hanging around you all day long and talking with you like I have. He just wanted to make sure none of the men got out of line with you was all."

Her eyes searched his, and he let them, knowing she was searching for the truth. "I can take care of myself." Her lashes brushed the tops of her cheeks. "But thank you, Jed. I could use a friend."

It amazed him how many times she showed her vulnerable side to him. Something the other men never witnessed. The thought touched him. "Well, you have one for as long as you like."

She smiled. "You, too." She sat back into the chair, looking straight ahead of her. "It's sure pretty here, isn't it?"

His focus followed hers. Aspen and pine trees surrounded the cabin, except for a small clearing where willow bushes outlined it. "Uh-huh. It sure is."

"When I was little—" she yanked her head his direction "—no comment from you about being little neither—" she grinned "—my ma and I used to come up here with Aunt Minnie and pick wild strawberries. Then we'd head back down to the house and make jam with them. Ma always said I ate more than whatever made it into them jars."

"What was your ma like?"

"Oh, she was a great ma. The best actually. She was always giving me hugs and telling me how special I was. Always listening to me whenever I needed to talk. We had some right fine talks, too, Ma and me." Her eyes brightened with the memories.

Jed wished he had memories as sweet as hers. But his mother and father were not the loving kind. Never had been. And it was pretty clear by now they never would be.

"Ma worked right alongside my pa. She could rope and brand a calf slicker and faster than anyone. Pa used to wonder how she did it 'cause she was little like me. I should say I'm little like her." Sunny turned her large brown eyes toward him. "People misjudged her the same as they do me. Ma didn't care none about it, though. Said God made her that way for a reason and that it wasn't right of folks to criticize what God had made. Whenever someone did take it upon themselves to do that, she just worked harder to prove them wrong, and she did, too. Ma could keep up with the best of them."

"Like you," Jed said, knowing his voice was filled with reverence and emotions he couldn't corral.

Her eyes softened with the smile she sent his way. "Thank you, Jed, for saying that. It's nice to have someone who understands me."

"I sure do." He stretched his long legs out in front of him and leaned back in the chair. "Whether you know it or not, we have a lot of things in common."

"Like what?"

"Well, you want to prove to the men that you're capable of running a ranch despite your size. And me...I want to prove to my father that I'm just as good as my brothers are. That I can make it on my own, too."

"Does he think you can't?" Surprise lifted her dainty eyebrows.

It hurt to talk about it, but she'd opened herself up to him, so he felt comfortable doing the same. That's what friends did after all. "My father thinks my brothers are the only ones who can make something of themselves. Father's always going on and on about my oldest brother, Daniel, and his big house, his children, his rich banker's daughter wife. And my brother Sebastian, who has a mansion up the street that's bigger than my parents' place. I think my father does it to provoke me into doing the same thing so he can be proud of me, too. But big-city life isn't for me. Shutting me up in an office all day long would strip the life right out of me."

"Same here. Oh, sure, I can cook and clean and do all them kinda things. Ma made sure of that. But I want to be outdoors. Working with cows and horses. Riding through the trees in the summer, hunting down strays or moving the cattle to fresh grazing. Even cleaning pens. That don't bother me none."

"See, I told you we had a lot in common."

They shared a smile.

"Well, it's getting late. Your uncle will be worried about you if we don't get back."

"Suppose you're right." They stood and Sunny gazed up at him. "No offense to your pa, Jed, but the man's wearing horse blinders or something, 'cause you're already someone he can be proud of." She stepped away from him and headed off the porch.

Her words touched Jed deeply. No one had ever said anything like that to him before. It felt good. Real good. He blinked the sheen of moisture from his eyes. "Lord, thank You for Sunny. May I be worthy of her friendship," he whispered before he left the cabin and caught up with her.

They made their way back down to the main house just as the mountains filled with shadow.

When they stepped inside, heat along with corned beef and cabbage met them.

Standing in front of the cookstove, Minnie turned toward them, holding a wooden spatula in her hand. "About time you two got here." She shook the spoon at them and winked.

"Where you been?" Emmett asked from his rocker near the fireplace.

Apprehension replaced the quietness inside Jed. Was Emmett upset? Did he think Jed was wooing his niece?

"I went for a walk up to the hunting cabin, and Jed came to fetch me."

"Keeping an eye on my girl. That's good." Emmett smiled at Jed with a wink.

Jed didn't know how to react to that. At times, if Jed wasn't mistaken, it seemed as if Emmett was throwing him and Sunny together on purpose. But that couldn't be. His job was to watch out for her and nothing else. Confused and unable to figure it out, he quit trying and joined Emmett in the living room.

Sunny offered to help her aunt in the kitchen, and the two of them busied themselves there.

Emmett glanced over his shoulder and then back at Jed. "So, how are the men treating Sunny? Are they being nice to her? They're not stepping out of line with her or anything, are they?"

"No, sir. They've all been perfect gentlemen." Well, except Cody. But the boy hadn't done anything other than tease her, and Sunny handled him just fine every time.

"You men ready to eat?" Minnie called.

"We sure are, sugar. I'm starving. Let's go eat, Jed."

"You're always starving," Minnie told Emmett with an affectionate smile.

Again Jed longed for the kind of relationship they had. If Sunny weren't off-limits, he would have pursued a relationship with her to see where it might lead, and even seen if she'd be willing to wait until he purchased his own place. But how would that work? She already owned a spread. One he knew without a doubt she wouldn't give up. And he couldn't abandon his dream of making it on his own either. He sighed. There were too many things against them. So he needed to stop thinking about her in that way. As hard as that might be.

They sat down at the table. Steam rose from the platter of sliced corned beef, baby onions, carrots and chunks of cooked cabbage.

Jed's stomach growled in response.

"I heard that," Sunny teased.

"Think everyone else did, as well. Come on. Let's eat, woman." Emmett smiled at Minnie.

Minnie popped him on the arm with a clean spoon. "Behave yourself, you ornery old coot." She kissed Emmett's cheek.

It amazed Jed how they didn't even try to hide their affection for one another. They were always hugging or kissing.

He slid a glance at Sunny, wondering what it would be like to hold her in his arms. To love her. Something he wasn't sure if he already did or not.

Jed's resolve to not think about Sunny and marriage was becoming increasingly difficult. During dinner Emmett and Minnie carried on about Sunny's wonderful traits. Sunny blushed under their praise, but Jed could tell it made her feel good, too.

When they finished the last of their meal, apple pie with cheese, Minnie and Sunny cleaned up the mess while he and Emmett retired to the rocking chairs.

It wasn't long before the women joined them.

"I was thinking," Minnie said. "In a little over two weeks, it will be Valentine's Day. Why don't we invite the neighbors over for an evening of fellowship and skating at the ice pond? It'll give us plenty of time to let them all know and for us to prepare."

Jed knew which ice pond she referred to. Near what used to be the old slaughterhouse where they'd dammed up a creek for an irrigation pond and left it full through winter just for that purpose.

"We haven't done that in a while." Emmett took his wife's hand and smiled at her lovingly and as if they shared a secret.

Sunny leaned toward Jed and whispered, "They met at a Valentine's skating party and married on one, too."

"Ah, I see."

"So what do you say, Sunny? Jed?" Minnie tore her gaze away from Emmett.

"Sounds good to me." Jed smiled.

Sunny clutched her tiny hands together. "Me, too. I haven't been skating in years. That sounds like so much fun."

It sure did. And Jed couldn't help but think about Emmett and Minnie falling in love over skating. He pictured himself and Sunny skating under the full moon, holding hands, having eyes only for each other. Sneaking away behind a rock to steal a kiss or two. And ending with Jed getting down on one knee, asking Sunny to marry him. And her saying...

"Jed, do you think that will work?"

He looked over at Minnie. He had no clue what she'd asked him, but he sure hoped it would work. His proposal, that was. If he ever got to offer one. A man could always dream anyway. And dream he would. Even Emmett couldn't deny him that.

Chapter Eight

Sunny didn't think Valentine's Day would ever arrive. But it finally had. She pulled back the vegetable-dyed quilt dressing her window and peeked out.

Lanterns hung on the fronts of the two sleds. Jed and Uncle Emmett were busy loading them, getting ready for the skating party.

Earlier, while the women had baked and cooked, the men had gone down to the pond and cleared the snow off the ice and dropped off a large load of firewood. Wood the ranch hands were now building a large fire with. A fire Sunny could hardly wait to enjoy. There was something about sitting around an outdoor fire on a cold winter evening, sharing a meal with friends and skating under the moonlight. Sunny shook with excitement just thinking about it.

She let the curtain fall back into place, scurried to her bed and sat down on the heavy woolen-pieced quilt that matched the window dressings.

After adding several layers of undergarments to keep warm, she slid her deep blue broadcloth skirt over her head and finished dressing. Excitement danced inside her at the prospect of the whole evening. It had been a long time since she'd last seen her aunt and uncle's neighbors. She could hardly wait to see the other ranchers again or to spend more time with Jed outside of working and sitting around with her aunt and uncle in the evenings.

She hurried into the kitchen and helped gather the rest of the food and eating utensils to load them into the sleds. She put on her Sunday-best gray woolen coat, gloves, boots and matching woolen bonnet. No cowboy hat this evening for her.

One step out the door and the cold sucked the air from her lungs, but she didn't care. A warm fire by the pond would soon knock the chill.

Jed and Uncle Emmett had the large black cooking kettle full of thick potato, cheese and onion soup already situated securely in backseat of the sleigh.

"Well, that's the last of it." Aunt Minnie handed the basket filled with a variety of cookies up to Uncle Emmett, who was standing in the sled.

"You ready to go, then, sugar?" Uncle Emmett hopped down.

"After I stoke the woodstove real good," Minnie said.

"I'll do that." Jed headed toward the house.

Sunny followed. "I'll help."

"Thanks. But I don't need any help."

"Now you sound like me." Sunny giggled.

"I do, don't I?" He grinned.

"I can hardly wait to get to the pond, so let me help so we can get it done faster."

Jed agreed. "By the way, you look very nice this evening."

"Thank you." His compliment warmed her more deeply than the penetrating heat from the cookstove.

Sunny took the cast-iron handle, raised the lid on the stove and arranged the pieces of wood inside it as Jed handed them to her. "You been skating before?" she asked.

"Uh-huh. Lots of times. You?"

"Yup. My whole life."

"I bet I can skate better than you."

Sunny expected something like that from Cody, not Jed, so as soon as she heard that, her attention darted toward him. A smirk covered his face. "Oh, you." She tapped him on his arm.

"You two coming?" Uncle Emmett stepped inside the kitchen.

Jed handed her the last piece of wood and moved away from her quicker than the time it took to blink. "That was the last piece." He brushed his hands off and headed outside.

"Shall we, Sunshine?" Uncle Emmett offered her his arm. Sunny wished it was Jed's arm she was being offered. Why did her brain insist on thinking those ridiculous thoughts? It was as if they were cobwebs clinging and determined to stay put.

Outside at the sled she placed her foot on the step. Uncle Emmett stopped her. "Why don't you ride with Jed, Sunshine?" He leaned over and, not bothering to keep his voice low, he said, "I want you two to take your *sweet* time and let this old married man have some time alone with his sweetheart on their anniversary."

"Oh. I forgot. Happy anniversary, Uncle Emmett." Sunny stood on her tiptoes and gave him a kiss on his cold cheek. Her aunt was already seated on the sled, so she grabbed her gloved hand and squeezed it. "You, too, Aunt Minnie."

"Thank you, precious." Aunt Minnie's attention shifted to Uncle Emmett. Their eyes locked. Love, plain and clear, passed between them. Like it always did.

Sunny silently moved away and joined Jed at the other sled. "Uncle Emmett wants me to ride with you. He told me to tell you that he wants us to take our time. It's their anniversary and he'd like some time alone with Aunt Min." She sneaked a peek at her aunt and uncle and smiled. It would be wonderful to still be in love with someone after all those years.

Aunt Minnie snuggled against Uncle Emmett, and her head rested on his shoulder as they pulled away. The horses' hooves clomped in the crusty snow, and bells tinkled with each bob of their heads.

The scene reminded Sunny of her parents and how many times she'd seen them snuggle and share looks overflowing with love like that. Joy wrapped around Sunny like a warm cloak on a cold day. How blessed she was to have two such wonderful examples of what a marriage could and should be like.

"Shall we?" Jed's voice called to her.

She faced him.

He offered her his hand.

Not one to usually accept help, she decided she would. But just this once.

She settled her hand into his. His large hand swallowed her small one when his fingers closed over the top.

A cozy feeling unlike any she'd ever felt before spread up her arm and settled into her heart.

Her eyes searched for Jed's in the lantern's glow, but his attention was on their hands.

Did he feel it, too? Whatever *it* was.

Seconds passed, then his bluebird eyes drifted to hers.

His eyes were filled with a softness she'd never seen in them before.

Only one sound at that moment could be heard—the beating of her heart, which seemed to have increased.

Goliath stomped his hoof, and Samson shook his head, showing their impatience.

Jed blinked, and the moment shattered. "We'd better get going." Why had his voice sounded deeper and broken just now? And why had that voice affected her so?

He cleared his throat and helped her into the front seat of the sled. This sled and the one her aunt and uncle had were different from the ones they used to feed with. These two had seats and sideboards.

Heated rocks at her feet felt nice, but not nearly as nice as the heat from Jed's touch only moments ago.

Jed draped the heavy bearskin over her legs, and the seat dipped when he lowered his bulky frame onto it. He picked up the lines and gave a swat on the horses' rumps.

Lanterns and the full moon cleared a path to the pond.

"Brrr. It's cold." She snuggled her coat closer to her, wishing she could snuggle against Jed instead.

Jed surprised her. He slipped his arm around and pulled her closer to his side. She looked up at him, but he kept his gaze forward. When they neared the site, he removed his arm and scooted over. Sunny didn't understand why he did that. But, then again, he probably didn't want to give anyone the wrong idea about the two of them. So why was that wrong idea suddenly feeling so very right?

At the ice pond Jed helped her down. She reached in back to help unload, but he stopped her. "Why don't you go sit down by the fire? I'll get this."

Strange how in that moment it felt like a kind and gallant gesture rather than him saying she couldn't handle it. "You sure?"

"Uh-huh."

He didn't need to tell her more than once. She was freezing. She hurried to the closest of the three blazing fires and sat on one of the logs circling the fire pit. Pine and aspen logs snapped and spit in front of her, making the area warm and cozy. Orange and yellow lit up the ground beneath her feet, and sweet, blessed heat surrounded her.

Uncle Emmett hung the cast-iron soup kettle on the hook hanging from a wrought-iron frame. Flames licked the bottom of the potbelly cauldron.

Minutes later the neighbors started arriving.

The Benson, Miller and Wright families greeted Sunny warmly. Then the women scurried off to set food onto the makeshift tables, and the children went off to play.

"Sure sorry to hear about your pa. He was a good man," Mr. Benson said. Mr. Miller and Mr. Wright agreed. "You still planning on keeping that ranch of yours?" Mr. Benson asked.

Sunny drew her shoulders up. "Yes, sir, I am."

He quirked a half-pitying smile at her. "You can't run that place by yourself. You know that, don't you?"

Here it comes again, she thought. Why didn't folks

just mind their own business and leave her to hers? She'd been around this particular mountain enough to know that wasn't likely to ever happen. So even though it was none of his business, she knew if she didn't answer him that Mr. Miller and Mr. Wright would badger her, too. "Yes, sir, I know that. I've got some money saved, and after I buy a few head of bred cows, I'll hire a couple of hands who are willing to come work for me for room and board until I sell the calves."

"You think you'll find two men who'd be willing to do that?" This time Mr. Miller chimed in, looking at her as if she were gone in the head.

Well, she wasn't. Pa had always told her she had a good business head on her. "Yes, sir. My pa did. When the ranch grew he paid them in cows and gave them a generous wage. I plan to do the same. They can raise their cows on my place for as long as they work for me."

"What happens when their herds get too large? You know you have to figure at least two or more tons of hay for each cow. Enough to feed 'em through the winter and early spring."

Sunny held her rising frustration at bay. Did these men think she'd woken up one day and decided she wanted to own a ranch? Well, she hadn't. She was born and raised on one, and Pa had taught her everything there was to know about ranching. Both the working and the business end. "Thank you, Mr. Benson, for that information, but Pa taught me that, as well. Amongst other things." She forced a smile on her face.

"Gentlemen, would you mind if I steal Sunny from you? I need her help." Jed spoke from behind her.

Sunny turned and a knowing look passed between them. This was one time she was glad Jed had come to her rescue. She was afraid if they continued badgering her, she might say something she'd later regret. Being disrespectful *wasn't* something her pa had taught her. She mouthed the words *thank you* to Jed.

"No, that's quite all right, Jed," Mr. Benson said.

When they turned to leave, Sunny heard Mr. Miller say, "She won't be running that ranch of hers by herself. It won't be long before her and Jed get hitched."

Sunny gasped, and her eyes went wide with horror wondering if Jed had heard them, too. Without turning her head she peered over at him. If he had heard them, he wasn't letting it show. For that she was truly grateful.

Jed led Sunny far away from the men. Crusted snow crunched under their feet. Children's laughter faded the farther they walked. When he'd decided to rescue her, he hadn't figured the men would take his gesture the way they had. Good thing Emmett wasn't around to hear their comment about him and Sunny getting hitched. Not that he would mind marrying Sunny, but he couldn't afford to lose his job. Or his dignity.

He shoved the crown of his cowboy hat farther onto his head. When Emmett had asked him to keep an eye on Sunny, had the man Jed respected stopped to think about how hard it would be on Jed? Didn't Emmett see how attractive his niece was to a man? To this man especially? Did Emmett think Jed's heart was made of steel or something?

Jed couldn't take too much more or keep this up much longer. His feelings for Sunny were growing with each minute he spent with her. Tonight, back at the ranch house, when he'd taken her hand to help her into the sled, he'd come far too close to kissing her. Good thing he hadn't, though. He refused to betray Emmett's trust.

Jed glanced over at her. Lands, she was easy on a man's eyes. Before he lost his heart to her completely, or did something he would regret, he needed to sit down and have an honest man-to-man talk with Emmett about all of this.

"Where we going?" Sunny's sweet voice from beside him tugged his mind back into the moment.

"I don't know. I hadn't gotten that far. I just wanted to get you out of there. I could tell the neighbors were making you uncomfortable."

"They sure were. Thank you, Jed."

Jed smiled. They were making progress. This time she didn't rebuke him, saying she could take care of herself. A fact he had no doubt about.

"I don't understand why everyone thinks I should sell my ranch. Why would I do that? I'm more than capable of getting it up and running again. And if I wasn't, I'd rather up and marry someone in order to keep it if I had to." She shoved her gloved hands into the large pockets of her coat.

If Jed wasn't trying to buy his own spread, he'd offer to marry her in order for her to keep her ranch. If he had to, he quickly tacked on. He had no doubt, however, that she was more than able to run the place herself. She didn't need him.

Besides, he wanted to buy his own spread, not inherit one through marriage, in order to prove to his father that he was every bit as capable as his brothers were.

"Sunny, that alone is something you need to decide. You know what you can and can't do. I personally have no doubt that you are more than capable of restoring your ranch back to its former glory. Don't let anyone talk you out of it, or into selling it." He huffed. "I just got through telling you not to let anyone tell you what to do, and what do I go and do? Tell you not to let anyone talk you into selling it."

She laid her hand on his arm. "Thank you for believing in me."

His gaze slid to hers and settled there. Didn't she know how that little gesture affected him? How her touch or her nearness affected him? Of course she didn't. How could she? He'd never told her.

"And for telling me what to do," she said through a chuckle.

His gaze snagged on hers and she winked at him. A wink that wasn't flirtatious, and yet he wished it had been.

Inwardly he groaned. He had to stop his mind from taking him down a trail that couldn't be traveled. At least not until he talked to Emmett. The idea of hurting the man or costing Jed his job twisted his gut. He needed to pray about having that talk with Emmett. And about a future with Sunny. If there ever could be one, that is.

The dinner bell clanged and echoed through the valley.

"Reckon we should head back to the fire and get something to eat." Sunny turned and headed that direction, and Jed followed.

When they arrived, everyone was gathered around the middle fire.

"Shall we pray?" Emmett bowed his head and everyone else did, too. "Father, we thank You for this gathering. Thank You for these people and thank You for this food. May our fellowship glorify You. In Jesus's name. Amen."

"Amen," everyone responded.

The women served their menfolk.

Sunny dished up a bowl of steaming potato cheese soup and handed it to Jed along with three buttered rolls.

"Thank you."

"You're welcome. After we get our food dished up, you want to join me?" Her inviting smile and her sweetness went straight to his heart. He wanted to enjoy her company as often and as long as he could. The way he justified it in his mind was Emmett said to keep an eye on her. And keep an eye on her he would.

"Uh-huh." He gave her a smile of his own.

They went and sat down by the least-occupied fire. Within minutes the other hands joined them. While disappointed, he figured it was for the best. At least their presence kept him honest and his actions completely respectable.

"Well, what do you know. There is a lady under all that boyish exterior after all. And a fine-looking one at that." Cody eyed Sunny like a mountain lion eyeing dinner.

Sunny glanced up at Cody, her appetite vanished.

"Give it a rest, Cody," Jed growled.

"Give what a rest?" Cody turned innocent eyes on his boss. "Complimenting your woman?"

George's spoon stopped midway to his mouth. Matt kept his head down but his eyes bounced between her and Jed. Sunny wanted to find the nearest cave to hide out in.

Jed sent Cody an intimidating stare. "Watch your mouth, Cody."

"It's the truth, ain't it? Anyone with eyes can see that it is."

George and Matt suddenly got very interested in their food, each taking one spoonful of soup after another and eating their rolls as if they hadn't had a meal in weeks.

Sunny couldn't believe what she was hearing. Cody was way out of line this time. It was one thing to pick on her, but to put Jed in the middle with something so ridiculous, well, she refused to let that slide. "I'm not anyone's woman. Jed and I are friends. Friends who respect one another. Something you know nothing about, Cody."

Cody didn't cow one bit. "What I do know is, is you should stick to dressing up in pretty dresses and acting like a lady rather than trying to play cowboy. Like I told you before, ranching is no place for a woman. Women can't do what a man can."

That did it. Sunny set her plate off to the side, stood and put both hands on her hips. "Tell you what, Cody. What do you say we have ourselves a little competition to see whether that's true or not?"

"What kind of competition?" Suspicion crowded his voice.

"Oh, let's see. Who can stay on a bull and an unbroken horse the longest. Rope a heifer the fastest. Pen three cows the quickest. And…" She paused, thinking for a minute. "Skijoring, too. Everyone in the county loves skijoring. Nothing finer than being pulled behind horses on a set of skis. The harder the course, the better."

"You? Ride a bull? As little as you are, that thing will devour you in a second." Cody frowned.

"I could say the same about you, Cody. You ride a bull? Hmm, we'll see. But then again, we won't. As tall as you are, you won't be able to ride it, those long legs of yours will straddle it."

"She got you again," George said through a titter.

Cody's eyes narrowed at George, then he looked at her. Sunny braced herself waiting for his comeback. "What is skijoring?"

Hmm. No comeback. That was an improvement. "You'll see. To make it more interesting, we'll invite the neighbors to see if they want to participate and we'll charge a small entry fee for each event. The winner will take home the purse for each event. What do you say? Or are you too chicken to ride a bull?"

"I say you're on. And I ain't afraid of no bull. Just you name the day and time and I'll be there."

"Before we do anything, let me clear it with Uncle Emmett and Jed first."

She looked at Jed, who had sat quietly through the whole exchange. This was one time she wished she could read his mind. Did he think she'd gone too far? If he did, he was sure in for a surprise. They all were.

Chapter Nine

Word about the competition spread quickly. Uncle Emmett had agreed to be the host as long at it took place before calving season in mid-March and it didn't interfere with their work. Convincing her uncle to let her participate in the events had taken a heap more talking but he'd finally agreed.

Over the past two and a half weeks, when the chores were finished, everyone had pitched in to prepare for the big day, including Cody. She figured the reason he had was to taunt her about what a fool she was going to make of herself, and how once she realized she couldn't do those things, she'd give up her ridiculous notion of ranching once and for all. Sunny smiled. If only Cody knew what she'd done.

On this third day of March, snow covered most of the high country and most of the ground, except around the corrals where the ground was bare, but that didn't stop the neighbors from showing up for the day's get-together. Some came from as far as five miles away and arrived two hours before the noon meal.

Everyone who wanted to participate in the events

signed up and paid their entry fees. Everything was going pretty good until the menfolk found out Sunny had signed up for all the events, too. Then they all gathered around her.

"Sunny." Mr. Wright looked at her. "We're concerned for your safety. We mean no disrespect, but you being a woman and all, a little one at that, we don't think it's wise for you to participate."

Sunny eyed each man. They all nodded their agreement. Her anger soared higher than the sky. The whole idea of this competition was to prove to Cody and men like him that she was more than capable. She silently willed herself to calm down, then drawing in a deep breath, she spoke as calmly as possible. "Gentlemen, I appreciate your concern, and I mean no disrespect either, but this competition was my idea."

A look of shock flew across each man's face.

"Well, if we'd a knowed you planned this here shindig and that you was plannin' on participatin', we'd a never come," one of the neighbor's hired hands tossed into the conversation.

"Well, if you're afraid of competing against a woman or you don't like the way this was set up, then please feel free to get your money back and withdraw from the competition. Because I have no plans of withdrawing from any of the events." She plastered on a "friendly" smile.

"Even the bull riding?" Mr. Wright asked. Concern dotted his face.

"Gentlemen, why don't we let Miss Weston decide what she can and can't do? After all, she is a grown woman." Jed stepped up alongside her, dressed in a black cowboy hat, a blue shirt that made the color of his bluebird eyes stand out even more, chaps, spurs and cowboy boots. He looked more handsome than a man had a right to look. Her heart leaped in her chest. "I, for one, am looking forward to seeing what the lady can do."

"Well, I ain't gonna compete against no woman," the same cowboy who'd spoken up earlier said again.

"That's fine, Herman. Then go see Mrs. Wright and she'll give you your money back and strike your name from the events you entered."

"Ah, come on, Herman. Don't ya wanna watch that cocky little lady fall flat on her face?" Adam, the burly moustached cowboy standing next to Herman, asked.

Like a raw blister inside a new leather boot, another round of anger rubbed against Sunny. She opened her mouth to let the man have it.

"Adam," Jed interrupted before she had a chance. "You and Herman need to get your entry money and leave. Now."

"Why? What'd we do?" Adam asked.

"I will not have you disrespecting Miss Weston like that. So you need to leave now."

Adam frowned, then removed his cowboy hat and bowed his head. "Sorry, ma'am. Meant no disrespect. I apologize for my comment about you being cocky." When he looked up at her, Sunny saw genuine remorse.

"Me, too," Herman added, then looked over at Jed. "If we mind our manners, can we stay?"

Jed looked down at Sunny, his eyes questioned hers. She nodded.

"Okay. But, I'm telling all you men right now, if any of you talk disrespectfully to or about Miss Weston again, you will leave immediately. Is that understood?"

Everyone agreed.

Sunny wanted to grab Jed and hug him. She'd always stood up for herself before, but as much as she hated to admit it, it felt real nice having someone else do it for a change. Someone she admired and had grown to care about. Deeply.

"Whenever you're ready to start, Miss Weston." Jed smiled at her.

In front of all these men, Jed showing his respect for her like that made her feel taller than a full-grown aspen tree.

"Everything's ready. Gentlemen, if you'll come this way."

She led them over to the course they had set up for the skijoring.

Eighteen people had signed up for the event. The contestants strapped on their snow skis. Several people were ahead of Sunny. Her turn finally came up. Jed got his horse, and Sunny grabbed the long rope tied to the back of Jed's saddle.

At her nod to the timers and Jed, he coaxed his horse into a gallop.

Sunny braced herself as she lunged forward on her skis. She held on tight to the rope as Jed's horse pulled her fast through the snow.

The first ramp came into view. Sunny shot up the snow-packed incline, flew in the air and landed safely on her skis several yards past the ramp. She wove back and forth through the short poles they'd put out to outline the course. Then she shifted her weight and headed toward the two upside-down L posts and grabbed the hoop hanging from each one.

Not missing either one of them, her insides pranced

like a proud filly. But she couldn't get too smug—she had one more jump to go.

She prepared herself as the second snowy slope came into view. Up she went, flying high in the air again, landing several yards from the ramp. She snatched two more hoops that were situated like the first two she'd gathered. She weaved back and forth over the last of the course. Past the finish line Sunny coasted on her skis up to Jed.

"Thanks for not taking it easy on me, Jed. That's some fast horse you have there."

"I knew you could handle it, Sunshine." Jed's smile was brighter than the sun bouncing off the snow. And the man had just called her Sunshine. No one else but her uncle and her pa had ever called her that. It seemed so personal, but she found she liked it. No, make that she loved it and wanted to hear him say it to her again. With any luck and a whole lot of prayer maybe she would, too.

When they got back to the starting line, several men congratulated her on her fast run. While that shocked the daylights right out of Sunny, it hadn't Jed. He just smiled at her as if he'd expected it.

Two more contestants ran the course before it was Jed's turn. They decided to use Jed's horse because the gelding was faster than hers.

"Don't hold back now."

"Wasn't going to." She winked at him, and her eyes widened when she realized what she'd done.

Jed grinned at her and gave her a wink of his own. Why did those winks of his make her heart flutter like a feather in the wind?

"Ready?"

"Yup. Whenever you are."

Jed nodded to the timers, and Sunny set the horse to galloping through the course, pulling Jed behind her. He never lost the rope, never fell and never missed any of the four rings like some of the other men had. So far he and Sunny were the only ones to get all four hoops. That was another thing that surprised her, because ski-joring was so well liked here.

At the end of the course he glided up to her. "Thanks for not holding back."

"You're welcome."

They looked at each other for a few moments, then Jed stepped back and said, "Let's go see what the last two contestants do, shall we?"

"Yup." They chuckled, and she pulled him back to the starting line.

Cody waited there with his skis on, while Matt sat atop Cody's horse, getting ready to pull Cody.

Side by side Sunny and Jed stood, watching Cody run through the course. He did really well until he missed the last ring.

Sunny found no joy in it.

After that event ended, they all removed their skis and forged their way to the table covered with food she and Aunt Minnie had spent days preparing. Twenty minutes after everyone's bellies were filled, they announced it was time for the next event.

Spurs clinked and chap fringe flapped as everyone headed over to the corrals where the roping event was all set to go.

Fifteen people had signed up for the roping event.

Uncle Emmett, Mr. Miller and a circuit preacher, Silas Yohansen, who was staying with the Millers, used the second hand on their pocket watches to time the event. They added their times and divided them by three.

Half an hour later, several men had completed the event.

Sunny was up next. She grabbed her coiled rope and built her loop to the size she needed. Her stomach jittered with excitement as she kept her eye on the heifer in the chute. The second the yearling darted from the opening, Sunny dug her heels into her horse, bolted after it, twirled her rope and threw the loop around the animal's neck.

Judging by the distance, she knew she'd roped the heifer the fastest so far. She hid her smile, waiting until it was confirmed and until after Jed took his turn. She loosened her rope from around the heifer and headed out of the corral and stood with the rest of the men.

"Lucky catch," Cody sneered from beside her.

"Well, let's see if you're as lucky as I am, then." Sunny draped her arm casually over her saddle horn in hopes of showing Cody he hadn't riled her. Even though he had, she wouldn't give him the satisfaction of knowing that. After all, she still hadn't gotten over his comments about her and ranching. Who was Cody to decide what she was to do or not do with her life? That was God's place, not Cody's, not these men's here and not anyone else's.

"Great job, Sunny." Jed winked at her, then rode into the corral. The wink wasn't flirtatious, but rather one of a shared secret that needed no words.

Sunny watched. Her stomach felt as if a million flying leaves were scattering about inside it. She prayed Jed would do good, but not as good as her, though. As awful as that thought was, she didn't feel real bad about it because unlike Jed, she had something to prove. Everyone here already respected Jed, including her.

The heifer darted out of the chute. Jed bolted after it, catching it with the first loop he tossed.

Sunny cheered, wondering how close their times were to each other.

Cody was the last roper. Inside the corral he gathered his loop and sent her a smug look as if to say *Just watch how a man does it.* Humph. A man who had been nothing but disrespectful to her. The heifer took off, and Cody chased it down. He threw his loop and missed.

"Go ahead and gloat," Cody said as he passed her.

This was a chance to put him in his place, but seeing how he looked lower than mud on a boot sole, she refused to make him feel even worse.

With the roping event finished, they ran the heifers out and brought in Uncle Emmett's small herd of wild mustangs he'd gotten last summer.

Twelve men had signed up for this event. Sunny made the count thirteen. Each horse had been numbered. Those numbers were put in a hat and each contestant drew a number. That number was not only for the horse they would ride but the order in which they would ride. Sunny happened to draw number one.

"You sure you don't want to change your mind?" Mr. Wright asked. "Them there mustangs ain't gonna take it easy on you."

"I'm sure, Mr. Wright." She laid her arm on his and looked him in the eye. "Thank you for caring, but I'll be just fine. You'll see."

The concern on the older man's face never let up.

"Trust me. I know what I'm doing." She leaned over

and for his ears only said, "I've done this for over fifteen years now."

He gave a short nod.

She'd had this same conversation with her uncle when they'd talked about the events that would take place. She'd shared how she'd done this many times before, also supplying the outcome of each ride.

To prepare for today's events she and the hands had spent the past two weeks earning the untamed horses' trust from the ground so they could put a saddle on them today and mount them.

Jed and Matt snubbed—wrapped the rope around the post—and blindfolded the horse Sunny drew. Sunny placed her blanket and saddle on the horse and climbed aboard. The black-and-white paint horse trembled underneath her. She knew exactly how that horse felt. While she'd done this many a time, each time her pulse quickened and her tongue went drier than a dead leaf.

She glanced at Jed. No fear showed on his face, only a look that spoke of the confidence he had in her, giving her the extra boost of self-assurance she needed to make this ride. She tugged her leather gloves on tight and clutched the rope reins attached to the horse's halter. "Ready," she said to the men holding the watches and to Jed and Matt.

They removed the blinders and released the untamed horse.

First the mare took off running, then she arched her back and crow-hopped, coming down hard on all four legs each time. When that didn't work in dumping Sunny off, the mare shot her front legs straight out and lunged in the air, dipping and swinging her neck. Sunny held on even tighter. The horse continued to buck, and Sunny's legs and knees ached from holding on so tight.

All of a sudden the paint stopped bucking, but Sunny knew the horse wasn't finished, she could feel it under her. With a quick shake of its head the mare went to bucking again, hard and fast. Sunny hung on until the horse took a sharp turn and Sunny went flying off, landing on her knees and hands.

Jed rushed to her. "You all right?"

She flashed him a smile. "Yup. I'm fine."

"You sure are."

At his words Sunny's heart bucked faster and harder than the horse she'd just ridden. She only hoped that meant he liked her as much as she liked him.

Jed offered her a hand up. She wanted to keep hold of that hand even after she stood, but she didn't. Sunny gathered her cowboy hat that had flown off sometime during her ride and settled it back onto her head.

The other men ran their turns. Only one other person had stayed on as long as she had and that was Jed.

Cody lost his saddle and was tossed off on the second hop. This time he didn't say a word to her when he passed her. It was the same way with the last event of the day, which was the bull riding. She'd hoped things would be different after he'd seen how well she'd done, but they weren't. She sighed. Well, she couldn't make someone see things how she saw them.

With the competition now over everyone got themselves something hot to drink, and those who'd entered the events gathered around the table where Uncle Emmett, Mr. Miller and Reverend Yohansen were seated, adding up the scores. When they finished, they announced the winners.

"First place in the skijoring goes to Jed. Congratulations, Jed." Reverend Yohansen handed him an envelope.

"Thank you." They shook hands.

"Congratulations." Sunny couldn't keep her admiration from showing on her face. And it hadn't even disappointed her that he'd won first place.

"Second goes to Miss Weston." Sunny stepped forward to receive her envelope from Reverend Yohansen and thanked him.

"Third place, Herman. Congratulations, Herman." The two men shook hands.

Sunny placed first in roping, first in riding the untamed horse and first in bull riding. Jed placed second in each of those three. Cody placed third in the bull riding.

When all the envelopes were handed out, the men gathered around Sunny and shook her hand, telling her what a great job she'd done. Some even apologized for doubting her abilities, for making fun of her and for criticizing her.

Then from out of nowhere Cody stepped up to her. She blinked the surprise away, not sure if he was there to apologize or to criticize her some more. He removed his cowboy hat and without looking up and in front of all these cowboys, he said, "Sunny, I owe you an apology. I was wrong about you." His eyes came up to hers. "You're one fine hand. And you showed this hand that size or gender doesn't matter. It's what's inside here that counts." He thumped his heart with his thumb. "You surely have what it takes and much more to make that ranch of yours into something special. Good luck with it, Sunny." He extended his hand toward her and offered her a timid smile.

Sunny shook his hand and gave him her best smile. "Thank you, Cody. Coming from you that means a lot."

Finally she'd earned Cody's and the other ranchers' respect. Funny thing was, it didn't feel as good as she'd thought it would.

Later that evening, exhausted from their long hectic day, Emmett and Minnie had gone to bed early. Jed and Sunny sat in front of the warm fireplace. His gaze slid to her, sitting with her eyes closed and her hands clasped on her middle, slowly rocking.

His admiration and respect for her grew more and more each day. She was the most amazing woman he'd ever known. The whole time she'd been at the Flying W Ranch, she'd worked right alongside the men, never once complaining about the grueling chores she'd been given. And she'd done them just as well as, if not better than, the men.

Today, watching her ride that bucking bull and untamed horse, roping that heifer in record time, running the skijoring course with ease and handling the men with grace when they deserved none, he'd realized that somewhere in the middle of it all, his admiration and respect for Sunny had turned to love. He could no longer deny it. He was deeply, hopelessly in love with the little spitfire from up the mountain.

His gaze trailed over her profile.

A yellow-red glow from the rising flames lit up her face, and her lashes brushed against her cheeks. She looked so peaceful. So beautiful.

Sunny opened her eyes and looked at him. He wanted

to look away, but felt powerless to do so. "Thank you for today."

"For what?" His voice came out low and broken, but she didn't seem to notice. If she did, she didn't say anything.

"For throwing the bull riding and untamed horse events."

Surprise belted him like an outlaw robbing the bank. "What? "I—I—" he sputtered. How did she know? He'd tried to hide it best as he could.

"No sense in even trying to deny it. I noticed what you did."

His heart raced. The idea of her being angry at him ate a hole in his gut. "Sunny, I didn't do it because I didn't think you were capable of winning. I did it—"

She leaned forward and placed her fingertips over his lips. He wanted to kiss the tips of those fingers one by one. Even more so, he wanted to kiss her lips with his own, but the time wasn't right. If it ever would be.

She removed her fingers from his lips and settled her hand on the arm of her rocker where for him it was much safer anyway. Not as tempting to hold and to kiss each finger. "I'm not angry, Jed. It's one of the sweetest things anyone has ever done for me. I only want to know why you would do that when that money would have brought you closer to your dream of owning your own place. Why would any man sacrifice his own dream for someone else's?"

He knew why, but he just shrugged. There was no way he could tell her it was because he was in love with her. Nor could he tell her that he wanted her for his wife and why that could never be.

Her hand rested on his arm. A warm tingling sensation rose up it and landed in his heart. He needed to move away but his heart kept him there with her. Jed was powerless to deny his feelings, but he knew the One who could help him, so he silently prayed. *God, have mercy on me* was all he could manage, though.

Chapter Ten

Sunny sat on her bed and re-counted her money. With the wages she'd earned over nearly two months, along with her small savings and the earnings from today's competition, she had enough to go home. Home. While she enjoyed living with her aunt and uncle, she couldn't wait to go back to the only home she'd ever known. Only this time her motivation was different. Strange how much it had changed even over the past twenty-four hours. Now it had nothing to do with proving herself to anyone. She was doing it for herself. For her love of ranching and that land. The only problem standing between her and doing that, though, was a handsome cowboy named Jedidiah Cooper.

Somewhere during her stay here she'd fallen deeply in love with him. She knew exactly when it had happened but at that time she'd refused to let him into her heart for fear he was like the men in her past. That fear had only gotten worse the day Jed had told her he wanted his own spread. The instant she'd heard that, her guard had come up, and she'd built a wall around her heart.

After today that wall no longer existed and she wasn't sure how she felt about it. Or how *he* felt about *her*.

Confusion grappled with her heart as she pondered the situation. Did his throwing the events and tossing away the earnings mean he really did care for her? Or was it some trick to get to her? To her ranch. She pinched her eyes shut and shook her head, hoping to rid herself of the mounting frustration.

She hated feeling this way about him, but she couldn't shake the past. She had loved Duke Graham. Or at least she'd thought she had until he had crushed her heart. It had taken a long time for her to get over him. She had thought Duke was a good person, too. But she'd been dead wrong. Even her pa had been fooled by the man.

Were Uncle Emmett and Aunt Minnie fooled, too? No! No! She shook her head again. Jed was different. Their conversation at the hunting cabin slipped into her mind and how he'd said he wanted to buy his own place so that he could prove to his father that he was as good as his brothers. He even had a place in mind. Somewhere on the Troublesome.

Duke had had no such ambition. His only goal was to marry Sunny so he could get his hands on her ranch.

Sunny stood and paced the floor. Long and hard, she pondered out the whole thing. How Jed had stood up for her many a time when Duke hadn't. How Jed helped her and never once made her feel inferior. How he had thrown two of the competition events so she could get first place and have a real shot at her dream. And how he behaved even when he thought no one was looking.

She stopped pacing. The decision was made—settled in her head and heart. Jed was worth the risk. Tomorrow she would tell him she loved him. She had to before she left for home.

Dressed in her flannel nightgown, she crawled into bed but couldn't sleep. She lit the oil lamp on her nightstand, leaned her pillow against the wall and picked up her Bible. It fell open to Psalm 138, and verse 8 snagged her attention. *The Lord will perfect that which concerneth me...* She closed her eyes and smiled. God was giving her the go-ahead and she knew it. She prayed for His guidance, for the words to speak and for the perfect opportunity.

She woke up hours later with her Bible still draped across her chest. Darkness filled her room. She lit the lamp, and with her stomach buzzing about as if hundreds of bees were inside it, she dressed quickly, taking extra care in her appearance, and headed down to the barn. She could hardly wait to talk to Jed. She only hoped it turned out the way she wished it would and that the morning went by quick. Her nerves couldn't take too much more waiting and neither could her stomach.

To keep her mind occupied, she went about doing chores, praying the whole time.

"We missed you at breakfast this morning."

Sunny froze at the sound of Jed's voice. The time had come for her to tell him she loved him. She closed her eyes and breathed one more soft prayer while she finished hooking up the horses to the tongue of the sled. Putting on her bravest smile, she stood to face him.

Jed stood only feet away with his bluebird eyes fixed on her.

Her heart leaped about like a frisky rabbit and her legs threatened to send her to the ground. Before that happened she slid around the rack and hopped onto the sled. Knowing the other men wouldn't show up for some time yet, she drew in a long breath, crossed her ankles and swung her legs back and forth as fast as her nerves were traveling, then blurted out, "Jed, I'm leaving."

"When?" The question was barely audible. Jed cleared his throat and tried again, fighting desperately to sound as if his heart wasn't about to yank him forward. "When are you going?" He waited, dreading her answer.

Her gaze dropped to her lap before coming up to him again. "Day after tomorrow."

He hadn't thought his heart could hurt this bad, but it did. It felt as if someone was taking it apart bit by torturous bit. Jed wanted to beg Sunny to stay, but he couldn't, and he knew it. He respected Emmett and couldn't bear telling the man who had shown such gracious loyalty to him that he'd fallen in love with his niece. Couldn't bear to see the disapproval on Emmett's face.

A man he'd come to love more than his own father.

A man who treated Jed with respect and never compared him to anyone else.

A man who believed in him enough that he'd given him not only a job of rank, but had allowed Jed to be a part of his family.

"Jed?"

At the sound of Sunny's voice coming from directly in front of him, he peered down at her. The urge to yank her into his arms and kiss her with all the love he had for her drove into him. As he battled not to, he gazed into her eyes without really seeing them or the softness or tenderness in them. Who was he kidding? He noticed it all. There was something different in those big brown orbs. Something he'd glimpsed now and again but didn't know what it was.

She looked all around and then her gaze stuck onto his. "I can't leave without telling you how I feel. I love you, Jed. I've tried not to, but I do. And I can't lie to myself about it anymore. I love you. There. I said it."

Jed's blood stopped flowing. No. No, it hadn't. It pounded in his ears loud, strong and fast. Sunny loved him? Had she really just said those words?

"Jed?" Her eyes searched his. "Please say something."

In one heartbeat he closed the short distance between them and cupped her face. His lips captured hers, never wanting to let them go. Let her go. He continued to kiss her and hold her and only pulled back when it was necessary to breathe.

"Does this mean you love me, too?" Her breathless whisper yanked him back to reality. His hands fell to his sides and she very nearly fell without him holding her up. Confusion coursed through her gorgeous eyes. "What's wrong?"

"I—" He raised his hat and shoved his hand through his damp hair before replacing it. "I love you, too, Sunny."

Her face brightened.

"But nothing can ever come of it," he hastened to add.

Sadness replaced the brightness. "What? Why not? If I love you and you love me…"

He didn't want to tell her what Emmett had told them. Didn't feel right about doing that. "I don't have enough money saved yet to buy my own spread. And until I do, I can't even consider having a relationship with you or anyone else."

"But, Jed, if you and I were to marry, you would have your own spread."

"No!" He not only shocked her with his harsh response but himself, as well. "I have to do this on my own, Sunshine. I have to prove to my father that I'm just as good as my brothers are. That I'm equally as capable of making my way in this world and providing a comfortable living for my wife and children."

"Jed." She laid her hand on his arm.

He wanted to snatch her hand up, hold it against his chest and never let go of it, but that wasn't fair to her to keep holding on when nothing could ever come of it.

"I completely understand how you feel." When she looked at him, there was a soft trust in her eyes that called to his soul. "I wanted to prove myself, too. To all those men and to all those ranchers at the competition. But once I did it, once I beat them at their own game, I can't explain it, but I really didn't feel no different than before. It's like I've come to realize it wasn't about them at all. It was about me. I needed to learn I was all right no matter what they thought. That what I do or what they think of me don't make me who I am."

She paused, still looking up at him. "Don't you see this isn't about your pa and whether or not he approves of you. You gotta be all right with yourself first. 'Cause if your pa never does approve of you and you don't let that go, you'll be miserable the rest of your life. Trust me, I know that one." The smile she sent him was definitely one of understanding and not judgment.

"You know what else?"

He couldn't wait to hear this one.

"I don't mean to sound like a preacher but I'm finally seeing that I cared more about man's opinion than God's. Not no more. Not since God and I had a long talk the other night. I now know I don't have to prove myself to anyone anymore. Because God's already pleased with me and that's enough."

Jed thought long and hard about what Sunny had said. The very thing that drove her all those years drove him, too. Only she wanted to prove to herself and to everyone else around her that though she was small and a woman, she was more than capable of doing everything they did. Whereas he wanted to prove to his father he was as worthy of his father's approval as his brothers were. All his life he'd struggled to gain his father's approval above anything else. Even above his Heavenly Father's approval. Jed slammed his eyes shut. *Dear Lord, what have I done?*

Sunny hadn't meant to hurt Jed, only to help him. Maybe she'd gone too far in telling him what she had. The fear of losing him yanked the breath right out of her. *God, help me here?* An idea dropped into her mind. Doing it would be the biggest risk she'd ever taken yet. But Jed was worth it. "Jed?"

His eyes slowly opened and torment filled them.

Not caring what he thought, she pulled him to her and ran her hands up and down his back in hopes of soothing his hurt. He let her and even seemed to respond to her if the muscles relaxing under her hands were any indication. That gave her a little bit of peace. "I didn't mean to hurt you," she whispered so as to not break the moment between them.

Jed pulled back and that moment left anyway.

"Sunny, I—"

Sunny quickly pressed her fingers to his lips. "Please, let me finish, okay?"

He nodded, so she removed her fingers.

"Because I know how important it is for you to earn your pa's respect and to prove not only to him but to yourself that you can, I have a proposition for you."

One brow spiked on his manly forehead, then dipped. "What kind of proposition?"

"I want to sell you my ranch. At a fair price, of course," she said, hoping her offering would give them both what they wanted. If not, in one single second, she just may have very well given up her whole future and the one thing that meant more to her than anything else. With the exception of Jed, that was.

Jed blinked and blinked again. "No, Sunny. I can't let you do that. Thank you for the kind offer, but I can't accept it. I have to do this on my own. You understand. I know you do."

Oh, she understood all right and her love for him grew even stronger. He had just proven what she already figured out to be true. He didn't want her for her ranch. Without thinking it through, she pulled his face down to hers and kissed him long and tenderly, allowing her mouth to show her love and gratitude, but most of all her respect for him.

He didn't pull away even though she felt his surprise. Instead his lips moved with hers, melting into them with their softness. Contentment streamed into her, knowing they would be together somehow. How? That, she didn't know. But she had faith in Jed, and even more now in God, and that was enough.

* * *

Reluctantly Jed stopped the kiss but continued to hold her. No one had ever loved him like Sunny did. No one had ever believed in him like she did. She had proven that just now by offering him the one thing that meant the most to her—her family's ranch. The love he had for her rose another notch.

There was no way he would let this woman slip from his life. She meant more to him than anything else in this world—even earning his father's respect. While he still wanted to buy a place of his own, he would even put that aside and move to her place just to be with her forever. Together they could restore it to its former glory.

Before he would ask her to marry him, though, he needed to talk to Emmett. He shifted her back and whispered against her lips, "I love you, Sunshine." He kissed her until he found himself holding her up.

He needed to have that talk with Emmett as soon as possible. "We need to hurry and get chores finished. I have something important I need to do."

She frowned and tilted her head. "What's that?"

He tapped her on the end of her nose. "You'll find out soon enough." With those words he unwound the lines, hoisted her onto the sled, hopped on beside her and gave the reins a quick slap on the horses' rumps. "Let's go, boys. And make it snappy."

Later on after the feeding was finished, Jed searched for Emmett and found him in his office. Jed's insides were shaking like a sailboat in a storm and his turbulent emotions were right there riding on the rough seas with it. Thoughts of marrying Sunny rocked him one direction, and trepidation and fear of losing Emmett's respect tossed him the other way. He reminded himself over and over again of Sunny's words about all of that as he stepped inside the room. "Emmett. We need to talk."

Emmett removed the spectacles from his face and placed them on top of the open ledger. "What's on your mind, son?"

Son? Whew. Did he have to call him that? Gathering the courage he needed, he looked Emmett square in the eye and said, "Emmett, I know you warned us about Sunny, and I know you will have to fire me now because of what I'm about to say, but it can't be helped. I've fallen in love with your niece."

Jed braced himself for Emmett's reaction, knowing his worst fears in life were about to be realized.

"Praise the Lord!" Emmett threw up his hands.

Jed blinked. Something he'd done a lot today.

"Me and Minnie were hoping and praying this would happen."

Shock rippled through Jed. "I don't understand. The day she came here you warned all of us about wooing her and—" He shrugged.

"I never meant you. I thought you knew that."

Now, how would he know that? He wished he had. Then all this time he could have courted Sunny right and properlike.

"Surely you know how much you mean to Minnie and me. We think of you as our own son. I'm sorry, Jed. I assumed you knew that warning didn't include you. Minnie and me hoped when you got to know Sunny you would love her like we do and even marry her." He stopped and eyed Jed. "You do want to marry her, don't you?"

The turbulent emotions stilled and Jed laughed out

loud. "I sure do! That is, if you will give me your blessing and your permission to ask her."

Emmett stood and the man he respected even more now grabbed his hand in a hard grip and pulled him into a hug. "Welcome to the family, son."

Jed had never felt this much happiness before. Not only had he not lost the love and respect of a man he loved and honored, he was about to gain a wife, too.

"Oh, thank you so much! These are wonderful." Sunny held the woolies chaps Jed had made for her up to her waist. "They're a perfect fit, too."

"Just like us, huh?" He winked and her heart skipped.

"Yup." She stretched on her tiptoes and planted a big kiss on Jed's cheek.

"Oh, no, you don't. You're not getting off that easy."

He took the chaps from her and tossed them into the back of the sleigh, then pulled her into his arms where she fit right nicely. He kissed her for the longest time. When he ended the kiss he helped her into the sleigh and climbed in next to her. Up the mountain trail they headed.

"This was a great idea, Jed. I haven't been on a sleigh ride in years." Sitting in her uncle's sleigh with the top down, Sunny looped her arm through Jed's iron one and snuggled up against him, resting her head on his firm shoulder.

Bells jingled and tack rattled as Rascal pulled the sled through the snow. Being here with Jed like this felt more right than anything else ever had in her life. And she was going to enjoy every moment of it.

Jed pulled the horse to a stop at the one place on the ranch that overlooked the small town of Kremmling.

Under the moonlit sky filled with twinkling stars, Jed pulled the heavy woolen quilt over both their legs and wrapped his arm around her. His solid-as-a-rock forearm muscle rested against the side of her neck. She reached up and intertwined his large hand with hers, then peered up at him.

He smiled at her. "I love you, Sunny." His whisper was husky and broken.

"I love you, too, Jed."

His lips touched hers. At first they were cool to the touch, but they warmed quickly. He raised his mouth from hers, but it hovered nearby. "So, you still want to sell me that ranch of yours?" His breath brushed across her lips.

Sunny's eyes widened. What? Here they were sharing a romantic moment and he wanted to know if she still wanted to sell him her place?

But he just quirked a smile at her, and amusement, not greed, danced in his eyes. "I was just thinking that if you do, then we can get married. What do you say?"

"Wh-what? Are—are you asking me to marry me?"

"Only if you sell me your ranch first." He winked.

"Buddy, consider it sold. It's yours." She grabbed him and kissed him hard.

"So that's a yes to marrying me?"

"Yup." This time *he* settled his mouth onto *hers* in what turned out to be the sweetest, most lingering kiss of them all.

Moments passed and Jed raised his head. Eyes filled with love touched hers, melting her insides with liquid warmth. "You do know that I was teasing you about the ranch, don't you? I don't care about the ranch. It's you alone I care about. You alone I want. And you alone that I love."

"I do know that. And I knew you were only teasing. I, too, don't care about the ranch. Only you and spending the rest of my life with you. That's the only thing that matters to me. I love you so much, Jed."

"I love you more." He smiled, then crushed her to him even closer in the gentlest of ways. This time neither he nor she initiated the kiss first—their lips met at the same time. Sunny never thought it possible, but even more love flowed through Jed's kiss, more than she had ever felt before. She willed her lips to do the same, and it must have worked because Jed's sigh was filled with contentment. Just the way love should be.

Epilogue

~❦~

They had planned on having the wedding at the Flying W Ranch, but Jed thought it only fitting that they have it on the ranch where they would start their lives together as man and wife. Sunny agreed right away and even thought it to be a right fine idea. She and Jed restoring the ranch back to its former glory together only seemed fitting, too.

Because neither of them wanted to leave her uncle in the lurch during calving season, they decided to delay their wedding until June 15. And boy was she glad they had. No snow. Only green meadows, fully leaved aspen trees, columbines, daisies and other wildflowers covered her ranch. Soon to be her and Jed's ranch.

"Oh, precious. You look so beautiful in your mother's dress." Aunt Minnie held her arms out and studied her. "That dark purple looks great with your dark brown hair and eyes." Her eyes misted. "You look just like your ma did the day she married."

Sunny's eyes turned moist, too. She wished her ma was here to see her get married. But she wasn't. With a quick swipe to her eyes, she pressed her shoulders back, determined to not feel sorry for herself and to instead focus on the other people she cherished in her life that were here with her on this special occasion.

"We'd better get going. Jed's waiting for you."

The short ride to the small lake on her ranch lasted forever. When the green water reservoir came into view Sunny's focus went to all the people seated on the tree-stump seats that had been set out in rows, and she was surprised at how many people there were and how far some of them had come.

Even Jed's family had shown up for the wedding. Tears had filled Jed's eyes when his pa had told him how proud he was of him. Her own eyes had filled with tears, too.

Thinking of Jed… Her attention shifted to her husband-to-be, standing next to Reverend Yohansen, who had made the trip here just for this special day.

"You ready, Sunshine?" Uncle Emmett met her and her aunt at the buggy. First he helped Aunt Minnie down and kissed her cheek before she scurried off to join the others. Then he helped Sunny down. In place of her pa, the man who looked so much like him would walk her down the aisle.

"I'm so happy for you, Sunshine," Uncle Emmett said as he led her toward the wedding area. "You're getting one fine upstanding man, and he's getting one fine outstanding gal. I have no doubt your marriage will be as wonderful as your parents' was and as your aunt's and mine is."

"I have no doubt neither that we'll be equally as happy. I've had very good role models. Thank you for that." She smiled, then turned her attention onto Jed standing at the end of the aisle.

Their eyes locked and held as she walked toward him. She was grateful for the sagebrush-cleared path; otherwise, with her not watching where she was going, the hem of her dress would have probably snagged on the bush and sent her flying.

When they finally reached Jed, Uncle Emmett handed her off.

Jed leaned over and his breath brushed against her ear, sending chills racing up and down her spine when he whispered, "You look beautiful, Sunshine."

"Even without my cowboy hat and boots?" she whispered back and winked.

"Yup."

They laughed.

He looped her arm through his.

They faced the pastor and spoke their vows to love, cherish and honor one another all the days of their lives. When Jed sealed it with a kiss, she knew it was also with a promise of many more to come. Despite all the obstacles set in their paths, somehow she had finally become the rancher's sweetheart.

* * * * *

Dear Reader,

This story is dear to my heart because I could relate to Sunny, only I wasn't trying to prove anything to anyone else, only to myself. Having rodeoed as a teenager, I loved horses and of course cowboys. When my cowboy husband decided to go into cattle ranching, I readily agreed. However, I didn't know then that I'd be working on the ranch, too. But I did it to please my husband and to help him out. After years of watching the other women who were born and raised on a ranch do a fabulous job at every phase of ranching— unlike myself—I felt completely inept and frustrated, so I eventually quit. It was the best thing I'd ever done because after that I discovered who I was, what I wanted to do and most importantly that God didn't create all of us to be ranch hands. We all have our individual jobs to do. Mine just happens to be writing, and I love it. So thank you, Dear Readers, for being a part of that love and for reading my stories.

God bless you and yours,
Debra Ullrick

Questions for Discussion

1. Having been made fun of most of her life due to her petite stature and love of ranching, Sunny felt the need to prove herself to those around her. Why do you think some people feel the need to do that?

2. Jedidiah had always felt like the outcast in his family, and in a way he was. His mother doted on his siblings and all but ignored him. How would you feel if this happened to you?

3. Jed strove to earn his father's approval, but office work wasn't for him, so he chose to follow his heart instead, even at the risk of never gaining that approval he craved. Was there ever a time that you followed your heart even against the wishes of your parents or someone else?

4. When Sunny finally gained the men's respect and approval, she thought she'd be elated but wasn't. Name a situation in your life when you thought that once you achieved a certain something that everything would change. Did it? If not, why?

5. In the past certain jobs were deemed unacceptable for women. Knowing that, how do you think you would have fared living back then? And what do you think you would be doing?

REQUEST YOUR FREE BOOKS!

2 FREE INSPIRATIONAL NOVELS
PLUS 2
FREE
MYSTERY GIFTS

Love Inspired.
HISTORICAL
INSPIRATIONAL HISTORICAL ROMANCE

YES! Please send me 2 FREE Love Inspired® Historical novels and my 2 FREE mystery gifts (gifts are worth about $10). After receiving them, if I don't wish to receive any more books, I can return the shipping statement marked "cancel." If I don't cancel, I will receive 4 brand-new novels every month and be billed just $4.49 per book in the U.S. or $4.99 per book in Canada. That's a saving of at least 22% off the cover price. It's quite a bargain! Shipping and handling is just 50¢ per book in the U.S. and 75¢ per book in Canada.* I understand that accepting the 2 free books and gifts places me under no obligation to buy anything. I can always return a shipment and cancel at any time. Even if I never buy another book, the two free books and gifts are mine to keep forever.

102/302 IDN FVXK

Name	(PLEASE PRINT)

Address	Apt. #

City	State/Prov.	Zip/Postal Code

Signature (if under 18, a parent or guardian must sign)

Mail to the **Harlequin® Reader Service:**
IN U.S.A.: P.O. Box 1867, Buffalo, NY 14240-1867
IN CANADA: P.O. Box 609, Fort Erie, Ontario L2A 5X3

Want to try two free books from another series?
Call 1-800-873-8635 or visit www.ReaderService.com.

* Terms and prices subject to change without notice. Prices do not include applicable taxes. Sales tax applicable in N.Y. Canadian residents will be charged applicable taxes. Offer not valid in Quebec. This offer is limited to one order per household. Not valid for current subscribers to Love Inspired Historical books. All orders subject to credit approval. Credit or debit balances in a customer's account(s) may be offset by any other outstanding balance owed by or to the customer. Please allow 4 to 6 weeks for delivery. Offer available while quantities last.

Your Privacy—The Harlequin® Reader Service is committed to protecting your privacy. Our Privacy Policy is available online at www.ReaderService.com or upon request from the Harlequin Reader Service.

We make a portion of our mailing list available to reputable third parties that offer products we believe may interest you. If you prefer that we not exchange your name with third parties, or if you wish to clarify or modify your communication preferences, please visit us at www.ReaderService.com/consumerchoice or write to us at Harlequin Reader Service Preference Service, P.O. Box 9062, Buffalo, NY 14269. Include your complete name and address.

All Laura White wants is a second chance.
Will she find it in Cooper Creek?

Read on for a preview of
THE COWBOY'S HEALING WAYS.

The door opened, bringing in cool air and a few stray drops of rain. The man in the doorway slipped off boots and hung a cowboy hat on a hook by the door. She watched as he shrugged out of his jacket and hung it next to his hat.

When he turned, she stared up at a man with dark hair that brushed his collar and lean, handsome features. He looked as at home in this big house as he did in his worn jeans and flannel shirt. His dark eyes studied her with curious suspicion. She'd gotten used to that look. She'd gotten used to people whispering behind their hands as she walked past.

But second chances and starting over meant wanting something new. She wanted to be the person people welcomed into their lives. She wanted to be the woman a man took a second look at, maybe a third.

Jesse Cooper took a second look, but it was a look of suspicion.

"Jesse, I'm so glad you're here." Granny Myrna had returned with a cold washcloth, which she placed on Laura's forehead. "It seems I had an accident."

"Really?" Jesse smiled a little, warming the coolness in dark eyes that focused on Laura.

"I pulled right out in front of her. She drove her car off the side of the road to keep from hitting me."

Laura closed her eyes. A cool hand touched the gash at her hairline.

"Let me see this."

She opened her eyes and he was squatting in front of her, studying the cut. He looked from the gash to her face. Then he moved and stood back up, unfolding his long legs with graceful ease. Laura clasped her hands to keep them from shaking.

A while back there had been an earthquake in Oklahoma. Laura remembered when it happened, and how they'd all wondered if they'd really felt the earth move or if it had been their imaginations. She was pretty sure it had just happened again. The earth had moved, shifting precariously as a hand touched her face and dark eyes studied her intently, with a strange mixture of curiosity, surprise and something else.

Will Jesse ever allow the mysterious Laura into his life—and his heart?

Pick up THE COWBOY'S HEALING WAYS
by Brenda Minton,
available in February 2013 from Love Inspired.